KT-164-086

MARY ANN IN AUTUMN

A Tales of the City novel

Armistead Maupin

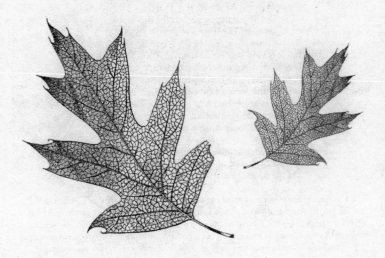

BLACK SWAN

TRANSWORLD PUBLISHERS
61–63 Uxbridge Road, London W5 5SA
A Random House Group Company
www.transworldbooks.co.uk

MARY ANN IN AUTUMN
A BLACK SWAN BOOK: 9780552777063

First published in the United States in 2010 by Harper
an imprint of HarperCollins Publishers

First published in Great Britain
in 2010 by Doubleday
an imprint of Transworld Publishers
Black Swan edition published 2011

A CIP catalogue record for this book
is available from the British Library.

Addresses for Random House Group Ltd companies outside the UK
can be found at: www.randomhouse.co.uk
The Random House Group Ltd Reg. No. 954009

The Random House Group Limited supports The Forest Stewardship Council (FSC®),
the leading international forest certification organisation. Our books carrying the FSC
label are printed on FSC® certified paper. FSC is the only forest certification scheme
endorsed by the leading environmental organisations, including Greenpeace. Our paper
procurement policy can be found at www.randomhouse.co.uk/environment

Typeset in 11.5/15pt Giovanni Book by
Falcon Oast Graphic Art Ltd.
Printed and bound by CPI Group (UK) Ltd, Croydon, CR0 4YY.

2 4 6 8 10 9 7 5 3 1

For Laura Linney

We shall not cease from exploration
And the end of all our exploring
Will be to arrive where we started
And know the place for the first time.

—T. S. Eliot

Mary Ann in Autumn

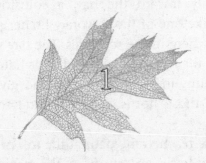

Single-family Dwelling

There should be a rabbit hole was what she was thinking. There should be something about this hillside, some lingering sense memory – the view of Alcatraz, say, or the foghorns or the mossy smell of the planks beneath her feet – that would lead her back to her lost wonderland. Everything around her was familiar but somehow foreign to her own experience, like a place she had seen in a movie but had never actually visited. She had climbed these weathered steps – what? – thousands of times before, but there wasn't a hint of homecoming, nothing to take her back to where she used to be.

The past doesn't catch up with us, she thought. *It escapes from us.*

At the landing she stopped to catch her breath.

Beneath her, the street intersecting with Barbary Lane tilted dizzily toward the bay, a collision of perspectives, like one of those wonky Escher prints that were everywhere in the seventies. The bay was bright blue today, the hard fierce blue of a gas flame. If there was fog rolling in – and there must be, given the insistence of those horns – she couldn't see it from here.

When she reached the path at the top of the steps, one of her heels got stuck in the paving stones. Yanking it free with a grunt, she chided herself for not leaving her Ferragamos back at the Four Seasons. Those stones, if memory served, had been used as ballast on the sailing ships that came around the horn – or so her landlady Mrs. Madrigal had claimed, once upon a time. Twenty years later the chunky granite blocks looked suspiciously ordinary, like the pavers in her driveway back in Connecticut.

As soon as she caught sight of the lych-gate at Number 28, a flock of wild parrots swooped low over the lane, cackling like crones. Those birds – or ones just like them – had been here when she was here, long before they became global celebrities in a popular documentary. She remembered how proud she had felt when she saw that film in Darien, and how utterly irrational that feeling had been, as if she were claiming intimacy with someone she had known slightly in high school who had grown up to be famous.

Those birds did not belong to her anymore.

The lych-gate was the same, only new. The redwood shingles on its roof had been crumbly with dry rot when she moved to the East Coast in the late eighties. Now they were made of slate – or a good imitation thereof. The gate itself, once creaky but welcoming, had been fitted with a lock and a buzzer and something under the eaves that looked like a security camera. So much for a quick snoop around the garden.

She peered through a hole in the lattice at what she could see of the house. The shingle siding had been replaced, and fairly recently. The trim around the windows was painted a hard, glossy black. There were now French doors opening onto the courtyard in roughly the spot where Mrs. Madrigal's front door had been. (Had anyone even thought to save that door with its wonderful stained-glass panels?) Most of the outside stairways, she noticed with a shiver, had been removed or modified to serve the transformation of an apartment house into – what was the official term? – a Single-Family Dwelling.

We had been a family, she thought. *Even in our separate dwellings.*

From this angle, of course, she couldn't see the little house on the roof, the funky matchbox studio Mrs. Madrigal's tenants had referred to as 'the pentshack.' Her guess was it no longer existed, given the extensive nature of this remodeling. It had probably been replaced by a deck – or another floor entirely – and she wasn't sure how to feel about that. Her memories of the place held both dread and delight.

Two blocks away, while looking for lunch, she found the corner mom-and-pop still intact, still called the Searchlight Market. Next door her old Laundromat had been stylishly renovated and a little too cutely renamed 'The Missing Sock.' It pleased her to find the original thirties' lettering still silvering the plate glass at Woo's Cleaners, though the place was obviously empty. The windows were blocked by pale blue wrapping paper, the very paper her laundry had once been wrapped in. Across the street, a pristine gallery of tiny *objets* had sprouted next to what had once been Marcel & Henri, the butcher shop where she had sometimes splurged on pâté, just to keep from *feeling* like a secretary.

And there was Swensen's, the ice cream shop at Hyde and Union that had been her consolation on more than one Saturday night when she had stayed in with Mary Tyler Moore. This was the original Swensen's, the one Mr. Swensen himself had opened in the late forties, and he had still been running it when she was here. She was about to stop in for a cone, just for old times' sake, when she spotted the fire trucks parked on Union.

Rounding the corner, she found dozens of on-lookers assembled beneath a big sooty hole on the second floor of a house. The crisis seemed to have passed; the air was pungent with the smell of wet embers, and the firemen, though obviously weary, were business-as-usual as they tugged at a serpentine tangle of hoses. One of the younger ones, a frisky Prince Harry redhead, seemed aware of his lingering audience and played to the balcony with every manly move.

We do love our firefighters, she thought, though she had long ago forfeited her right to the Municipal We. She was no more a San Franciscan now than the doughy woman in a SUPPORT OUR TROOPS sweatshirt climbing off the cable car at the intersection. She herself hadn't used a cable car for years, yet every handrail and plank was as vividly familiar as her first bicycle. This one had a light blue panel along the side, marking it as a Bicentennial model. They were built the year she'd arrived in the city.

She waited for the cable car to pass, considering something that eventually sent her into Swensen's to address the middle-aged white man behind the counter.

'I used to order something here,' she said, as winsomely as possible, 'but I can't remember the name of it. It was thirty years ago, so you may not . . .'

'Swiss Orange Chip.'

'Excuse me?'

'Chocolate with orange bits, right?'

'Yes!'

'That's Swiss Orange Chip.'

17

She gaped at him. 'How on earth did you do that?'

He shrugged. 'It's the flavor people can never remember the name of.'

'Oh . . . right.' She gave him a curdled smile, feeling irredeemably average. 'It's really good, at any rate.'

He made her a sugar cone with a single scoop. Without tasting it, she carried it half a block to Russell Street, the little alley off Hyde where Jack Kerouac had been holed up for six months in the early fifties, working on a draft of *On the Road*. Her first husband, Brian, had brought her here when they started dating, since the place held great significance for him. Standing before the A-frame cottage like a pilgrim at Lourdes, he had told her only that Neal Cassady had lived there, and she, God help her Cleveland soul, had asked if that was one of David Cassidy's brothers. He was gentle about it at the time – he wanted to get laid, after all – but he wouldn't let her forget it for years. Had she paid more attention to that moment and what it said about both of them, she might have saved them from a marriage that was pretty much doomed from the start.

Now, according to the daughter they had adopted, Brian was out living his own version of *On the Road*, driving his beloved Winnebago from one national park to another, apparently more at ease with life than he had ever been. He was seven years older than she, which made him sixty-four now, an age that could only be darkly ironic to a boomer who was finally facing it. *Will you still need me? Will you still feed me?*

Leaving the Cassady cottage, she headed down the street with her ice cream, finally reuniting with the dark citrus tang of Swiss Orange Chip. The taste of it, as she had suspected, swept her back on a tide of subliminal memory to a much younger self.

It was the taste of a lonely Saturday night.

Back at the Searchlight she bought a turkey sandwich and ate it by the tennis courts in the leafy little park at the crest of Russian Hill. For a moment she considered taking the cable car to the Wharf for an Irish coffee at the Buena Vista, but that would only delay the deeply unpleasant mission at hand. She had told her Mouse she'd explain everything as soon as she hit town, and since she'd been sobbing the last time they talked, postponement was no longer an option. But how she dreaded putting it into words.

She dug her iPhone out of her shoulder bag and dialed his number. It rang six or seven times before he picked up: 'Mary Ann?'

'Yeah.'

'Thank God. I was starting to worry.'

'Sorry . . . I just needed . . .' She let the thought trail off. She had no earthly idea what she had needed.

'Are you at the Four Seasons?'

'No. Russian Hill.'

'Why'd you go there?'

'I don't know. Dumb idea.'

'Do you wanna come here?'

'You're at home?'

'Yeah. Ben's at the dog park. We'll have the place to ourselves.'

That was something of a relief. Ben was a lovely guy, but what she had to say would be hard enough to share with *one* person.

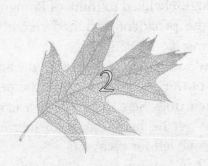

The Politics of the Park

The dog park was a fenced-in parcel of packed sand next to the Eureka Valley Recreation Center on Collingwood Street. When Ben reached the gate, Roman was already straining on his leash in anticipation of the free-for-all awaiting him. There were at least a dozen dogs today, among them two of Roman's favorites: a frisky ridgeback named Brokeback and a Portuguese water dog who, except for a smudge of white on his chest, was almost Roman's double. Ben often had to explain to strangers that Roman wasn't a Portie but a black Labradoodle, one of a growing number of poodle hybrids (golden doodles, schnoodles, even Saint Berdoodles) to be found around the Castro these days. But he hated it when people called them 'designer dogs.' He liked to think of Roman as a mutt – a term the president-elect had recently used to describe himself.

Ben found something reassuring in the anonymous fellowship of the dog park. Most of the people who brought their dogs here didn't know each other on the outside, yet he had seen them hug each other when someone left for vacation.

Their offhanded intimacy defied boundaries of race, gender, age, sexual orientation, and – every now and then – mental health. And even the serious crazies somehow seemed less so when immersed in the loving lunacy of dogs. It was a temporary cure for everything.

Ben sat down on a bench that would not have looked out of place in a formal English garden. There were half a dozen of these along the perimeter fence, the result of a beautification effort led by Sister Chastity Boner, a dog-loving member of the Sisters of Perpetual Indulgence. Winter had been a long time coming this year – not to mention the rain – so he settled against the bench and gorged on the remains of autumn. There was a bolster of fog already rolling over Twin Peaks, but it had yet to smother the sun. The abstract mural on the south wall of the rec center was still ablaze with color, and the frolicking dogs were still casting long shadows on the sand.

A heavyset old man in a navy blue parka sat down next to Ben on the bench. 'Roman's had a haircut,' he said.

Ben nodded sheepishly. 'We let him get too rasta. The groomer had to take him down a lot more than usual.'

'Looks good,' said the old man. 'Very sporty.'

'Thanks, Cliff.' He knew the guy's name because Cliff was often here with his dog, a shivery little piebald terrier named Blossom, who, for some peculiar reason, fascinated Roman more than most of the other dogs in the park. 'I think he's a little embarrassed about the haircut,' Ben added. 'He'd rather be shaggy.'

'Aw, look. He's forgiven you already.'

Roman had his nose wedged in Blossom's butt.

'That's what I like about 'em,' said Cliff. 'They get on with things and don't hold a grudge. They don't dwell on the past.'

'No, I know. He ate my Sonicare this morning and hasn't given it a second thought.'

'Your what?'

'My electric toothbrush.'

The old man smiled, exposing a row of teeth that could have used a toothbrush some time ago. 'Our unit had a dog in 'Nam. Little brown mutt the mamasan brought to our hooch one day. Plannin' on eatin' it, I guess. Sweet little guy. We made him our mascot for a coupla months, until they transferred us.'

'What do you think happened to him?'

'I *know* what happened to him. Chief petty officer shot him.'

'Shit.'

'Had to. We couldn't take him with us. He woulda starved. Or got eaten.'

Ben sighed. 'I guess so.'

'Did you notice our latest addition?' Cliff asked.

Ben followed the old man's wobbly finger to a glossy red fire hydrant sitting squarely in the middle of the sandy plain. 'What's it doing there?'

Cliff shrugged. 'For the dogs to pee on, I guess.'

'It's a joke then.'

'Maybe, but it's a real fire hydrant. Bolted right into the ground. It was here when I came in this morning.'

'It's fucking dangerous,' said a woman who'd been eavesdropping on their conversation. She was roughly Ben's age – certainly no older than forty – with garish Amy Winehouse eye makeup to compensate for her skeletal Amy Winehouse limbs. 'Karma is clinically blind, you know. She could knock the shit out of herself.'

Ben didn't know which of these dogs was Karma, but he saw the woman's point. The hydrant was an immoveable iron stump, and these dogs yielded to nothing once they got going. Why compromise their safety for some kitschy human effort at witticism?

'Anybody know who did it?' Ben asked.

'Not me,' said Cliff, almost as though he were a grade-schooler who'd been asked to snitch on a friend. Cliff kept his profile low when it came to the politics of the park. He was friendly enough, but usually limited his talk to the dogs themselves, avoiding all discussion of their owners. Ben sometimes thought of him as 'Mr. Cellophane' from *Chicago*. *'Cause you can look right through me, walk right by me, and never know I'm there.*

'I have my suspicions,' said Amy Winehouse, persisting in her investigation of the Great Fire Hydrant Mystery. Now she was aiming her caked turquoise lids toward a cluster of dog owners chatting in the middle of the park.

The group included a chubby Asian teenager, a middle-aged white woman in an Obama sweatshirt and a pair of look-alike ginger bears dispensing treats to their Jack Russell. Ben felt a peculiar sympathy for the culprit, whoever it was. He (or she or they) must have believed that the others would be deeply amused by the fire hydrant.

But this was the wrong crowd to be second-guessing. The hardcore regulars saw the park as an extension of their homes, fiercely debating every change that came along. When, for instance, the new redwood planters were installed along the fence, there were those who fretted that smaller dogs might get cornered there by the larger ones. The exact distance between the planters and the fence was a subject of grave deliberation for weeks. Ditto the contents of the planters, since some of the prettiest flowering trees dropped blossoms that were potentially poisonous. ('But only if eaten in large quantities or boiled into a tea,' Ben's husband had explained – and Michael, after all, was a gardener. 'There's nothing to sweat until you see a Doberman with a teapot.')

The ginger bears had left the others, and Ben realized they had done so to watch their Jack Russell tentatively approach the fire hydrant. There was a glimmer of dad-like pride on their faces as the dog began circling the alien totem, obviously as baffled by its presence as the humans were. When he finally headed off without lifting his leg, the ginger bears were noticeably crestfallen, though Ben did not remark upon it.

It occurred to him that Michael would probably have suspected these guys from the get-go. Michael was a bear himself, though not exactly a member of their fraternal order. He had once remarked that the most hidebound of bears, the ones who invoked manhood in beards, suspenders and long johns, had a penchant for cramming their homes with juvenilia: mid-century cookie jars and Disney figurines under glass domes.

That corny fire hydrant certainly fit the profile.

'Well,' said Ben, slapping his knees as he rose from the bench. 'Time to hit the road, I guess.'

A cloud passed over Cliff's face. 'Don't go on my account. I can sit anywhere.'

Ben felt bad for the old guy, who, for one reason or another, always seemed on the verge of apology. 'No, I'd love to hang out. I've just got shopping to do. We're cooking for a friend of my partner's tonight.' Ben usually called Michael his husband but had gone with the less threatening word in deference to Cliff's age and the likelihood that he was straight. Michael wouldn't approve, but Ben saw it as good manners.

'Well,' said Cliff. 'Cook him something nice.'

'It's a her, actually.' He decided to make it more interesting for Cliff. 'Maybe you've heard of her. She had a TV show here in the late eighties. Mary Ann Singleton?'

Cliff blinked at him in mild befuddlement. 'She still lives here?'

Ben shook his head. 'She's been back East for years. She's just visiting. You remember the show?'

'Sure. Went to it once even, sat in the audience. Got her autograph. Not personally, but . . . her producer took it.'

'No kidding? Small world.'

Roman appeared and nuzzled the leash in Ben's hand. 'I guess that's my cue,' he said, grateful for another excuse to get out of there.

Delano's Market was just around the corner from the

dog park, but Ben took Roman all the way back to where the car was parked on Eureka, so he could drive into the market's basement entrance. This was one of the few occasions when he'd leave Roman in the car, having heard too many stories about dogs being snatched for use as 'bait' in dogfights. It sickened him to think that such cruelty could happen here, but it did, and not infrequently. In fact, one of Roman's playmates at the park, a nervous little boxer named Mercy, had been rescued during a dogfight bust in the Excelsior.

Leaving a window cracked, Ben locked the Prius and headed up the stairs to the market. Just before he reached the top, his cell phone tingled against his thigh, so he retrieved it from a tangle of bio-degradable poop bags and checked the readout.

It was Michael's gardening assistant, a cub named Jake Greenleaf.

'Hey there,' said Ben.

'Hey, Ben. You seen your hubby? He's not picking up, and one of our clients is looking for him.'

'He should be at the house,' said Ben.

'He's not answering, if he is.'

'Then he must be with Mary Ann.'

'Who?'

'You know . . . the one who came out when Anna had her stroke.'

'The hot Connecticut mess?'

Ben chuckled. 'Whatever.'

'What's she doing here?'

'I dunno. It's all very mysterious.'

'Well, if you hear from him, tell him Karl Rove's got a bug up his ass again.'

'Will he know what that means?'

'Oh, yeah,' said Jake. 'Oh, yeah.'

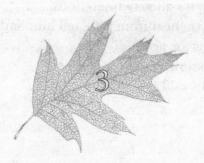

Solid Proof

The nastiest clients, in Jake's opinion, were not the rich ones but the ones who used to be rich, the ones who made a huge wad during the dot-com boom and lost it in a big way. Downsizing, as they liked to call it, had turned them into assholes who couldn't afford a driver anymore but still wanted a gardener to boss around.

Like this client – the one who looked like a younger Karl Rove – who came charging out of his house the moment Jake returned his cell phone to his backpack.

'Did you reach him?'

'Not yet. I left a message.'

The client grunted and rolled his eyes.

Jake had tried to be nice to this loser, but the guy

was always such a dick. He never asked for Jake's opinion about anything. When Michael wasn't around, in fact, he barely spoke to Jake at all. Jake was just a day laborer in Karl Rove's eyes, not a junior partner in the business, and these failed dot-commers always had to talk to the boss.

'Here's the deal,' said Jake. 'This is my specialty. I've been doing rock gardens for Michael for over three years. If you wanna turn that fountain back into a planter you're gonna need drainage, and that means we're gonna hafta hammer a hole in that concrete. You can talk to Michael, but he'll just tell you the same thing—'

'I don't doubt that, Jason—'

'Jake.'

'Whatever . . . Jake.'

'I spoke to Michael's husband,' Jake said evenly. 'He's dealing with a family emergency.' It wasn't the truth, but it was sort of the truth and easier than explaining that Michael's favorite drama queen had just rolled into town with a fresh steaming load of drama. Besides, Michael was pushing sixty and having serious issues with one of his rotator cuffs. He had earned the right to some downtime, whatever the reason.

Jake lifted the jackhammer off the ground, letting it swing from his hand gunslinger-style. 'Want me to keep going?'

The client nodded sullenly. 'Yeah . . . just have Michael call me.'

31

'No problem.'

Napoleon headed back toward the house, then stopped and turned with a mean little smirk on his face. 'You might wanna . . .' He tapped his forefinger against his cheek. 'Your beard is splattered with something.'

He knows, thought Jake. *He knows and he's having fun with me.*

Jake's free hand shot to his beard and made an exploratory search. 'Oh . . . the jackhammer. Hit a wet spot. Hope it wasn't cat shit.'

He was trying to show that he was indifferent to mud and beyond humiliation by this douche bag, but the wildfire raging across his face told another story. He hated those telltale blushes. They came less often these days, but when they did, they came with a holy vengeance. And that wasn't who he was anymore. Or at least who he wanted to be.

Maybe it's the testosterone, he thought. Maybe the hormone intensifies what's already there – like it does with hair growth and muscle mass. Wouldn't that suck bigtime? It didn't seem likely, but he could ask about it on Wednesday at the Lou Sullivan Society. There might be other guys there with similar experiences.

If you can manage to keep from blushing, dude.

The client went back into the house. Jake finished his jackhammering and lost himself in the arrangement of rocks on the slope. He had picked out these rocks himself at the stone yard in Berkeley. They were rough and honey-colored, streaked with purple and rust, and he enjoyed finding their kinship to each other as he embedded them in the soil. They were like pieces of a puzzle that he was building and solving at the same time. When all the rock was in place, he would have the entirely different satisfaction of tucking moss and soft grasses between the cracks. That was the icing on the cake.

It didn't matter that he was doing this for a douche nozzle. This rock garden was Jake's when all was said and done. He would photograph it, remember it, imagine it years from now as a mossy ruin from an earlier time – *his* ruin – since the guy who builds something owns it forever. Even after Karl Rove had died or moved away, this mighty tumble of golden stone would still be Jake's, solid proof of his days on earth.

He had said something like that the week before at Lou Sullivan. Not before the group or anything – he was way too shy for that – just gabbing afterward with a hot trans dude named Rocco, who had already announced his taste for men. Jake had hoped to impress him with his devotion to his work, but ended up sounding like a total garden geek. It didn't help that a butch bio guy was lurking nearby pretending to swig on a Snapple but obviously ready to pounce on Rocco as soon as Jake was done boring him to death with horticulture. He left just after that, choosing solitude over disgrace.

He was no good at meeting people. Even at a support group for trans folk he felt like a visiting Martian. He had thought that would change once he'd made the leap, but so far, claiming another gender – even the one that came naturally to him – had merely offered new ways to feel alienated, new opportunities for humiliation. His hookups with bio guys had been one-night stands at best; the only good that had ever come from that had been meeting Michael and thereby landing this job. A lot of bio guys were just in it for the novelty, losing interest altogether once their curiosity was satisfied. As for other trans guys, they were either cruising the Lone Star for liquored-up bio bears or flirting with the femme dykes down at the Lexington Club. They weren't looking for Jake.

Still, his drive for completion never waned. In fact, once he'd begun the testosterone, the urgency for the surgery had grown even greater. So he was saving his money, biding his time until the day of deliverance. He was barely past thirty, anyway; the man of his dreams could wait until the plumbing was adjusted. For the moment, at least, *he* was the man of his dreams, and everything else was needless distraction.

Besides, there were matters far more pressing than finding a partner. Like, for instance, how to pee believably. That was less of an issue in San Francisco, where people were used to surprises, but he dreaded the thought of being clocked at a urinal in, say, Bakersfield or San Leandro. Michael, after all, often sent him off on shopping forays to nurseries in the suburban boonies. So Jake had sent away for something called a Freshette – a funnel-and-tube urination device used by bio women on camping trips.

He had worn this thing in his boxer briefs for several days before realizing – on a bus full of school kids, no less – that the funnel looked like some sort of weird domed erection. So he'd trimmed the Freshette down to a less disturbing size before threading its tube through the shaft of a small cushiony dildo he'd found at Good Vibrations. They called it a 'packer,' he learned that very day, and it was just what he needed: something believable to pull out of his fly when privacy was impossible.

He was getting there.

For three years Jake had been living in the Duboce Triangle with someone he thought of as his 'tranmother.' Anna Madrigal was in her late eighties but still getting about. She'd had a stroke a few years back, remaining in a coma for several days, but she'd recovered and since that time had seemed as blissfully fearless as the sole survivor of an air disaster. Her energy was flagging, but she could still be found plodding around the neighborhood in kimono and sneakers, a look that could sometimes border on bag lady. Jake knew better. Anna had a decent nest egg from the sale of a house on Russian Hill, where, once upon a time, back in the seventies, she had been Michael's landlady.

Anna treasured her independence, so Jake never called himself her companion or caregiver, though that's how he saw it – and proudly. The old girl was something of an icon among local trans folk, so he found it something of a privilege to keep an eye on her and do her heavy hauling. But mostly, of course, she was just good company.

And that was the reason he headed home for lunch that day. The drive from Pacific Heights to the Duboce Triangle and back again would eat up most of his lunch hour, but he needed a serious dose of Anna, however small. His heart sank when he entered the flat and she wasn't in her favorite armchair by the window.

'Yoo hoo,' he called, using the silly greeting she sometimes used. He had never done that before and surprised himself with the sound of it.

There was no answer, so he went down the hall toward the bedrooms.

'Anna . . . I brought us sandwiches from the corner.'

Still no response. Her bedroom was empty, so he figured she was out on one of her constitutionals. It served him right, of course, for not calling first, but he'd always enjoyed the way her face lit up when she received unexpected company.

He headed to the kitchen for a glass of juice. There, beneath a shaft of afternoon sunlight, he found her. She was lying on her side on the floor, her face turned away from him. Her old cat, Notch, was perched solemnly on her hip, as if standing guard. Jake felt the blood rush from his face as violently as it could rush in.

'Oh, no,' he murmured, moving closer to her body. The cat rose to its feet, still balanced on Anna's hip, and arched its back lazily, completely indifferent to whatever the fuck was going on. Jake, meanwhile, had forgotten how to breathe.

'Oh, Jesus,' he said. 'Jesus—'

'No call for that,' Anna said sternly.

Jake gasped with relief and went to her side, squatting so he could see her face. Notch leaped from her hip and strode briskly away. 'What happened?' asked Jake.

'Just having a little snooze.'

'*On the floor?*'

'It's nice down here. The linoleum's so smooth and cool. I see why Notch likes it.'

He considered, then dismissed, the possibility that Anna had finally lost her mind. 'You fell, didn't you?'

'Maybe a little bit.'

'When?'

'Not that long ago. Who knows? I've been sleeping.' She extended her hand. 'Give us a lift, dear.'

'No . . . wait . . . you may have broken something.'

'Don't be melodramatic. I'm not in pain. I was just catching my breath, and I fell asleep.'

So Jake helped her sit up for a moment before scooping her in his arms and rising to his feet. She was a good four inches taller than he, but surprisingly light, an armful of velvet and bones. As he carried her down the hall, he caught the scent of her perfume, which he remembered was called Devon Violets. The name had always puzzled him, since violets – at least the ones *he* knew about – didn't have a scent.

'Where are we going?' asked Anna.

'To the armchair. To eat our sandwiches.'

Looking up at him, she chortled. 'I feel like Scarlett.'

He didn't get it. 'Johansson?'

'No, child . . . O'Hara.'

'Who's that?'

'Oh . . . that *is* depressing.'

'What do you mean?'

'Nothing, dear. Just being silly.'

Anna pecked at her sandwich but gobbled up the black-bottom cupcake he had brought as an after-thought. He had read somewhere that old people eventually lost their more refined taste buds, so that only really sweet things held their interest in the end. He wondered if that was true, and if he should start finding ways to make main courses seem more like dessert. He was a crummy cook, though – or at least a fairly disinterested one; Anna was much better in the kitchen than he would ever be.

'That was lovely,' said Anna, dabbing at the crumbs on her chin with the tissue she kept tucked in her sleeve. 'Very thoughtful of you, dear.'

'I have to get back soon,' he said. 'Michael's not working.'

'Oh, no. His shoulder?'

'No . . . well, it's still hurting him, but . . . he's spending the day with his friend from Connecticut.' Anna's watery blue eyes blinked at him, absorbing the news. 'Mary Ann's in town?'

'Mmm.'

Anna drew back, frowning a little. 'Why do you say it like that?'

'I didn't say anything. I said "Mmm".'

'Yes, dear . . . but your *tone*.'

Jake shrugged. 'I just think . . . she's kind of a pain.'

Anna seemed to take this personally. 'You've met her only once.'

Jake remembered it well. Mary Ann had flown into town (in her husband's private jet, no less) when Anna was already deep in her coma. It was a nice enough gesture, Jake supposed, but Mary Ann would never have known about Anna at all if Michael hadn't tracked her down. Sure, she must have been nervous about facing friends she hadn't seen for decades, but beyond that there was something off-putting about her: a certain aloofness that made Jake feel instantly judged and dismissed.

Since that time Mary Ann and Michael had been talking a lot on the phone. According to Ben, who shared Jake's assessment of this woman, Mary Ann would call to unload at least four times a week. And it was always about her: her distant husband and unappreciative stepson, her dead dream of being a network anchor, her really lousy night at the country club. To hear Ben tell it, Michael rarely got a word in edgewise.

'It's not like I hate her,' said Jake. 'I'm just not real big on her.'

Anna regarded him soberly over her teacup. 'Do you know why she's here?'

Jake shook his head. 'Ben doesn't even know. Whatever it is, she was saving it for a face-to-face with Michael.'

'Which is when?'

'Now . . . I guess.'

The old lady nodded methodically, her beach-glass eyes fixed on the sycamore across the street. Jake wondered if she was hurt, if she felt left out of the loop. Mary Ann had been her darling once upon a time, her ingénue on Barbary Lane.

Anna fidgeted with a strand of snowy hair before tucking it behind her ear.

'I wonder if Shawna knows,' she said quietly.

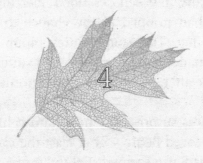

The Puppy Stuff

That morning, of all mornings, Shawna had seriously considered changing her hair. The Bettie Page look had served her well, but it just didn't pack the same wallop anymore. These days the Mission was awash with wannabe Betties in glossy black page-boys and crimson lipstick. Last week, in fact, when Shawna was shopping at a clothes-by-the-pound shop on Valencia Street, the chick who weighed her seed-pearl sweater set could easily have been her double. To say nothing of that über-obnoxious woman on last season's *Project Runway*. Clearly it was time to throw in the bangs.

She was finishing her frittata when she got the tweet – four words screaming obscenely from her

BlackBerry – BETTIE PAGE IS DEAD. One of Shawna's fans, the self-described Piercing Diva of Dubuque, had jumped at the chance to share the news with her. The iconic fifties pinup who had somehow made naughty so nice had suffered a fatal heart attack after a bout with pneumonia. She was eighty-five.

Shawna was surprised by how hard it hit her. She had always loved Bettie – or at least the *idea* of her – but Bettie had also seemed slightly unreal, a human-size Minnie Mouse in the Disneyland of desire. Now all she could see was an old woman who'd been living with her brother somewhere in L.A. She remembered Bettie's three divorces and her struggles with schizophrenia and how she'd regretted tossing out her fishnet stockings after she found Jesus and went to work for the Billy Graham Crusade. Mostly she remembered how Bettie had avoided cameras after her 'rediscovery' in the nineties, striving to protect her myth. That myth was finally safe. Now that she was dead.

Shawna rose from the kitchen table with a sigh and went to the rose-tinted mirror at the end of the hall. She studied herself soberly for a moment, checking her lipstick, testing the silken weight of her pageboy in her hands. *What now? Do I hang on to this pelt out of respect for Bettie or abandon it for the same reason?*

She would think about that later. Her blog needed attention (not to mention her advertisers), so there was really no time for reinvention. Besides, she was meeting her boyfriend for lunch, and he might have some thoughts on the subject.

For the fourth time that month Shawna met Otto at the Circus Center. This was a yellow-brick building on Frederick, an old high school gymnasium, very Deco-looking, with huge metal-frame windows that filled the room with soft gray light as acrobats practiced on the trapeze. Shawna sat in the top row of the bleachers, as far away from the action as possible, since she hated the thought of embarrassing Otto in his element.

Otto was actually his real name, though he'd lengthened it to Ottokar for his professional handle. The original Ottokar had been emperor of Bohemia – something Otto had learned from a Tintin comic book. He was a lanky, lion-maned man who rode a beat-up bicycle, when he wasn't riding a unicycle, and carried coffee-stained paperbacks in his knapsack. The night they met (the night Iron & Wine came to the Café du Nord) they'd talked mostly about the music, learning next to nothing about each other. Shawna liked that – not because she was in any way ashamed of her work but because Otto had come to their hookup with none of the usual expectations. He'd never even heard of Grrrl on the Loose, much less followed a blog, so her raffish online persona had never worked its cheap tricks on him. This guy wanted the girl – not the Grrrl – and that made all the difference to Shawna. Bettie Page, poor thing, should have been so lucky.

When Otto told her he was a clown – came out to her, in effect, with a mortified grimace as if he'd just confessed something horrendous – her heart had gone out to him. She'd tried to show him she was totally cool about it, that she understood his art form beyond the kitschy creepiness of Ronald McDonald and Bozo the Clown. She'd told him about her passion for Fellini and how her gay uncle Michael (who wasn't *technically* her uncle) had introduced her to Cirque du Soleil when she was seven years old.

But all the while she'd been fixated on something else: a report she'd once written for her blog about a local group whose fetish was fucking in clown costumes. She had witnessed this phenomenon herself one rainy night on Minna Street, though it had struck her as more of a stunt than an actual fetish. ('Call me old-fashioned,' she would later write, 'but when I feel something red and round and hard, I don't want it to be a nose.') She had left the party early, apologizing to the host, having learned nothing beyond the obvious reality that lube and greasepaint were not each other's friends.

Of course those people had just *pretended* to be clowns. Otto was the real deal; he approached his craft with a dignity that bordered on the sacramental, especially when he made his rounds at schools and nursing homes. She respected him for his charity work and admired his expertise with unicycles and bowling pins, and generally found him to be sweet and a great deal of fun in the sack, but she never started taking him seriously – much less gazed into his heart – until she met Sammy.

Sammy was a life-size monkey puppet who rode on Ottokar's arm. In the routine Sammy would poke teasingly at Ottokar until the clown became angry and smacked the monkey in the face, knocking him to the ground. Aghast at what he had done, Ottokar would scoop Sammy into his arms, where, like a simian pietà, Sammy would hang as limp as the rag that he was. Ottokar's frantic efforts at reviving Sammy would eventually succeed (to the audible relief of the audience) only to be undone when the clown stumbled and fell, crushing the monkey under his weight. For a long time all the audience could see was Ottokar's inert form. Then, limb by skinny limb, Sammy would appear again, pulling himself from beneath the body of his friend.

What was it about this bit that had endeared Otto to her? Had it simply shown he was a nice guy, a compassionate person, or was it something to do with his irony, his weary grasp of life's betrayals? Whatever it was, her defenses had fallen on the spot. Her previous lover, a Brooklyn lighting designer named Lucy Juarez, had worn Shawna down with her melodrama and free-range jealousy. Lucy had been the ultimate buzz-kill, in fact, the final nail in the coffin of Shawna's two-year New York experiment. She had moved East to sell a book (or a 'blook,' as Lucy had once snidely called it, since almost all of it had come from the blog) and partly to show her doting single dad that it was time for them to pursue separate lives. But her dad had long ago hit the road in his RV, and Brooklyn, for all its pioneer charm, was starting to wear a little thin. When she packed her bags and headed back to San Francisco, she felt no shame about it whatsoever, only a determination to simplify her life and cut out the neurotic bullshit once and for all.

Maybe, come to think of it, that's why Otto had seemed so right.

He was in the ring now, walking on stilts, except they were more of a cross between stilts and skis, and he could bounce on them, like some sort of alien marsupial. Shawna remembered that he was trying out an act that he was taking to Pier 39. He was wearing his 'civvies,' as he liked to call them, loose jeans and a ragged gray T-shirt. His only piece of clown gear was the nose itself – that inevitable fucking red rubber ball. She watched him for at least fifteen minutes, enjoying the flirty moves of his muscles, before he spotted her in the stands and raised his arm in a solemn salute.

Ten minutes later, having finally shed the stilt-ski

contraptions, he sat down next to her and pecked her on the cheek, still wearing the nose.

'Hello, Mr. Kar.'

'Hey, Puppy.' She had once made the fatal mistake of sharing this childhood nickname with Otto, so he felt called upon to use it from time to time. She found that somewhat endearing, in spite of the seriously heavy shit it dredged up for her.

'I brought sandwiches,' she said, patting the plastic bag next to her. 'I thought we could go to the park. Ever been to the AIDS Grove?'

He shook his head. 'Can't say I have.'

She smiled faintly. 'I know it sounds morbid. Like . . . Cancer Valley or something, but it's incredibly gorgeous right now and I think you might—'

'Hey. I'm there.'

So they walked into the park through the Stanyan Street entrance, passing the usual array of bongo players, children, and homeless people until they arrived at the AIDS Memorial Grove, a sunken dell full of redwoods and winding paths. They ate their lunch on the curving stone bench next to the Circle of Friends, where hundreds of names were engraved in ever-expanding circles, like ripples from a stone thrown into a pond.

'Are these all dead people?' Otto asked, munching on his sandwich.

'Not all of them. Some are just donors. See . . . there's Sharon Stone over there.'

Otto screwed up his face. 'That's kind of confusing, isn't it? How can you pay your respects to them if you don't know who's dead and who isn't?'

She agreed with him and told him so. How badly, *really*, did Sharon Stone need to see her name in print? Wasn't there a friend – or even some stranger – she could have memorialized instead? And Calvin Klein, for fuck's sake. Why did he have to put his name here, of all places, when it was already on half the asses in the country?

She rose and moved closer to the circle, squatting so she could point to a name.

'Here's one I know about for sure.'

Otto leaned forward to read it. 'Jon Fielding. You knew him?'

She shook her head. 'He died before I was born. He was Michael's partner.'

He was struggling to place the name, so she helped him out. 'You met him at the farmers' market. The gay guy I call my uncle?'

'Oh . . . yeah. With the young . . . uh, husband.'

'Very good,' she said, smiling at him.

'Hey, I'm from Portland, okay?'

She laughed and looked back at Jon's name. 'He was hella handsome. I've seen pictures of him. My dad really liked him.'

She could see his wheels turning for a moment. Then, hesitantly, he said: 'So your dad is gay, too.'

'No. He just . . . lived among them.' She was

amused by the anthropological sound of that, like some overly serious voiceover on the Discovery Channel. *Brian Hawkins has explored the darkest reaches of San Francisco, where for many years he lived peaceably among the homosexuals.*

'Well . . . that's cool,' said Otto.

'Yeah. I had some fierce uncles.'

'What about your mom?'

Shawna shrugged, since they had talked about this before. 'She was a flight attendant or . . . whatever they called them. She died when I was born.'

'I meant your adoptive mom.'

'She left when I was five. Left *us* . . . me and my dad. I really don't know her.'

'You haven't seen her since then?'

'Oh, I've seen her. She came out several years ago when my friend Anna was sick. And I went to see her once in Connecticut when I was still living in Brooklyn.'

'And?'

'She was married to a retired Republican CEO and lived in a big house on a golf course. The sandwiches she served – I swear to you – had the crusts cut off.'

Otto winced sympathetically. 'Do you know why she left in the first place?'

'A job in New York, my dad said. I don't remember it. She was a local TV personality. She had a show here called *Mary Ann in the Morning.*'

'Aha. So that's where you got it from.'

'Got what?'

'Being a personality.'

She felt her face turning hot. 'I'm not a *personality*! Where did you get that? Don't call me a personality.'

He smiled in appeasement. 'I just meant . . . media in general. And you moved to New York and all . . . for professional purposes . . . like she did.'

Shawna grunted. 'I wasn't following in her foot-steps, believe me.'

'I do, Puppy. I believe you.'

'And while we're at it, could you lay off the Puppy stuff? I told you that in the weakest possible moment, and I really hate being called that.'

'Sorry . . . I thought your dad called you that.'

'Only because Mary Ann did.'

'And that would be . . . ?'

'The woman we're talking about.'

'Right. Got it. No more Puppy.' He seemed to be puzzling over something.

'What?' she asked.

'I thought you couldn't remember her.'

'I can't. Not really.'

'But you remember Puppy?'

'My dad told me that when I was a teenager. To convince me she didn't have ice water in her veins.'

Otto shrugged. 'Sounds like she liked you a *little*.'

'Sure,' said Shawna. 'Just not enough to keep her here.'

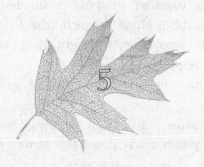

The Truest Alarm

The first thing Mary Ann looked for at Michael's house was the new construction at the end of the garden. Like the rest of the house, this Lilliputian structure was cedar-shingled and one-story, with latticework on the street side, which was already threaded with roses. Michael had referred to the place as a 'cottage' in a recent phone conversation, but that was really stretching it. It was barely as big as one of those 1920s Model T garages that people here turned into gardening sheds. Its shingles were still raw and blond, having yet to know the rains of a Northern California winter. All in all, it was kind of sweet.

The rest of the compound seemed unchanged since her last visit. (She thought of it as a compound, since it was really three old 'earthquake shacks' that had been strung together to make a higgledy-piggledy house.) Climbing from the taxi, she found herself unexpectedly buoyed by the sight of her old friend's deftly feathered nest. Unlike the old house on Barbary Lane, this one still harbored someone she loved.

Michael must have been looking out for her, because he was halfway down the garden path when the taxi pulled away. 'Babycakes,' he called, opening his arms to her. In three years his salt-and-pepper hair had lost most of its pepper, and his stomach beneath his untucked green polo shirt had become a sturdy dome that approximated an early pregnancy. She remembered Michael telling her the belly was caused by his HIV meds. Lipodystrophy, he called it. Likewise the grooves in his cheeks, which she might have described as rugged had she not known differently. Only his smile was unchanged.

She leaned against him for a moment, accepting his warmth in silence.

Finally, she pulled way. 'This is sweet of you.'

'C'mon.'

'I'm so fucked up.'

He gave her an ironic smile. 'I'm gonna need more than that.'

'You'll get it. Trust me.'

He led her into the house. Once he had settled her on the couch, he brought out a cheesecake, which prompted him, naturally, to make a forced joke about *The Golden Girls*. She wondered if some of that belly might be attributable to natural causes.

'This isn't my usual practice,' he said, apparently reading her mind.

'It looks yummy,' she said. 'Can I pass for now?'

He looked more bewildered than offended. 'Sure . . . of course. Would you rather vaporize?'

'Do what?'

'I told you about it, remember? Very little smoke, just cannabis-flavored air. It's a great buzz, and it saves your lungs.'

The last thing she needed right now was something that would make her story more vivid than it already was. 'You wouldn't have any vodka, would you?'

'You bet.' He headed back to the kitchen with the cheesecake, stopping at the door. 'Cranberry or tonic?'

'On the rocks would be fine.'

'Should I make one for myself, or do you want me sober?'

'Whatever you want,' she said absently. 'It doesn't matter.'

Michael returned with two glasses of vodka – one on the rocks for her, one with cranberry for him. She took a sip of hers without waiting to toast him, since it would have felt weird at a time like this. Then she widened her eyes to approximate delight and offered her own bit of stalling: 'It's wonderful about Obama, isn't it?'

He agreed with her less exuberantly than she'd expected. 'Yeah . . . pretty amazing.'

'But?'

'C'mon . . . it was 'Yes, We Can' followed by 'No, You Can't.' '

'Oh you mean . . . the proposition?' She knew how clumsy this sounded the moment she said it, but she couldn't remember the number of the damn proposition and she didn't want to sound disinterested. 'What a heartbreak that was.'

'More like a rat-fuck.'

'I should have mentioned that first. I've just been so preoccupied . . . to put it mildly. It didn't *un*marry you, did it?'

'Who knows? There's gonna be a ruling in the spring.'

Michael and Ben had been married for the third time in August. The first wedding had been performed at City Hall but was thrown out by the state courts. The second had happened at a B&B in Vancouver but was valid only in Canada. The third one Michael had referred to as the 'shotgun marriage' since he and Ben had rushed to say their vows before the November election, when the voters would have their say.

'Well,' she said lamely, 'I'm sure it'll take eventually.'

'Like a flu shot.' He gave her a half-lidded smile.

'If only,' she replied ruefully.

'If only what?'

'There were an inoculation against marriage.'

Michael's brow furrowed. 'Are we still talking about me?'

She took a long slug of her drink, set it down and turned to face him.

'I'm leaving Bob,' she said quietly. 'I've left him.'

Michael nodded slowly, seemingly unsurprised.

Had she been that obvious? She knew her late-night phone calls to Michael had sometimes been protracted rants, but they had mostly been non-specific, focused on the tedium of life in Darien or the tedium of life in general. She had hardly talked about Bob at all. 'How did you know?' she asked.

He shrugged as if it were obvious. 'You never talked about him. Happy people talk about their spouses.'

'Do they?'

'Did you just get bored or something?'

'No . . . well, a little, but I could've dealt with that. He was decent enough most of the time and . . . you know, a good provider.'

'As they say,' Michael added, and Mary Ann could have sworn she detected the shadow of a smirk. She wondered if he saw her as a spoiled suburban house-wife, someone who had long ago sold out everything for a man who could 'provide.'

'So what was the problem?' he asked.

She took another slug of the vodka and set it down. 'I caught him fucking someone.'

'Well . . . that would do it.'

'Someone I know, in fact. My life coach.'

'Your *life coach*? Whatshername, you mean? Calliope?'

She nodded dolefully.

'The woman you want to be when you grow up?'

She winced. 'I don't think I put it *quite* that way, but . . .' She didn't bother to deny it; that was *exactly* the way she had put it, and Michael knew that better than anyone. She had raved about Calliope for hours on end – her womanly wisdom, her impeccable sense of style, her absolute commitment to Mary Ann's fulfillment.

Michael's lip flickered in a way that she recognized all too well.

'Go ahead and laugh,' she told him.

'Sorry . . . it's just a little—'

'No. It's a scream. You think I don't know that? Remember how she was always chastising me for my wudda/cudda/shudda? "Stop with the wudda/cudda/shudda, Mary Ann!" Well, she wudda and she cudda and she did.'

Michael smiled, but his eyes were glassy with sympathy.

'Maybe,' he offered tentatively, 'it was just a one-time thing. Maybe it wasn't even serious.'

She shook her head. 'It was serious. Venice is always serious.'

He frowned. 'You were in Venice?'

'*They* were in Venice. I was in Darien.'

'Then how could you walk in on them?'

'I *didn't* walk in on them. We were Skyping.'

His expression told her nothing.

'You know what that is, right?'

'Of course . . . Oprah uses it. I'm just trying to visualize this.'

'Bob thought it would be nice if we could see each other when he was on the road. He's on a ton of boards all over the world.' She could feel angry tears assembling behind her eyes, but held them back, knowing they'd be better spent later. Michael, meanwhile, was tugging methodically on his silver mustache, already deep in speculation.

'Anyway,' she continued, 'he was in Venice at the Gritti Palace – supposedly meeting with this group of investors – and I had something really important to tell him, so we Skyped for about fifteen minutes, and he blew me a kiss good-night, and the stupid son of a bitch forgot to turn off the Webcam.'

Michael parenthesized his head with his hands, waiting.

'It was kind of sweet at first . . . strangely intimate. He drifted off and I could watch him snoozing on this beautiful hand-painted bed with a gorgeous view of the Grand Canal. Then Calliope came into the room with an armful of Dolce and Gabbana shopping bags and crawled onto the bed with him.'

'Fuck me,' said Michael.

Mary Ann nodded. 'That's more or less what she

said.' She picked up the glass again and polished off the remains with a grimace. 'The sick part is, I couldn't stop looking. I watched until the bitter goddamn end. Like some crummy porno with a flatassed old man pounding away on a Botoxed crack-whore.'

Michael blinked at her. 'His ass is flat? You never told me *that.*'

'Mouse . . . can we stay on the subject.' The ancient nickname just tumbled out of its own accord, now that she was finally coming clean.

He picked up her glass. 'Want another one?'

She shook her head. 'That was enough, thanks.'

He set down the glass and slipped his arm across her shoulder. 'You know . . . I can't say I'm terribly surprised.'

'I can't, either. He hasn't been . . . you know . . . *present* emotionally for several years. The sex wasn't much to speak of, but we weren't that young anymore and I just thought we were entering . . . the cozy stage. I was kind of relieved, to tell you the truth.' She realized too late that she had said this to someone her own age who – to hear him tell it, at least – was having the best sex of his life. She hoped he wouldn't bring that up.

'So what was it you called to tell him?'

It was uncanny, after all these years, how Michael could still find his way so deftly to the epicenter of her pain.

'That I was worried about being pregnant,' she replied.

His mouth opened slightly, and he made a little huffing sound that didn't quite qualify as laughter. 'You're kidding, right?'

His disbelief was understandable, but it still felt like an act of petty cruelty. She couldn't help but sound wounded. 'It does happen, you know, to women my age. It's rare, but it happens. Even when we've been through menopause.'

'So *were* you pregnant? *Are* you?'

'No,' she said quietly. 'It was . . . a false alarm.' What an odd way to put it, she thought, since what she was feeling now was the truest alarm imaginable. An unwanted pregnancy, however inconveniently late in life, paled in comparison.

'But why would you even think you were—'

'I was bleeding, Mouse. I thought I was getting my period again.'

The room was so incredibly still that she could hear, from somewhere in Michael and Ben's kitchen, the sound of a dripping faucet. Or more likely one of those aerated water bowls for dogs, given the way these guys seemed to dote on their Labradoodle.

When she finally spoke, it might have been someone else.

'I have uterine cancer.'

After a moment, Michael just said: 'Shit.'

'I know this isn't fair to you, Mouse. There was just

no one else I could tell. Darien's too much of a hornet's nest and—'

'Sweetie.' Michael slipped his arm across her shoulder, trying to pull her closer, but she felt herself resisting. She still wasn't ready to collapse yet. He sensed this and released her after a squeeze or two. 'Bob doesn't know, then?'

She shook her head. 'He's probably still freaked that I might be pregnant.'

'Shouldn't you tell him—?'

'God, no.'

'He hasn't come home yet, I take it?'

'No.'

Now she was wondering if Bob and Calliope were still at the Gritti or if they'd taken their act to some other romantic venue, someplace to the south, maybe, sunny and by the sea. If only she had muted the Skype – or just turned the damned thing off – as soon as she had seen what was happening. Now, for the rest of her days, she would have to live with those voices, gruff with lust, then oh-so-achingly tender, voices that were already cutting into her like knives when that clueless young doctor told her the news.

She turned and looked at her old friend.

'Mouse, if you can't do this, just say so.'

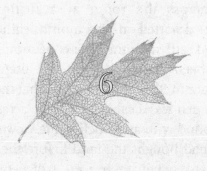

Not To Be Alone

Normally, with groceries in the car, Ben would have headed straight home, but he wasn't sure how much time Michael needed with Mary Ann, and he didn't relish the thought of walking in on whatever drama was unfolding. So he headed over to his workshop on Norfolk Street and finished staining a stair-step *tansu* that was slated for delivery on Monday. Roman, as usual, was thrilled to be there, feverishly prowling the shop for the mice that were known to live behind the walls. The place had once been an appliance repair shop, so even with the addition of whitewash and fiberglass skylights, it hovered on the funky side of dilapidated. Ben loved it, though, loved its rich aromas of cedar dust and linseed oil and the quiet afternoons he spent here, alone with his craft.

As he brushed the stain onto the *tansu*, he gazed wistfully across the room at a rustic fireplace surround he'd started on nine months earlier. He and Michael had settled on the pine-cone motif, since the piece had been intended – was *still* intended – for their fireplace in Pinyon City. Except that there *was* no fireplace, much less a cabin; just three acres of rocky, sloping ground with an unbelievable view of a Sierra range. He had bought the land before the economy began to tank, when there were still people in the market for museum-grade furniture. He'd envisioned their own secret Eden, where Michael could grow old in the bosom of nature and he, Ben, could have ready access to snowboarding. He'd pictured rocking chairs on the deck and hikes up the canyon with Roman and occasional trips into Pinyon City for drinks at the corner saloon.

For the moment, of course, building *anything* was out of the question, since Ben could barely manage the mortgage on the land. Michael was in similar straits – still paying the mortgage on the city house – and his shoulder was threatening to put him out of commission for a while. There were hopes that this new administration might be able to fix the economy, but even the most optimistic observers believed that it would take a while – years, even. All things considered, not a time to go further into debt.

Still, there was no reason they couldn't enjoy the place now, cabin or no cabin. They could pitch a tent there (at least in the summertime) and wake up beneath the pines with the scent of sage in their nostrils. Michael, of course, could get grumpy as hell on camping trips, but that was mostly at public campgrounds where the crowds made him noticeably misanthropic. 'I didn't come to the wilderness,' he had once announced a little loudly at a campground in New Mexico, 'for the chance to shower with America.'

But this would be different. This would be their own turf, where they could stake a sort of spiritual claim just by spending some time there. As for showering, they could do that down the road at the state park, preferably at a time when America wasn't around. The important thing was to *be on that land*, leave their mark. Burn a little sage, maybe, make a little love. The property wasn't visible from the access road, so maybe they could find a talisman here in the city – a big stone raven or a rusty iron Quan Yen – that they could plant there on the mountainside as proof of their intentions, even when they weren't around. He loved the idea of finding it there every time they came back.

Pinyon City had become their version of the future. 'We'll get that for Pinyon City,' they would say when they spotted a woolen blanket in a garage sale or a set of rugged dinnerware, and they would buy that thing, whatever it was, and stuff it into the coat closet to await its eventual alpine destiny. Some of these items had been absorbed by the city house, like the rare Indian basket that Michael surprised Ben with on his birthday. Michael had tracked it down on the Internet, ordering it from a private collector in Reno. Roughly the size of a grapefruit, it was woven from pine needles and red gum – a reliable indicator that its maker had lived not far from their homestead-to-be. They had already picked the very spot it would occupy on the mantelpiece that Ben was building. It would have made it there, too – a perfect symbol of their reverence for the land and its culture – had they not displayed it on the coffee table in full view of a teething Labradoodle.

Ben stayed at the workshop until the skylights turned dove-gray with dusk. He drove home through the Mission, where the traffic was predictably sluggish and snarled, then double-parked at a boutique pet shop in the Castro to pick up a brand of organic dog food they didn't carry at Delano's. By the time he reached Noe Hill, the sky was already doing its crazy purple thing. He stopped at the gate to admire it, then studied the house with a sense of palpable apprehension. Had she left or were they still in the thick of it?

Roman led the way, dragging Ben on the leash, delirious at the thought of an imminent reunion. Michael, as it happened, was sitting on the sofa, apparently alone, rummaging through a box of old snapshots. The dog had been trained not to jump on his masters, so he did a little river dance instead, hopping on his back legs in an unashamed exhibition of his poodle ancestry. 'That's right,' said Ben. 'There's Dad. Give Dad a kiss.' This was already a ritual with them; the dog always got the first kiss.

Ben leaned down and pecked Michael's mouth, which tasted of pot smoke, despite Michael's cherished belief that his vaporizer had magically eliminated all that. He worried sometimes that Michael smoked too much. There were days when he came home and found his husband too buzzed and chatty to connect with. At such moments Michael could lose his train of thought completely, though he usually tried to cover it up. What would happen, Ben wondered, when this chemical forgetfulness merged with the ordinary sort that comes with aging? Unless, of course, this *was* the ordinary sort.

He sat down next to Michael and leaned his head against his shoulder.

'Is Mary Ann—?'

'Back at her hotel,' said Michael.

'Oh.' Ben made an effort at sounding sincere. 'Sorry I didn't get to say hello.'

Michael wasn't buying it, of course. 'I wish you liked her more.'

'I don't *dis*like her. She's just . . . kind of a mess, and . . . it gets to be too much sometimes.'

'In what way?'

'C'mon. She calls here three or four times a week.'

'That was just *last* week.'

'No, it wasn't. It's been going on for ages, and you're on the phone for hours sometimes. It feels like she's living with us, Michael.' When his husband said nothing in response, Ben added: 'Not to sound jealous or anything.'

Michael lifted his head and planted a peck on Ben's shoulder before righting himself with a grunt. 'We just have a history, you know. We've been through a lot of shit together. I can't just cut that off.'

'I'm not asking you to.'

'I know that.'

'So what's going on with her?'

Michael released a resonant sigh. 'She has cancer. That's why she's here. She's having a hysterectomy.'

Ben scrambled for the right thing to say. There was plenty of reason for sympathy, of course, but he found himself weighing his words with miserly care, wary of what was coming next. 'Why isn't she having it . . . closer to home?'

'She's leaving Bob. She doesn't want to be any-where near home.'

'She's leaving him now? Shouldn't she at least wait until she's—'

'She caught him fucking somebody. She saw the whole thing on Skype. She's humiliated and hear-broken and scared shitless about the cancer. She's just trying to take care of herself right now. So she got the fuck out of there.'

Ben knew better, of course, but he couldn't help fixating on entirely the wrong part of that explanation: 'How do you see that on Skype?'

'Sweetie . . .' Michael laid his hand tentatively on Ben's leg before taking the leap. 'She asked if she could stay in the cottage.'

Ben nodded slowly, his suspicions confirmed.

'It wasn't easy for her to ask,' Michael added. 'More than anything . . . she doesn't want to invade our privacy.'

Ben adopted a tone that he hoped would sound compassionate yet practical. 'Then why not take a hotel or rent a condo? She's not, you know . . . hurting for cash. The cottage is barely big enough for that bed, and . . . she'll need her own privacy, won't she?'

'She needs not to be alone, Ben. That's what she needs. She doesn't have a home anymore.'

Ben knew already there was no point in resisting. He had no deep sentimental connection to Mary Ann, but Michael's conscience – and, yes, Ben's own – made this huge inconvenience inevitable. 'How long does she want to stay?' he asked.

Michael shrugged. 'The surgery is in two weeks, so . . . I guess at least that long and . . . a little bit longer.'

'Will the surgery take care of it? The cancer, I mean?'

'They won't know until they . . . get in there.'

Ben laid his hand on Michael's knee, signaling the

end of the discussion, then stood up. 'Call her, then
. . . unless you've already agreed to it.'

His husband shook his head. 'I was waiting to hear
from you.'

That had to be less than the truth, but Ben
appreciated the effort.

While Michael was in the bedroom talking to Mary Ann
on his cell phone, Ben gave the cottage a once-over in
preparation for her arrival. The sheets on the bed had
not been changed since some friends from Nevada City
had crashed there over Halloween, so there were still
traces of green Hulk makeup on the pillowcase.

Ben stripped the bed, then hauled everything to the
laundry room before tackling the cramped cottage
bathroom. The toilet and sink were relatively clean,
but the floor of the fiberglass shower stall was tinted
the same lurid green as the pillowcase. He got on his
knees and scrubbed it ferociously – a little harder
than needed, in fact – while he fretted over the sea
change that would soon be coming to their domestic
life. He valued their daily rituals and hard-earned
independence and, frankly, didn't want them fucked
with. He knew that was selfish, and that charity, in
this case, literally began at home, but he couldn't
shake the ungenerous feeling that someone had just
stolen his husband.

Back at the house, he found Michael stuffing the
sheets into the washer.

'I'll get that,' Ben told him, already trying to atone for his thoughts.

'That's okay. I've got it.'

'If you need Clorox, it's on the top shelf.'

'Great.'

'Where is that fancy goat soap the two Susies gave us for Christmas last year? I thought we could put it in her bathroom.'

Michael turned and gave him a sleepy, appreciative stoner smile.

That night, after catching two inscrutable episodes of *Lost* on Apple TV, they turned in earlier than usual, leaving the lights on for a while as they scratched Roman's belly in unison. The dog was sprawled between them, dark limbs flopping, as big and goofy as a chimpanzee. For Ben, the moment had a wistful quality, since this cozy family unit would be altered dramatically come morning, when their guest would return with her expensive luggage. There was no point in kidding himself; he would just have to make the best of it and accept this altered reality as something that mattered to Michael.

'Where did you meet her again?' Ben asked, trying to take an interest. 'At Anna's apartment house?'

'Mmm. Well . . . actually . . . the first time was at the Marina Safeway. She tried to pick up a boyfriend of mine.'

Ben wrinkled his nose. 'While you were there?'

'I was . . . you know, somewhere else in the store. She looked crushed when I showed up, poor thing. She had her heart set on him.'

'Was she just clueless? Or was he really butch?'

'Butcher than me, you mean?' Michael grinned. 'Still is, to tell you the truth. He was a Marine recruiter. I saw him at the Alameda Flea Market a few years back. He still looks pretty good. Totally your type. Big ol' furry chest.'

Ben was touched when Michael made the effort to acknowledge his 'type.' He would even do it on the street sometimes when a burly daddy passed their field of vision, Michael muttering a sultry 'ten o'clock' under his breath until Ben spotted the party in question. Since these men were rarely of interest to Michael – he was drawn to the younger and smoother, like Ben – the gesture was all the more impressive. He was like a beachcomber collecting shells for his beloved, when the shells meant nothing to him.

Which was not to say that Michael couldn't be jealous. Once, they ran into a playmate of Ben's on a trip to P-town. Ben found his husband sulking like a teenager in bed that night, nursing a corrosive dread of abandonment that could only be assuaged by Ben's patient insistence that forever, fuck it, meant forever. Their twenty-one-year age difference had been one of the nicer spices in their libidinal stew, but age itself could be a source of panic for Michael.

Sometimes, in fact, Ben wondered if Michael's generous daddy-spotting was just his own way of tagging and releasing his fears.

Ben scooched closer, sandwiching Roman between them as he stroked Michael's arm, soothing two creatures at once. 'Didn't it bother you when she moved away?'

'What do you mean?'

'You thought you were dying, right? *She* thought you were dying.'

'It was complicated, babe. She and Brian were on the rocks, and . . . she got this job offer in New York . . . and she'd already watched Jon die in the worst kind of way . . . and she couldn't handle going through that again.'

'So she ran away.'

Michael shrugged. 'Sort of.'

'Seems like a pattern.'

Michael's stony silence showed Ben he had gone too far, so he changed his tone – and the subject. 'She had a TV show here, right? Was she famous?'

'Oh, yeah. Her face was on the side of buses. She had a morning talk show. Sort of like Oprah, but . . . you know . . . *local*.'

Ben noticed that Michael had italicized the last word with a telltale widening of the eyes. 'Not great, huh?'

'It was okay. She was fine, but the show could be a little lame. You know, cooking segments and D-list celebrities. I don't blame her for wanting something more.'

'Which didn't happen in New York, I take it?'

'The cable channel folded before they could get the show off the ground. She was cut adrift and ended up doing infomercials and shit. Then she worked for a fancy party planner, and that's where she met her husband, apparently. At a party.'

And life got a lot easier, thought Ben.

'I don't think she married him for the money,' Michael added clairvoyantly. 'I think she loved him. She loved his son, too. She helped raise him.'

'Where is he now? The son.'

'At NYU. Freshman year. She was already feeling like an empty nester when the Skype thing happened.'

It was an opening, but Ben didn't take it; he could get the details later when the time was right. Instead, he proposed that they take Mary Ann to Pinyon City, where the crisp air and snowcapped peaks might lift her spirits before the surgery – or maybe even help with her recuperation. They could rent their usual house by the river and pay a ceremonial visit to their property. Assuming, of course, she would want to.

'I think she'd love it,' said Michael, who, like Ben, believed Pinyon City could fix anything.

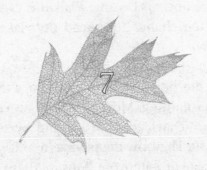

Somebody to Hang With

'So where goes my wandering boy tonight?'

Jake was pulling on his flight jacket at the door when Anna asked the question. He knew that 'wandering boy' was just one of her old-school expressions, but it still made him feel irresponsible. Anna let him live there for nothing, even paid him for his help sometimes, so he was always wondering if he was living up to his side of the deal. 'I'll be on my cell,' he said reassuringly. 'I can be home in no time.'

'Don't be silly, dear. I was just being nosy.' Anna cupped her hand against his beard and gazed intently – embarrassingly – into his eyes. 'Marguerite and Selina have invited me up for a nice Italian dinner. I'm well taken care of.' The upstairs neighbors had been, until recently, the flatmates of Jake and Anna, so, when the upstairs became available, everyone had welcomed the chance to spread out. Jake certainly had, anyway.

It wouldn't have killed him to tell Anna where he was going, but he knew from experience that it took too much explaining. Most old-time San Franciscans – his boss Michael, for one – could be really rude about Pier 39. They saw the place as a tourist trap and a serious waste of waterfront. Most of them had never even been there, either, never seen what a good time it could be. They didn't know shit about the fire jugglers or the cool aquarium or the funny 'Gumpisms' scrawled on the tables at Bubba Gump's Shrimp Company. They called it corny, most of them, without ever having seen it.

Jake found Pier 39 a welcome relief from the Castro. The ghetto, for all its acceptance and security, made him feel like all eyes were upon him, since, for the most part, they *were*. If they weren't sizing him up for sex, they were judging his believability or resenting him for denying the honest butch dyke they thought he should be. At Pier 39 Jake was just another guy in the crowd. His manhood could be casual there, an easy assumption shared by everyone. It was like being back in Tulsa at the mall – only safer.

And Jake had a major thing going with the sea lions. On evenings like this he would ride his bike all the way down Market Street to the Embarcadero just to grab an hour with those jokesters at the pier. Their raucous barking calmed his fears like no other music, and there were more of them now than he'd seen all year, since winter brought more herring. Hundreds of sea lions were sprawled on the wooden rafts provided for their comfort, while the humans watched from the rail, making noises of their own.

'Oooh . . . look at that fat one!'

'Is that one a girl or a boy, Mommy?'

'Awesome! He just knocked that other one into the water!'

'Aren't they supposed to be at Seal Rock?'

The last question had come from a round-faced young blond guy in a red hoodie, standing next to Jake. It was just one of those things that people said in a crowd, mostly hoping to feel part of the crowd, expecting an answer from anyone or no one.

'They used to be out there,' Jake answered, 'but they started hauling out here in 1989.'

The guy turned to him and frowned. 'Hauling what out?'

'That's what they call it. Hauling out. What they're doing right now. Getting out of the water so they can . . . you know, breed and all.'

'Oh.'

'Some people think the earthquake drove them into the bay, but there were already a few of them here by then. They were probably just getting away from their predators, since Orcas and Great

Whites don't come in this far. They took over a dock that used to be here, so it got kinda testy for a while.'

'Why?'

'Look at 'em. They're ginormous. And stinky. And dangerous if you get in their way. Some of the old dudes weigh almost a thousand pounds.'

The blond kept his eyes on the raft, where, in the deepening twilight, the sea lions were stacked on top of each other like enormous sacks of flour.

'So cool,' he said reverently.

'Word,' replied Jake.

The next time he saw the guy, Jake was down the pier in the left-handed store buying a pocket spiral notebook. He wasn't consistently left-handed, so he didn't need most of the things they sold, even their super-cool Bahco pruning shears. Writing was pretty much the only thing he couldn't do right-handed, and since he liked to take notes on the job (like his hero, Capability Brown), he'd always hated those left-handed spirals. The clerk was putting the notebook in a bag when Red Hoodie got in line behind him.

'Dude,' he said pleasantly, catching Jake's eye.

'Oh . . . hey.'

'That for you?'

'Who else?'

'Awright!' The guy held up his hand for a high five, so Jake followed through in what he took to be a moment of left-handed brotherhood. As a man, he had never before high-fived with a guy. He would have been too embarrassed to initiate it himself, and no one else had ever offered, maybe because Jake was shorter than most guys and it would probably have looked stupid. This guy was short himself, so they could pull it off.

'What did you get?' Jake asked.

'Just some scissors.' He held them up with a Boy Scout smile. 'I had to cut some poster paper last week and got me some serious blisters.'

Jake nodded. 'You a teacher or something?'

'Nah . . . it was just for . . . a project.' He looked uncomfortable as his eyes darted around the store. Jake wondered if he was seriously into crafts or something and too embarrassed to admit it. 'This place is cool,' said the guy.

Jake nodded. 'The first of its kind in the world.'

'Where are the other ones?'

'Fuck if I know, dude.'

He had expected to get a laugh, but the guy just flinched and lost his smile for a moment. 'We sure don't have 'em back home,' he said, recovering. 'I can tell you that much.' He handed a $20 bill to the clerk, waited for the change, and thanked her nicely. 'Where's good to eat around here?'

For a moment Jake didn't realize that the question was directed to him. 'Oh . . . well . . . I like Bubba Gump's, but that's kinda for special occasions. I usually just get something at the Pier Market and eat

it on a bench somewhere. They got good crab sandwiches. The chowder's pretty good, too.'

'Could you show me?'

'Sure,' said Jake. 'I'm goin' there anyway.'

Though neither of them had suggested it, they ended
up eating together.

They had waited in line together, so it had just
made sense to look for a bench together. They found
one at the edge of the performance area and sat on
either end of it, eating their crab sandwiches while
they watched a tall, skinny clown with a monkey
puppet.

'He's really dope,' said the blond kid.

'Yeah. He is.'

The kid extended his hand. 'I'm Jonah, by the way.'

'Jake.'

'My girlfriend would love this. She's big on clowns.'

'Oh yeah? You should bring her here some time.'

Jonah shook his head. 'She's back at home. I'm just
here for . . . work.'

'Missin' her, huh?'

'Oh . . . man. A month is too long.'

Jake could see the raw truth of this in Jonah's face.

'It's the best thing in the world,' Jonah added.
'Loving a girl like that.'

There was nothing more to be said about that –
especially on Jake's part – so he underscored the
sentiment with a respectful silence.

Jonah, meanwhile, seemed to have embarrassed himself.

He tossed his sandwich wrapper in a can and looked out at the bay for an easy way to change the subject.

'So what's that island out there?'

Jake grinned. 'That's no island, dude. That's a motorized vessel.'

'C'mon. It's got palm trees and a beach . . .'

'I wouldn't lie to you, man.'

'. . . and a lighthouse! I'm a country boy but—'

'No, dude, I swear. This wack boat builder built it back in the seventies. He's parked the thing all over the bay. They call it Forbes Island.'

Jonah snorted. 'Because it's an island!'

'No, because Mr. Forbes built it. Or Forbes Somebody, I forget. They run it as a restaurant now. You eat under the water and look out through port-holes at the fish.'

'You've seen this yourself?'

Jake shrugged. 'I YouTubed it.'

'How do you get out there? Or does it come to you?'

'There's a shuttle. It leaves from the dock down here.'

'We gotta do this!'

'Dude, we just ate.'

'I mean some other day. If you want to, I mean. I've got another week here. I could use somebody to hang with.'

Even before his mention of the girlfriend, Jake had decided that Jonah wasn't gay. There was something in his eyes – or maybe a lack of something – that made him seem unavailable. For Jake this was as much a relief as a disappointment, since the prospect of sex always brought with it the need for full disclosure. Besides, there was something more valuable to be gained here: a brotherly bond with another guy that took for granted their common masculinity. He had longed for such a friendship when he was a teenager in Tulsa, but the visuals had made it impossible. Now, he had a shot at it.

'What the hell,' he said, clapping Jonah on the shoulder. 'You're on.'

Anna was sitting up with a book when Jake returned. She was wearing her green satin kimono – the one with the coffee stains that Jake had tried like hell to get out. The lamplight made a little halo around her head. He wondered how long she'd been there.

'How was dinner?' he asked.

She looked up from her book. 'Oh . . . my dear. It was lovely. Marguerite made . . . what do you call them?'

Jake shrugged. She was always asking shit like this.

'Oh, you know . . . those little potato dumplings . . .'

'Au gratin.'

'No . . . . they're Italian. You know.'

80

'Nucky? I can't pronounce it—'

'Yes, yes . . . close enough.' Anna smiled. 'That's what they were.' She took off her purple reading glasses and folded them up, tucking them efficiently into the sleeve of her kimono. 'How was your evening, dear?'

Jake surprised himself by coming clean: 'I met somebody.'

'Ah.' It was amazing how much she could pack into that sound.

'It's not like that.'

'I see.' She switched off the lamp to relieve her eyes. 'Then what is it like?'

'Who the hell knows? It's no big whoop. We're just gonna eat out on Forbes Island.'

'Should I know where that is?'

'It's this . . . floating island thing next to Pier 39.'

She nodded slowly, wordlessly, at the mention of the dreaded tourist trap. 'Well,' she said finally. 'That side of town can be lovely.'

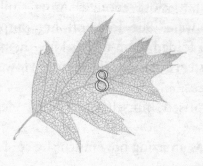

Signing

Shawna was dawdling over a plate of fried artichoke hearts at Pier 23 Café, a funky waterfront roadhouse she had loved ever since her dad took her there for her thirteenth birthday. These days, it was a handy waiting room when Otto had a gig at Pier 39. She could avoid the tourists, have a beer or two, and be pleasantly pissed by the time her inamorato was done with his clowning. Otto enjoyed the walk from Pier 39 – the release it offered from all those people – and Shawna liked how she felt (not to mention how she looked) amid the film-noir grittiness of the café. Tonight, as a freighter droned dolefully on the black satin bay, she was glad she hadn't cut her Bettie bangs just yet.

'Excuse me, I know you must hate this . . .'

Shawna looked up to find what she expected: a typical fan of her blog – early twenties, male, slightly geeky – approaching her with extreme care, as if she were a skittish creature in a forest. Or maybe some bad-ass dominatrix.

'You're Grrrl on the Loose, right?'

She smiled, giving her stock answer: 'That's the blog, not me.'

'Good title, though.'

'I don't know. Those three *r*s are getting tired, aren't they? I may have to put them to bed.' She gave him a friendly, jaundiced glance. 'Hope you'll still read me.'

'My girlfriend loved your piece on eco-friendly sex toys. This is her.' He pulled the poor woman forward to present her. 'You friended her on Facebook.'

'Ah . . . right.' *You and five thousand other people*, she thought as she shook the woman's hand. 'Nice to see you in the flesh.'

The couple laughed nervously, as though Shawna's off-handed response had been riddled with innuendo. Why did they always expect her to be dirty? She prided herself on writing about sex in a healthy, joyful, unapologetic way, but people were determined to cast her as the Duchess of Smut. That was still on her mind when Otto strode into the café. As she waved him down, an idea was assembling in her head.

'That for me?' he asked, eyeing the beer she'd bought for him.

'If you play your cards right.'

He grinned and gulped half the glass before sitting down.

'How were the hordes?' she asked.

'Hordey.' He took off his backpack – the one that held the monkey puppet and some of his clothes – and set it on the floor beside him. He'd made an effort to clean up, but there were still traces of clown white in his smile lines, and his big, honey-colored mane was a matted, scraggly mess. 'Picked up some cash, though.'

'Cool.'

Otto snatched an artichoke heart and popped it into his mouth.

'You wanna order something?' she asked.

He shook his head. 'I had a burger at the pier. Mostly I wanna go back to your place and cuddle the fuck out of you.'

'Okay.' She smiled crookedly, loving the sentiment in spite of his wording. 'I wanna ask you something first.'

'Shoot.'

'You know how lately I've been sort of disenchanted with the blog?'

'Not really.'

'Well . . . I have. I think it's kinda run its course. I mean, I think I've done some good, but I'm tired of being Debbie Dildo, you know?'

Otto shrugged. 'You're good at it.'

'Thanks, but . . . it gets to be limiting after a while. I think I wanna open it up, talk about life in general . . . you know, the petty shit and the big issues we all have to deal with. Something substantive. I think my readers would follow me, and I would really—'

'Go for it. What's stopping you?'

'Well . . . I need you to tell me it's okay.'

'Why?'

'Because I might be writing about us. In part, at least.'

'Oh.' A cloud passed over his face. 'Like . . . using my name and all?'

'Yeah, unless . . .' She decided to keep it light. 'You're not wanted for something in ten states, are you?'

He wouldn't pick up on the gag. 'I like my privacy, Shawna. I love what we have, but . . . I don't know about sharing it with strangers.'

'You just performed on a pier with a ton of strangers.'

'No,' he said quietly. 'That was Ottokar. Or Sammy sometimes. But it wasn't me. That's why I'm able to do it.'

That made sense, in a way, but she suspected his fears ran deeper than that. 'I wouldn't be writing about our sex life,' she said. 'I wouldn't be as . . . specific as—'

'It's not that.'

'Then what?' She was starting to feel hurt, and, worse yet, sounding that way. 'Are we just not . . . that serious?'

Otto saw her mortification and grabbed her hand across the table. 'Listen, ladylove . . . if we weren't serious I wouldn't give a shit *what* you put in that blog. I just don't want to feel self-conscious about what we have. I don't want to be weighing my words all the time. I don't want to think of us as . . . you know . . . material.'

Anyone else who'd called her 'ladylove' would have received, at the very least, a derisive snort, but Shawna found it sort of sweet. It was possible Otto had picked up that expression the summer he worked as a knight at the Renaissance Pleasure Faire, but she preferred to believe it had sprung, freshly minted, from his uncorrupted heart.

She decided not to press him further about the blog. He didn't read it anyway, and they weren't on record as being a couple. She could call him her boo or something similarly vague and still do the kind of writing she wanted to do. He was right about the potential for self-consciousness in such an enterprise. It was better just to let the words flow, as she always had, and let Otto be Otto. The less he knew the better, really.

On the way home to the Mission, they were stopped at a light under the freeway overpass when a homeless woman in a dirty red tracksuit approached the car with a ragged cardboard sign that read YOUR MAMA WOULD GIVE A DAMN. Shawna wondered how well that actually worked, if most people saw their mothers as pillars of generosity and therefore felt inspired to give. It was original, anyway, and it made her smile.

She dug around in her bag for a loose bill, with no success. Otto saw what she was doing and pulled out his wallet. 'Is five enough?'

'Make it twenty,' she said. 'I'll pay you back.'

'She's a junkie. See those sores on her neck.'

'And your point is?'

'I'm just sayin'.'

Shawna rolled down the window and held out the twenty. The woman took it without a word, then pulled up the leg of her sweatpants so she could stash the offering in her sock. Shawna caught a glimpse of putrid gray flesh, a constellation of sores. The woman's face, by contrast, was a fiery red-brown, sun-ravaged and grimy. She looked to be anywhere between thirty and sixty. The awful agelessness of the streets.

'The world is fucked,' the woman announced.

'You got that right, sister.'

The woman cackled, showing broken teeth and rotten gums. 'You got you a man in there?'

'I do,' said Shawna, casting her eyes toward Otto. 'I got me a man in here.'

The woman leaned down and spoke through the window. 'You be nice to her, ya hear?'

Otto looked flustered, so Shawna jumped in: 'He is. He's very nice to me.'

'I had me one for a while.'

'A man, you mean?' Shawna couldn't help grinning. The woman might as well have been talking about a parakeet.

'Yep,' said the woman. 'When I was about your age.'

'Oh, yeah?'

'I was prettier'n you, too.'

'I'm sure you were' was all Shawna could think to say.

'A whole *lot* prettier.'

'Hey, watch it,' Shawna said jovially, 'or I'll take my money back.'

'You do, bitch, and I'll cut you.'

Otto was obviously aghast, but Shawna caught the twinkle lurking deep in the woman's red-rimmed eyes. 'Not if I smack the shit out of you first,' she said.

This elicited another cackle. 'You're all right, kid.'

'I don't know about *that*.'

'Nah. You're my kinda lady. Nothin' scares you, does it?'

It was an interesting question. 'Not the usual things, I guess.'

'Good for you. Us girls gotta be brave.'

'I guess we do, yeah.'

The woman raised her grimy fist in a show of

solidarity with Shawna before trudging farther down the traffic island in search of another handout.

'How does it get that bad?' Shawna asked Otto.

He just shrugged. 'Heroin.'

'That can't be all of it.'

'You'd have to ask her.'

The light changed and Shawna drove away. She felt a shameful rush of relief as the woman grew ever smaller in the rearview mirror. *That's why the homeless beg at stoplights*, she thought. *It's as much for us as it is for them. We're shielded from the horror by glass and steel, and we can make a clean break as soon as the light changes.*

'She was nice,' Shawna offered.

'It's her routine. It's part of signing.'

'Signing?'

'That's what they call it. When they hold out those signs.'

'How do you know that?'

'Because I work the streets, too.'

She snorted. 'The mean streets of Pier 39.'

'She's living for the next fix, so she does what she has to do.'

And we drive on, thought Shawna. *We drive on and do nothing.*

'What's the matter?' asked Otto.

'Nothing. Everything. She said it herself: the world is fucked.'

'You wanna go back? Offer her a hot shower and a place to sleep?'

Otto knew the answer to that already.

'I could write about her,' Shawna said feebly.

Otto gave her a sly sideways smile. 'And who would that help?'

She turned her eyes back to the road. 'Bite me, clown boy.'

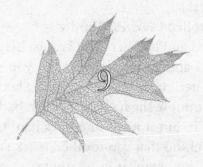

Lady Parts

The cottage seemed even smaller on the inside, which was fine with Mary Ann. The last thing she needed was room for rattling around. She'd had that in spades back in Darien, and that cavern of a house, minus husband and stepson, only amplified her despair. She wanted to feel cozy now – confined, even – and here, in this doll's house of a room, with the guys just across the garden, she could be alone but not alone.

She was touched to see how they'd prepared for her arrival: a Mason jar of pink tea roses by the bed and a little wooden crate of artisanal goat soap on the dresser. There was even a Quan Yin – a jade one with a sweet smile – though that might have always been

91

there. She set down her suitcase with an appreciative sigh. 'Perfect.'

Michael rolled his eyes. 'Hardly.'

She turned and laid her head against his chest. 'No, Mouse . . . I appreciate it more than you can know.' He patted her shoulder awkwardly. She wondered how much trouble she had caused. Ben had *seemed* all right about it, but it was sometimes hard to read the emotions behind that gap-toothed Huck Finn smile.

'You can put your suitcase there,' Michael said, indicating the only patch of unoccupied floor in the room. 'And there's a rod in the bathroom where you can hang stuff. If there's not enough room, let me know. We can hang it in the house.'

She assured him she was fine, that she planned to live as simply as possible during her stay, that all she needed was access to their washer and dryer and maybe a shelf in their refrigerator. It felt good, actually, to pare down her life like this.

'We're vegetarian these days,' Michael told her.

'You *are*? Since when?'

'Six weeks, maybe.'

'You never mentioned it.'

He shrugged. 'I don't wanna be an asshole about it.'

As long as she'd known him, Michael had been a bacon-double-cheeseburger kind of guy. This had to be Ben's influence. 'Do you just . . . disapprove of meat?'

'It disapproves of me. I asked Ben to take me to this

Brazilian steakhouse on Market Street for my birth-day, and we ate, like, half a barnyard – cows, chickens, pigs, *and* their internal organs – and three days later I had a major attack of gout.'

'Gout?' The word sounded so archaic. 'Like Henry the Eighth?'

'Yeah . . . most of those bloated old British kings. And Mel Brooks, for God's sake! At least that's what Wikipedia says. I'm in elegant company.'

She smiled. 'How does it . . . you know, manifest itself?'

'Mine was in my big toe. It felt like broken glass under the skin. It hurt whenever my toe touched the sheet. So I figured it was time to change my diet.'

'I remember when you ate nothing *but* meat for years. Meat and cheese and strawberries with heavy cream.'

'The Atkins Diet,' said Michael. 'The gateway to gout. The thing is, I was already starting to get grossed out by the idea of animal flesh. I was chopping chicken breasts into smaller and smaller pieces. And I saw this documentary where they were prodding a half-dead cow with a forklift, and it just revolted me. So . . . I thought I should listen to that. Plus Ben and I both have high cholesterol, so vegan made sense.'

'*Vegan?* I thought you said vegetarian?'

'Ben's doing vegan. I have to have my cheese. And I buy those cartons of egg whites. We're not fanatical about it. We can stock up on meat for you, if that's what you'd like. We can go to Trader Joe's together and get what you need.'

She wasn't prepared to commit to vegetarianism, even briefly, so she kept it vague. 'You know me. I'm happy with my yogurt and half a sandwich.'

'That's why you're still so skinny and pretty.'

It was such a lovely thing to say, and there was really no way to keep the tears back. 'I'm sorry,' she said, wiping her eyes. 'I swear it won't be like this.'

'Oh, c'mon.'

'What?'

'Of course it's gonna be like this. We're saying good-bye to your uterus. We'll need a few tears for that if we're gonna have a proper send-off.'

He had summed up the situation with his usual charming candor, but it was the sound of 'we' that made her terrible burden suddenly seem lighter. *We'll need a few tears for that.* She had almost forgotten the sweet solace of the first-person plural.

She kept things light to keep from crying again. 'Don't tell me there's a ritual or something.'

'For what?'

'Sending off your uterus.'

He rolled his eyes. 'Yeah, twelve crones in purple robes smear your body with patchouli oil and dance the sacred Farewell Womb Dance. Jesus, woman!'

She laughed. 'Well, you never know. Not around here.'

'You've been in Connecticut too long.'

'Tell me about it.' She pecked him on the cheek. 'Go to work, Mouse. I'm gonna settle in. Maybe take a nap.' She was already savoring the thought of snoozing on those sun-warmed sheets while hummingbirds idled in the window.

'I left the house open,' Michael added, 'in case you wanna hang out there. Watch TV, read a book or something. Just lock up if you decide to head out. You know the neighborhood. There's shopping in both directions . . . down on 24th or the Castro.' He paused, considering something. 'You're okay with walking, right?'

She nodded. 'I'm not feeling anything so far . . . if that's what you mean.'

'I guess that *is* what I meant.' He fell tellingly silent for a moment. 'So you've got the doctor lined up and all?'

'I did. I mean . . . my doctor in Darien hooked me up with somebody at Mount Zion but . . . he's not gonna work out.'

'Why not?'

She shrugged. 'He's got a penis.'

Michael absorbed that. 'You want a lady handling the lady parts.'

'Is that silly?'

'Not at all. I totally get it.'

She'd felt sure he would say that, but it helped to hear it anyway. 'I thought I might call DeDe and D'or,' she told him. 'See if they can recommend somebody.'

'I dunno.' A mischievous glint came into his eye. 'That could very well involve twelve crones in purple with patchouli oil.'

'C'mon, Mouse. They're the least New-Agey lesbians I know.'

'How many lesbians do you know these days?'

He had always loved teasing her like this, making her seem more out of it than she actually was. It was part of their ancient ritual. 'We have lesbians in Darien,' she told him. 'There's one on the board of the country club. She's a Bush Republican.'

He smirked. 'So to speak.'

To her amazement, she heard herself giggling. Michael could still do that for her, she realized, still make her feel that giddy release. For a fleeting moment, they might have been back at Barbary Lane, holed up together in his room on a dateless Saturday night, wisecracking their troubles away. And how minuscule those troubles had been.

Michael pecked her on the cheek. 'I'm outta here.'

'Go. Make pretty things grow.'

As he crossed the doorstep he pulled out the key and handed it to her with a decidedly tentative look. 'Maybe I shouldn't bring this up.'

She felt an instant tightening in her belly. 'Go ahead.'

'You know Shawna's back from New York, right?'

Mary Ann had guessed as much from Shawna's Web site, where recent entries had focused on San

Francisco. She avoided Shawna's blog, for the most part, since she was put off by the material. The last time she checked, Shawna was writing about a high-end spa somewhere back East that offered sperm facials to its clients. (And not in the crude vernacular sense, either – actual facials made of sperm from who-the-hell-knows-where.) Mary Ann didn't need this information from anyone, much less from the only Shawna she had ever known, the little girl with whom she'd sing along to Billy Joel on the drive home from Presidio Hill School. It was too much for her. She was far from being a prude; she just couldn't make the trip from there to here.

And it worried her sometimes that Shawna might suddenly decide to get personal in the blog. There was already an autobiographical element to her work, and sooner or later she would get around to her rocky childhood and the selfish adoptive mother who left when she was five. Shawna saw herself as an artist, and that's what artists did.

'I had a feeling she was here,' she told Michael.

'Do you want me to say anything about . . . what's going on with you?'

'No . . . please. I don't want her to feel she has to do anything.' She flashed on the hideously uncomfortable afternoon she had spent with Shawna in Darien. Shawna had taken the train from the city and had made an earnest effort at bridging the gap, but they had both begun to squirm before the day was over.

They were different people with different histories and no valid reason, biological or otherwise, to relate to each other.

'Should I tell Anna?'

'I'd rather you not tell anyone, Mouse. Not until it's over, anyway.'

'No problem. She probably knows you're here, though.'

'Why?'

'Because Jake already knows . . . and Jake rooms with Anna.'

'Oh . . . right.' *This town*, she thought, *this tiny little town*.

'I'll keep the details quiet, though.'

'Thanks, Mouse.'

'Get some rest. I'll be back by six. Ben wants to cook for us.'

She watched him shamble across the garden to his truck, a portly silver-haired figure in faded green overalls, the closest thing she had to a knight in shining armor.

She asked herself, in light of her history, if she was once again running to a man for her salvation, but the question evaporated almost as soon as it materialized.

After unpacking, she took a quick shower, put on her pajamas and crawled into bed, sleeping lightly for an hour or so, drifting in and out of consciousness to the white noise of lawn mowers and distant car alarms. There were moments, as she lay still like that, when she thought she could feel something pernicious stirring inside of her, announcing its presence. The doctor had said she might not feel anything prior to the surgery, so this could well be a product of her own neurosis, a morbid variation on hysterical pregnancy.

Or not.

She recognized the irony of equating her cancer to a pregnancy, since women who had never given birth were more likely to contract the disease. *Use it or lose it* was the phrase that had popped into her mind when the doctor explained this to her, though she hadn't dared say it out loud. It was too on the nose, too terribly true, to be spoken.

It would be easy enough to blame her childlessness on Brian, her first husband, since his sperm, for some reason, wasn't capable of making babies, but the truth was she had never felt the urge to raise a child. Her temperament just wasn't suited for it, and (to her credit, she thought) she had admitted that limitation more freely than most women. If her old high school friend Connie hadn't died giving birth to Shawna, Mary Ann could have passed up motherhood altogether and been none the worse for it. But Brian was over the moon about this freak shot at fatherhood, so she had bowed to his dream.

Restless now, she got out of bed and went to the toilet. She ordered herself not to look at her pee but found herself doing so anyway. There was a wriggly thread of red running through it, like a worm embedded in amber. She shuddered and shucked off her pajamas, heading straight to the shower again, as if she could just wash it away. She was sorely ignorant about all of this, and that ignorance, she realized, had been her legacy.

In her mother's day, a hysterectomy had been an act of stealth, a 'woman's problem' to be whispered about, and then, of course, only among women. To Mary Ann the very sound of the word – hisssterectomy – had suggested a secret uttered under the breath. There was shame involved when a woman lost her God-given purpose in life, so (even after having two kids) Mary Ann's mom had told everyone she knew that she was visiting her older sister in Baltimore. Mary Ann's dad had stayed home with the kids for four days, feeding them TV dinners and pacing the family room like a caged panther.

When her mom finally returned, looking sorrowful and weak, Mary Ann had assumed this was the awkward aftermath of a brief marital breakup. That explanation had made the most sense to her, given her father's panic in her mother's absence, and the fact that both of them had been yelling a lot more than usual. Mary Ann had fretted over them until the following summer at their cabin in Michigan when, one night before bed, the truth was finally passed down, mother-to-daughter, like treasured heirloom jewelry.

How, then, could she draw on the memory of her mother's experience, when she'd been kept in the dark about it? She had no way of knowing if her mom had felt this fragile in her own body, or how extensive her cancer had been, or if it had even been cancer. Like so many bodily mysteries in Mary Ann's life, she would just have to wing it. There was no practical wisdom to be gleaned from her Greatest Generation mom, the woman who had once described periods to her preteen daughter as 'the bitter tears of a disappointed womb.'

Back in the bedroom, Mary Ann found DeDe Halcyon-Wilson on her BlackBerry and dialed the number. DeDe answered on the second ring.

'Well, hello there. This is a nice surprise.'

She'd known DeDe for a long time. She had worked for DeDe's dad at his advertising agency and, several years later, had broken the story when DeDe and her lover D'orothea escaped from Jonestown via Cuba with their twin children in tow. The story had launched Mary Ann's television career and forged a bond between her and the ex-socialite heiress that had proven resilient despite years of neglect and a continent between them. They had remained firmly on each other's Christmas card list and had accidentally reunited several years earlier at a charity golf tournament in Boca Raton. Stuffy old Bob hadn't known what to make of the Halcyon-Wilsons with their Hillary buttons and their easy elegance, but Mary Ann had received them like long-lost sisters.

It felt like that now, she realized, only stronger. 'Oh, God, DeDe, it's so good to hear your voice.'

'Same here, missy. Hang on . . . lemme get D'or. She's out in the garden with the grandkids.'

'Grandkids?'

'I know. Tragic, isn't it? Where did the time go?' A certain breathlessness in DeDe's voice told Mary Ann that she was already loping through the garden. Mary Ann could picture that garden easily, or at least how it had looked thirty years earlier when DeDe's mother, then doyenne of Halcyon Hill, had summoned Mary Ann to the estate to break the news of her daughter's socially embarrassing return from the dead. DeDe and D'or and the kids had just arrived in Miami in a boatload of gay Cuban refugees.

And now those kids had kids! 'Who do they belong to?' she asked DeDe. 'The grandkids, I mean.'

'Both of them. Anna and Sergei have two of their own, and Edgar and Stephen adopted a seven-year-old last year. Where the hell is she? D'or! There you are. Get your svelte butt over here! It's Mary Ann! Yeah, *that* Mary Ann.'

All this joyful fanfare – and the squeals of children in the background – made Mary Ann wonder if she should do this on the telephone. But she couldn't afford another moment's delay if she was going to change doctors in midstream.

'DeDe, listen, I wanna come visit you guys, but I need—'

'Mary Ann! Girlfriend!' D'or was on the phone now, apparently in the very midst of all those screaming children. 'It's a friend, Milo . . . no, nobody you know . . . go play with Juniper . . . she needs you at the space station. I'm sorry, Mary Ann. How the hell are you? *Where* the hell are you?'

'I'm here,' she responded feebly.

'In Hillsborough?'

'No, up in the city.'

'Is Bob with you?'

'No, that's part of why . . . listen, it's wonderful to hear your voice, but . . . could you maybe ask DeDe to take the phone to a quieter place? There's something kind of important I need to—'

'Gotcha. No sweat. Talk to you later, doll. Whatever it is, we'll fix it.'

If only.

When the sun dipped behind Twin Peaks, she went for a walk around the neighborhood, mostly to lift her spirits. Like Russian Hill, this side of town was etched with bowered stairs and secret alleys, and she'd always been a pushover for that kind of charm. Back in Connecticut, whenever she'd grown homesick – or whatever the word might be – it wouldn't be the bridge or the pyramid or the cable cars that would call her back to San Francisco; it would be the raw *essence* of the place, its DNA, something that was everywhere but nowhere: a snippet of bay filigreed with trees, or a row of houses on a fogbound hillside, glowing like fairy lights buried in angel hair.

She made herself wander for an hour. She tried to pretend that her pain wasn't portable, that she was still capable of starting over, still the sort of woman who could be saved by geography. Never mind that it hadn't saved her for many years. Not on her trips to Paris or Prague or St. Barts. Not during her six months in cooking school in Tuscany or even her volunteer work with Habitat in New Orleans after Katrina. A mess who traveled was, ultimately, just a traveling mess. Travel might be broadening for a while, but sooner or later it just narrowed your illusions about what you could be.

On the way home she stopped to catch her breath on the steep street flanking Michael and Ben's house. There was an old guy across the street who was doing the same thing, so she felt a moment of senior solidarity with him, though he was much older than she was and didn't notice her standing there. He seemed to be admiring the new cottage, the one where she was living now, and that somehow made her happy. She considered engaging him but settled on solitude, holding back until he was gone.

A Force For Good

Pasta made the most sense, Ben decided, since they were cooking for Mary Ann that night, and it was best not to overwhelm her with one of his all-veggie extravaganzas. Nobody thought pasta was weird. He could make a nice penne dish with a little Gimme Lean sausage and his basil-and-cashew pesto. He had Googled 'vegan + uterine cancer' at his Norfolk Street workspace that morning to find what he had expected: a documented correlation between cancer and animal-food consumption. A vegan diet could not in itself cure cancer, the experts said, but it could limit the places where cancer could live. That was good to know if Mary Ann's cancer had yet to spread beyond her uterus.

Leaving his workspace with Roman just after four, he drove to the Whole Foods on Potrero Hill and shopped for dinner. (Michael, like many, had always called this market 'Whole Paycheck,' which was certainly true enough, but Ben couldn't resist the scope of its organic inventory.) When Ben returned to the parking garage, Roman was sitting up in the front seat with a look of quizzical pathos on his face.

'What is it, Mr. Doodle? You wanna go to the park?'

The dog reacted with disproportionate glee, panting his reply.

'No,' said Ben, sensing a misunderstanding, 'not the beach . . . the *park*.'

Roman just looked puzzled now.

'You like the park. All your friends are there. Don't you wanna see Mercy? And Blossom and Cliff? And Crazy Amy Winehouse Lady?'

Ben knew he was babbling like a lunatic – to a dog, no less – but he felt no shame about it. Most people were babbling these days, some of them into a headset, others just tweeting into the void, into the gray ether of faceless strangers. At least he knew Roman was listening. At least he knew Roman was trying his best to understand.

That's what Ben liked about the dog park. It was nothing if not a constant effort at direct communication. Even the people there were actively engaged in the practice. Today, for instance, seven or eight of them had pulled their white plastic chairs into a circle and were shooting the breeze like old men on the porch of a country store. All of them, in fact, *were* male, and most of them could easily fit someone's definition of old. Not a problem for Ben, of course, except that one of them, a writer named Gabriel Noone, who told stories on NPR, had come on to Ben in the locker room at the Y, and Ben, put off by the guy's needy posturing, had politely declined. Better to go it alone today.

So he sat on one of the benches against the fence while Roman went nuts with a scrappy Boston terrier. He didn't remain alone for long, however, because Cliff came into the park with Blossom, spotted Ben and Roman, and began making his way slowly toward the bench. The old man was wearing a faded green car coat that Ben recognized from previous visits. He used its many pockets to store dog treats, tennis balls and assorted squeaky toys – all for the enjoyment of Blossom and her friends.

Seeing Cliff, Roman parted company with the Boston terrier and made a beeline for the old man's pocket. 'Well, look at ol' Roman come running.'

'Make him sit for it, Cliff. Don't let him jump on you.'

'Okay then, sit,' the old man told Roman. 'No . . . stay . . . sit. That's a good boy. You want another?'

'Just one more,' Ben said. 'Otherwise he'll never leave you alone.'

The dog was sitting attentively, waiting for the next

bonanza, when a nerve-jangling scream made him jerk his head toward Collingwood Street. At that end of the park the cyclone fence was four times taller than elsewhere and covered with canvas panels, not only to keep balls from escaping but presumably to shield the neighbors from the undesirable sight of dogs at play. It was therefore impossible to find the source of the scream – even when another one came, followed by a string of explosive words:

'I'M ONTO YOU, YOU FUCKIN' MISERABLE PIECE OF SHIT! YOU THINK YOU CAN GET AWAY FROM ME, MOTHERFUCKER? YOU COCK-SUCKING SORRY-ASS EXCUSE FOR A HUMAN BEING!'

'Uhoh,' said Cliff, cocking an eyebrow at Ben. 'She's back.'

'Who is it?'

'Some schizo. She comes by here from time to time. Her brain is fried. I'm surprised you've never seen her.'

'Or *heard* her, at least.'

'THAT'S RIGHT YOU, YOU FUCKIN' BASTARD. I'M ONTO YOU. THE WORM WILL TURN, YOU SCUMMY SON OF A BITCH! THE WORM WILL TURN! EAT SHIT AND DIE, MOTHERFUCKER! YOU HEAR THAT?'

By now Roman had abandoned the treats altogether and moved between Ben's legs for protection. The men in the circle of chairs all had nervous smirks on their faces, but they were obviously trying not to look toward the big canvas wall.

'Who's she talking to?' Ben asked.

The old man shrugged. 'Somebody in her head, I suppose. Whatever you do, don't make eye contact or she'll try to come in. She's got a hunting knife strapped to her leg. I've seen her pull it on people.'

'I can't see her anyway,' said Ben.

'Nah, look . . . she's pulled the canvas back.'

Ben shot a quick furtive glance in that direction. The sidewalk was lower than the fence at that point, so all he could see was the woman's head and upper body: a beet-red fist of a face above what appeared to be a filthy red tracksuit.

Then she dropped the canvas and disappeared from sight again.

Ben had an armful of groceries when he returned to the house, so, as soon as the door was open, Roman wriggled past him and bolted toward the human who was dozing in the window seat. He licked her face extravagantly, causing her to wake with a small cry of alarm. 'Roman, no!' Ben yelped, though the damage was already done.

Mary Ann sat up, swiping at her face. 'It's okay,' she said. 'That's more action than I've had in months.' She had changed into sweats, Ben noticed, and her face was completely free of makeup. Her short silver hair suited the shape of her head, he thought, and her fine-boned prettiness had carried her gracefully to the brink of sixty.

'I'm sorry,' she said. 'I shouldn't have been here.'

'Why not?'

'I have my own perfect little house, for heaven's sake.' She reached for one of the grocery bags. 'Let me help with that.'

'No,' he said. 'I've got it. And you sleep wherever you want.'

She followed him into the kitchen. 'Let me help unload, at least.'

'Sure,' he said, since her need to feel useful was obvious. He wondered, somewhat guiltily, if she had sensed his reluctance about this new living arrangement. 'The pantry's right there,' he told her. 'All of this packaged stuff goes on the top two roller shelves. It's sort of free-for-all, so don't worry about placement.'

'Man after my own heart,' Mary Ann replied with strained jocularity. She removed the pasta bags and packaged soups from the canvas carryall and began to transfer them to the pantry. They were both silent for a while, grateful for the chance to bury their awkwardness in mindless activity.

Finally, Ben said: 'I'm sorry about . . . all of it.'

She gave him a wan smile. 'Thanks.'

'I think you're being remarkably strong.'

'Either that. Or I'm in shock.'

'Have you found a doctor?'

'Not yet. I've got a friend working on it.'

'Do you have many of those here?'

'What? Friends?' She shook her head. 'Not

anymore. I mean . . . it's been a long time. I wouldn't even know how to find them.'

'You should get on Facebook.'

'Oh . . . God no, Ben. I hate the Internet.'

'Why?'

'People get so ugly. I used to read the *Chronicle* online back in Darien, just to . . . you know . . . because I liked seeing the names of familiar places. But I was always tempted to read the . . . What's that part where the readers write in?'

'The comment board?'

'Yeah. They're so depressing. All those bitter people gloating about someone else's death or calling someone ugly or just being really hideous to each other. I couldn't handle it. It wasn't the San Francisco I remembered.'

Ben handed her a bundle of kale. 'That's because they're from Chico.'

She laughed. 'Not all of them, surely. Where does this go?'

'Bottom bin in the fridge. The thing about Facebook is that it's friendly. Most people use their real names, and you can block anyone who's being an asshole. In my experience people are usually nice . . . even a little bit corny sometimes.'

She squatted to stuff the kale into the vegetable bin, then looked up at him with a crooked smile. 'Perfect for the old lady, in other words.'

He chuckled. 'I didn't mean *you* were corny. I just

thought you might enjoy the experience. It brings back the past like you wouldn't believe. All sorts of people.'

'That's just it. Do I really want that?'

'Why not?'

She stood up again. 'I've pretty much kept the friends I wanted to keep. If you lose someone along the way, there's usually a good reason, isn't there?'

'What about fans, then? There must be a lot of them.'

'*Fans?*'

'Michael says you were a big star here back in the day.'

She rolled her eyes conspicuously, but he could tell that she was pleased. 'I had a local show. I was . . . you know . . . somebody for a while, but 'star' is pushing it.' She paused for a moment, then asked: 'What's this about, Ben?'

He was asking himself the same question. Sure, he was trying to lift her spirits, but his other motive was undeniably self-serving. Mary Ann might not be so dependent on Michael, Ben figured, if she had a wider network of supportive friends.

'I just thought you'd enjoy it,' he said. 'It's been fun for me, and—'

'I wouldn't even know how to do it. I'd probably—'

'Well, that part's easy. I could set it up for you in a few minutes. If you wanna use my computer, you could . . .' He cut himself off, suddenly wary of overselling it. 'Sorry, I get like this. Just tell me to shut up.'

She smiled and began folding the empty canvas bags on the butcher-block island. The act was so methodical and matter-of-fact that she might have always been tidying things away in this kitchen. 'Where do these go?' she asked.

'Just leave them. I keep them in the car.'

She arranged the bags in a stack and gave them a nervous pat to indicate that she was done. Without looking up, she said: 'I know how invasive this is.'

He was thrown, so he feigned confusion. 'What?'

'Me being here. Leaching off your happiness.'

Now she was gazing directly at him, waiting for his response. Where had this come from anyway? Could Michael have said something to her?

'C'mon,' he said finally. 'You're not leaching off anything. We're happy to have you.'

'No, Ben, that's sweet, but . . . I'm sort of borrowing your husband.'

He shrugged. 'Then make sure to give him back.'

She laughed. 'Well . . . okay . . . deal.'

He picked up a tub of Earth Balance and tucked it into the butter bin on the refrigerator door. 'I get it, Mary Ann. I know why you need him.'

She seemed to study him for a moment. 'Where on earth did he find you?'

He gave her a heavy-lidded smile.

'Oh, that's right,' she said. 'The Internet.'

'I'm telling you, it's a force for good.'

'I'm not looking for a man, if that's what you're thinking.'

'I didn't think you were.'

'Could you set it up on my laptop?'

'Set up what? Oh . . . sure.' He was amazed how quickly she'd capitulated. 'Of course.'

'Is now a good time?' she asked.

Ben felt an unexpected sense of accomplishment when Mary Ann broke the news to Michael over dinner that night.

'Ben got me going on Facebook, Mouse.'

Michael set down his fork and looked at Ben. 'No shit.'

'I thought she'd enjoy it,' Ben said evenly, wondering if Michael, for one reason or another, might think this was a bad idea.

'It was kind of liberating,' said Mary Ann. 'I used my maiden name and listed myself as single on the profile. They had a box that said 'It's Complicated,' but it really wasn't complicated at all, so I just said single. It was like a quickie Mexican divorce.'

Michael grunted. 'That guy deserves a quickie Mexican hit man.'

Ben was jarred by this response, and it must have showed.

'I mean it,' said Michael, stabbing his salad as if there were vermin hiding in it. 'I've been thinking about it. No fate is too cruel for that douche nozzle.'

Mary Ann smiled at the terminology. Ben recognized it as one of Jake's expressions, so Michael must have just been saving it for the right occasion.

'You know what you should do?' said Michael. 'You should talk about the Skype thing on Facebook.'

Mary Ann winced. 'Right, Mouse. Why not share my humiliation with the world?' She turned to Ben. 'He told you about that, I guess.'

Ben nodded.

Michael said: 'I don't mean mention it directly. Just the occasional veiled reference. So he knows that you know.'

'I'm sure he's not on Facebook,' said Mary Ann.

'Yeah, but his friends might be.'

A stifled groan from Mary Ann.

'I'm just sayin'. You could have some fun with it. Make 'em sweat a little.'

'Sweetheart,' said Ben, admonishing his husband with a look. Michael had a way of working a gag until it screamed bloody murder.

'The thing is,' said Mary Ann, 'I'm not even positive that he doesn't *already* know that I know.'

'What do you mean?' asked Ben.

She shrugged. 'He could have done it on purpose.'

Michael looked annoyed. 'Well, of course he did it on purpose!'

'I mean, left the Skype on.'

'No!' Michael looked genuinely aghast.

'Bob's not good at confrontation,' she said. 'Not about the tough stuff. He might have just decided to show me rather than tell me.'

'C'mon, babycakes. No one could be that vile. Hadn't you just told him you might be pregnant?'

Ben wasn't sure he'd heard this correctly. 'I'm sorry . . . what?'

'My cancer symptoms,' Mary Ann explained quietly, looking at Ben. 'I didn't know what was happening yet.'

He still wasn't sure what she meant, so he nodded and left it alone. He could see from her face that the conversation was beginning to get to her.

'Anyhoo,' said Mary Ann, chirping away the darkness, 'I have twenty-six friends already.'

Michael seemed confused. 'Oh . . . on Facebook, you mean.'

'Yeah. Ben friended me, and some of his friends recognized my name from my TV days.'

'That's because they're old,' said Michael.

Mary Ann batted her eyes in half-serious indignation. 'Excuse me?'

'I didn't mean it that way.'

'What other way could you mean it?'

Though Michael didn't deserve it, Ben let him off the hook. 'He was being jealous,' he told Mary Ann. 'That comment was for me, not you.'

'His Facebook friends are older gentlemen with facial hair . . .'

Ben grinned at Mary Ann. 'He's exaggerating. A few of them maybe . . .'

'. . . and they all look like me . . . fleshy features, big bellies. It's totally unsettling.'

'So?' said Mary Ann with a shrug. 'You're his type. What's so unsettling about that?'

'Thank you,' Ben mumbled through a mouthful of bread.

'It would be much more unsettling,' Mary Ann added, 'if they were all cute little twinkies or something.'

'Don't be so sure,' said Michael. 'Now that I know what his type is I have to worry about whether I'm the best version of that type. Not to mention what will happen when . . . you know, I'm no longer that type.'

Mary Ann rolled her eyes so Ben could see it. 'He's always been like this, you know.'

Ben nodded. 'I kinda figured.'

'When things are going great, he finds a way to make it not count.'

'Hey,' said Michael. 'Gang up on me, why don't you?'

'I'm not saying a word,' said Ben, exchanging a private smirk with Mary Ann.

It was a moment of bonding he had not really expected.

An Underlying Agenda

So here they were, at last – sitting underwater on a floating island in San Francisco Bay – a wack place to eat dinner if ever there was one. But something about the way the waiter had just crooned the word 'gentlemen' as he handed them their menus had turned their excellent adventure into an embarrassing dinner date.

Or so it seemed to Jake. He wondered if Jonah was feeling the same discomfort over the assumption that they were a couple. It was Jonah, after all, who'd insisted on this goofy outing to Forbes Island, so he was the one whose motives were suspect. At first Jake had written off the evening as a boyish whim, but now there was something brightly expectant in

Jonah's eyes that hinted at an underlying agenda.

'May I show you our wine list?' the waiter asked, while a solitary, bewhiskered fish idled in the murk beyond the porthole.

Jake glanced at Jonah, who shook his head. 'I'm good with ice water.'

'Same here,' said Jake, relieved that he'd been spared the ordeal of wine selection. He was sure that duty would have fallen to him, since he was the one with the beard, and Jonah, weirdly enough, seemed even younger than his twenty-two years now that he was spiffed up in a blue blazer and a white shirt.

When the waiter had left, Jonah pulled an iPhone from the breast pocket of his blazer and summoned a photograph. 'That's Becky,' he said, showing it to Jake.

The girl was a toothy brunette with flat, shiny hair. She was standing in front of a sign that read HOME OF THE LOBOS.

'Smokin',' said Jake, though she wasn't especially.

Jonah returned the phone to his blazer. 'She works at the chamber of commerce. We've been together since high school. How 'bout you?'

'How 'bout me what?'

Jonah smiled. 'Is there a girl in your life?'

Jake hesitated, looking for a way to be as truthfully misleading as possible. 'There used to be,' he said at last, 'but no more.'

The kid frowned in sympathy. 'That's too bad.'

'Thanks, but . . . it wasn't a good fit.'

Jonah nodded solemnly. 'You'll find the right one.'

'So where's the chamber of commerce? Where your girlfriend works. What town?'

'Oh . . . teeny tiny little place. Snowflake, Arizona. About six thousand souls.'

'Where it snows a lot.'

'Well . . . a fair amount, but that's not the reason. It was founded by a guy named Snow and another guy named Flake. Back in the 1870s.'

'Dude . . . shut up.'

Jonah smiled. 'My last name is Flake.'

'Seriously?'

'There's a bunch of us in Snowflake. People tend to stay put.'

Suddenly, the name rang a bell for Jake. 'There's a movie about that town. I saw it on TV back in Tulsa. Some logger who said he got abducted—'

'—by a UFO. Yeah, that was Snowflake.'

'That was some scary shit. They probed him with these creepy metal doohickies. Were you living there when that happened?'

Jonah shook his head. 'I remember the movie. The abduction was before I was born. My cousin was town marshal back then. He thought the whole thing was a hoax.'

'Marshal Flake.'

Jonah hesitated, seeing the smirk on Jake's face. 'Actually, yeah . . . Marshall Sanford Flake.' He managed a sheepish smile. 'Told you I was a country boy.'

Jake was instantly remorseful. 'No, man, it's cool. I grew up in the suburbs of Tulsa. I would have given anything to live somewhere that interesting.'

'When did you move here?'

'About four years ago. Just picked up and left. Got tired of working at Wal-Mart.'

'So what do you do now?'

'I'm a gardener. Actually, a partner in a gardening firm.' It was stupid, but he couldn't help bragging a little. For some reason, he wanted to impress this green kid from the hinterlands.

'And it doesn't . . . you know . . . get to you?'

'What? Gardening? I love it.'

'No . . . this city . . . the people and all.'

Jake was pretty sure he knew what Jonah meant, but played dumb. 'How so?'

'You know . . . San Francisco values . . . that sort of thing.'

Jake shook his head, remaining as poker-faced as possible. 'Nope. No problem so far.'

The kid nodded rhythmically, as if keeping time with the silence between them.

The waiter returned with their meals – salmon for Jake, a rack of lamb for Jonah. Jake welcomed this temporary relief from conversation, since there was already a whiff of uneasiness in the air. He was making appreciative noises about the salmon, when he realized that Jonah's head was bowed discreetly in prayer.

'Oh . . . sorry . . . I didn't . . .'

'You wanna join me?'

'That's okay. I'll just . . . you go ahead.'

So Jonah kept his head bowed while his lips moved in silence for a few more awkward moments.

'Sorry,' said Jake, as soon as Jonah had picked up his knife and fork.

'No biggie. You were thanking Him in your own way.'

'I always thank the salmon.' Jake was joking, but not completely, since he often made an effort to be appreciative when a helpless creature had died for his sins.

Jonah chewed a mouthful of lamb before speaking again. 'You're not a Christian, then?'

Jake shrugged. 'I was raised one.'

'But?'

'I dunno. I couldn't buy it anymore.'

Jonah looked him directly in the eye. 'You know, dude . . . that's why they call it faith.'

'Believing what you know ain't so.'

A cloud passed over the kid's face.

'Mark Twain,' said Jake. ' "Faith is believing what you know ain't so." '

'Oh.'

The kid was looking more and more like the

bug-eyed fish pressed against the porthole, so Jake kept his tone as gentle as possible. 'I just don't think that anybody's up there. I don't believe in life after death. I wish I could, but I can't. I think if there's a heaven, it has to be here and now. We're the only ones who can make it happen.'

'I understand,' Jonah said softly. 'That's why I do what I do.'

Jake just blinked at him.

'I'm a missionary, Jake.'

'No kidding.' For a moment, Jake thought of the classic image, picturing the kid in a pith helmet and jungle khakis. 'To where?'

'To here . . . for now.'

'Here? San Francisco?' It took him a while, but Jake finally saw the cold, gray light of dawn. 'Oh . . . you're a Mormon.'

'We actually prefer—'

'Right . . . sorry . . . the Latter Day . . . whatever. You came here for the election, then? To work for Prop 8?'

The kid nodded.

'Canvassing or something? Going door to door?'

'Yes.'

Jake could feel his face flashing red – a sure sign that he was beginning to lose control – but he made no effort to temper his reaction. 'How did that work out for you? After you'd won, I mean . . . after you'd taken away people's rights in a state you don't even

123

live in, for fuck's sake. Did you feel you'd done some good in the world?'

Jonah seemed to think about that for a moment. 'Truthfully . . . no.'

'Wow. Imagine that.'

'I'm not sorry it passed, because I truly do believe that marriage is between one man and one woman. But I never felt that I'd connected with another soul. Made a real difference, you know. I never had that one-on-one. And when I saw you standing there watching the sea lions, and you seemed so kind-hearted and decent and . . . I don't know, like a regular guy . . . I felt like I had to reach out to you, because I could help.'

'And how would that be?'

'Look, Jake . . . I thought I might be gay myself until I met Becky.'

'Excuse me?'

'Maybe I'm totally out of line here, but I'm pretty good at telling when somebody's—'

'You're talking labels, Jonah. Around here we don't put labels on people.' This was completely untrue, Jake realized – San Francisco was obsessed with labels – but he had to say something, and this was all he could manage in the heat of the moment.

'Let's put it this way,' said Jonah, lowering his voice as he looked around the room. 'You sleep with guys, right?'

After a moment, Jake replied quietly: 'Yeah. Not often enough, but . . . yeah.'

'And do you know why that is?'

Jonah's wooden, seminar-style questioning annoyed the hell out of Jake. 'Because I'm attracted to them?'

'Yes,' said Jonah, missing the sarcasm completely, 'but *why* are you attracted to them? I'll tell you why. *Because you're trying to complete your masculinity.* Someone, at some point in your life, said you weren't man enough, and you believed them, and that's why you think that being with another man will somehow—'

'Jonah—'

'Hear me out, dude. You're one of the manliest guys I've ever met. Not just in appearance but . . . your manly heart and your compassion. You're the real thing, dude. You're man enough for any woman.'

By this point, Jake had lost track of his emotions. He felt flattered, insulted, humiliated and validated all at once. Without making a spectacle out of it (since several of the other diners were already glancing in their direction), he pulled his wallet from his back pocket and removed three twenties, tucking them under the butter dish.

'What's that for?' asked Jonah.

'I gotta go. That should cover my portion.'

'C'mon, dude—'

'You mean well, Jonah . . . but you don't have a clue what you're dealing with.'

'If this is about Prop 8—'

'It's about everything, Jonah. It's about all sorts of shit you don't know about in Snowflake. The world isn't as neat as you think. It's not your fault. It's everybody else's fault.' Jake pushed back his chair and stood up. 'That includes me, for what it's worth.'

Jonah gazed up at him in forlorn confusion.

Without looking back, Jake headed directly for the stairs, only to remember, as he climbed into the cool night air, that there was no instant escape from this phony island. He stood beneath the phony lighthouse and the real palm tree and waited for the shuttle to arrive, fretting at first that Jonah might follow him out there, then fretting because he did not. He imagined the kid sitting alone in the midst of all those strangers, heartsick that he had failed in his holy mission. He considered going back, but he knew there was nothing he could say that wouldn't make it worse. He was well beyond saving by anyone.

An hour later, back at the flat, Jake was in bed when Anna appeared in the doorway in her Chinese pajamas. She had been fast asleep when he got home, so he couldn't imagine how she could have heard him crying from the other end of the hall.

'Is there something I can do, dear?'

'No. I'm fine. Go back to bed.'

'I've had a lot of practice at listening.'

'I know. It's okay.'

She turned to leave, then stopped abruptly, wobbling a little as she did so. 'Maybe this Sunday we can go to the new science museum in the park.'

'Sure. That would be nice.'

'I hear they have green things growing on the roof.'

'I've heard that, too.'

'Good night, dear. You're a man among men.'

It was pretty much the same thing Jonah had said, but this time the compliment actually meant something.

The Elusive Leia

Shawna's homeless woman had begun to haunt her. That's how she thought of her now – as *her* homeless woman – since the poor creature had a way of materializing at the oddest times, though never in the actual flesh. Shawna would flash on her scalded face in the midst of an Almodovar film at the Sundance Kabuki, or down at the Rainbow Grocery when she was scooping rice from the bulk-foods bin. Once, she even dreamed about the woman, dreamed that the two of them were dining at the Cliff House, gossiping like old friends as they admired the sunset, though – as dreams had a way of doing – it wasn't the sleek new Cliff House but the funky old one with the greasy photographs and flocked wallpaper that Shawna remembered from her childhood.

What bothered her most was that she didn't know the woman's name. Her image was becoming clearer all the time in Shawna's promiscuous imagination, but she still lacked identification, that all-important peg on which to hang her humanity. How could you even survive, Shawna wondered, when no one bothered to learn your name?

She drove back to the underpass one foggy afternoon in the hope of a reunion, but the only person there was an old hippie with a sign reading GULF WAR VET. While waiting at the light, Shawna lowered her window and signaled him with a $10 bill.

'Excuse me,' she yelled.

The guy put down his sign and came hobbling toward her. As he took the bill, he examined it at length. 'Money looks fake these days, don't it?'

She smiled but passed on the discussion, conscious of how little time she had. 'I was wondering if you know a woman who sometimes signs on this corner. Red tracksuit. Forty or fifty years old, maybe.'

The guy nodded so slowly she couldn't tell if it was a response or a tic.

'You do know her, then?'

'She ain't here.'

'I see that. Do you know where she might be?'

'You could try the traffic island on South Van Ness.'

'Do you know her name?'

The guy shrugged. 'We call her Leia.'

'What do you mean, you *call* her that?'

'Like Princess Leia.'

'But . . . why?'

'I dunno. It's a nickname. Ask her.'

The light turned green, signaling an end to their conversation. 'Thanks a lot,' she said, extending her hand. 'My name's Shawna, by the way.'

The guy just looked at her hand for a moment, as if it might somehow contaminate him. 'Good for you,' he muttered, before shuffling back to pick up his sign.

Shawna looked for the woman at the traffic island on South Van Ness, but she was nowhere to be found. There were several other signers working the island, but Shawna balked at the thought of interrogating another stranger about the elusive Leia.

That night, when she and Otto were eating at Weird Fish in the Mission, she told him about her abortive search, knowing already that he would question her motives.

'Is this about your writing?' he asked.

'No. I mean, it *could* be eventually, but it's not about that now.'

'Then what?'

'I dunno. I just feel like . . . I'm *supposed* to find her. I know how fucked-up that sounds, but . . . she's in my consciousness now.'

'What was it? Her sparkling personality?'

She shot him a peevish look.

'Hey, I'm just trying to nail this down. You should've told me earlier.'

'Why?'

'Because I saw her this afternoon. Down at the Civic Center.'

'You're kidding? What was she doing?'

He shrugged. 'Trying a case at the courthouse.'

'*What?*'

He smiled like a naughty little boy, then popped a French fry into his mouth. 'You gotta learn to tell when I'm teasing.'

'No. You gotta learn to not be full of shit. Where was she? What was she doing?'

'She was sleeping in a cardboard box.'

'Seriously?'

'Well . . . as seriously as you can sleep in a cardboard box.'

Now she was really exasperated. 'Why are you making light of this?'

'Because, ladylove . . .'

'Don't call me that. Not while you're being an asshole.'

'Shawna . . . listen.' Otto's tone remained calm, maddeningly enough. 'I think you're getting a little ooga-booga about this. I see these people every day, and most of them are seriously loony and dangerous. It's not as quaint and Dickensian as you think.'

'Did I say that? Did I say it was quaint and Dickensian?'

'Okay. Fine. Sorry.' He held his hands up in placid surrender. 'Want me to show you where she is?'

She was surprised by the offer, until she realized the reason for it. 'You don't want me going down there on my own.'

'That's right. I don't.'

'Okay.' She gave him a half-smile to show that he was back in her good graces. 'I can live with that.'

'When do you wanna go?'

'When do you think?' she replied.

They found parking on Grove Street, not far from City Hall, then cut across the plaza toward the library, passing the organic garden that Mayor Newsom had installed to demonstrate his support for sustainable agriculture. The rustic split-rail fence around the garden stood in ludicrous contrast to the grim-faced granite buildings in every direction. In the daytime, the plaza struck Shawna as a black-and-white movie; at night, even the shadows seemed to have shadows.

'What were you doing here, anyway?' she asked Otto.

'There was a matinee up at the Opera House. Sammy and I were working the crowd outside. We came down to Burger King afterwards.'

It unsettled her when he spoke of the monkey as if they were a couple, but she never let herself say that. Sammy, after all, was why she had fallen for Otto.

'By the way,' she said, 'they call her Leia. As in Princess Leia.'

Otto looked puzzled for a moment. 'Oh . . . the woman, you mean?'

'Yeah. It's her nickname on the street.'

'Did she use to wear her hair like that or something?'

'Who knows?'

'Well, it's appropriate.'

'Why?'

'Because,' said Otto melodramatically, 'I am about to take you to a galaxy far, far away.'

They followed Grove past the library into the heart of the Tenderloin, entering an extended hellscape of junkies and whores. This was always a shock to Shawna. You would never guess that some of these streets stretched all the way across town to Russian Hill with its cable cars and postcard views of the bay. To make the two-mile journey from there to here was to witness firsthand the gradual degradation of a city's soul.

Instinctively, Shawna moved closer to Otto. 'I thought you said she was in the Civic Center?'

'Well . . . two or three blocks away.' He turned and looked at her earnestly. 'Do you wanna call it off?'

'No. Do you?'

Otto just smiled dimly and kept walking. Ahead of

them, on the corner, was a vacant lot with a low wall of concrete blocks on two sides, presumably to keep people from parking there. To Shawna it looked like a deserted construction site, or maybe the rubble-strewn remains of a demolition. A billboard on a neighboring building depicted the eyes of an elegant dark-skinned woman gazing over the rim of a whiskey glass, with a tagline that read THE NIGHT KNOWS WHAT IT WANTS. The cold white light from the billboard made it easier to spot Leia's box, but, mercifully, stopped just short of it.

The box wasn't huge – refrigerator-size, Shawna guessed. There was certainly room enough for some-one to lie down in there, though who that someone might be was currently obscured by a layer of black garbage bags. Shawna stopped about ten feet from the box, wary of frightening the resident, and shot a quick glance at Otto.

'What should I do?' she whispered.

He shrugged. 'Say hello, I guess. You're asking *me*?'

Otto was obviously pouting, but she didn't have time to humor him. She had already noticed several scary-looking knots of men on the other corners. The Orpheum Theatre was just down the street, re-assuringly armored in neon, but this was one of those neighborhoods where you knew to stride briskly, eyes fixed straight ahead, if you had somehow made the mistake of passing through. And here they were, stopping.

'Excuse me,' she called. 'Leia?'

There was no response. The garbage bag didn't stir.

'I met you down by the freeway last week. I gave you some money.'

'There's nobody there,' said Otto.

'You don't know.'

'If she's sleeping, then I wouldn't disturb her.'

Shawna moved closer. 'Leia?'

'Don't, Shawna.'

She was reaching for the garbage bag when it flew back of its own accord, fanning a rotten-sweet stench into her nostrils. The person whose home she'd just invaded sprang up like a crazed jack-in-the-box, making Shawna yelp. It wasn't Leia, though; it was a pockmarked Hispanic guy in a stocking cap.

'Shit. I'm so sorry. I was looking for Leia.'

He propped himself up on one elbow. 'What you want with her?'

'Just to help.'

'She's down the alley. I'm saving her place.'

Shawna shuddered to think that this wilted cardboard coffin required 'saving' for anyone, but she knew the guy was telling the truth. She had just spotted Leia's YOUR MAMA WOULD GIVE A DAMN sign in the weeds behind the box.

'Which alley?' asked Otto, stepping forward.

The man pointed across the street. 'Over there next to the blue beer sign. But don't go down there.'

'Why not?'

'Just don't.' The man lay down again, pulling the plastic bag over himself.

Shawna turned to Otto. 'We have to.'

'No, we don't.'

'Well, I am.' She strode across the lot, stepped over the concrete-block wall, then turned back to Otto. She realized she'd put this peace-loving guy in a terrible spot, and, most of all, she didn't want it to look like she was testing his loyalty. 'It's all right,' she said. 'I'll be careful. I just wanna look.'

She crossed the street and walked half a block to the mouth of the alley. She could hear Otto's footsteps behind her – or what she assumed were his footsteps – but she didn't look back for fear of engaging him again. This was *her* craziness, not his.

The alley was barely ten feet wide and lit only by a window in the neighboring residence hotel. Even from out on the sidewalk it stank of piss. Someone halfway down the alley was sitting on the ground under a blanket, rocking rhythmically back and forth. In the far distance another figure, this one only in silhouette, was pressed against a wall with odd formality, like someone about to be executed. His stillness was mesmerizing; it took Shawna a while to notice that someone was kneeling in front of him.

'She's got a trick,' whispered Otto, slipping his arm around her waist.

'Jesus!' She jumped more than she would have liked.

'That's good. Your reflexes still work. C'mon.'

'Wait.'

'I mean it, Shawna. No more of this. I'm manning up here.'

She turned to him with a crooked smile. 'Really?'

'If you wanna get killed over a blow job in an alley—'

'Shhhh.' She took his arm to silence him. 'We're leaving, okay? We can wait for her back at the box.'

'We're not waiting anywhere. We're heading straight back to—'

The end of that thought was amputated by a scream from the alley.

'Fuck,' murmured Shawna, swiveling to look down the murky passageway. The silhouetted figures at the end had now become a single writhing mass. The person under the blanket was yelling 'shut up' repeatedly, like a mantra, still rocking back and forth.

Then came another scream, even more horrible than the first, prompting Otto to sprint down the alley toward the sound. 'Wait,' yelled Shawna. 'Be careful.'

I dragged the poor guy here, and now he's going to be killed.

She headed into the alley, though more cautiously than Otto had. 'We're calling the police!' she yelled. 'Leave her alone!' She hoped this wouldn't further inflame the situation, but it was all she could think to do. Then she heard the abrasive clatter of an overturning garbage can and watched as a man bolted into the street at the other end of the alley. To her abject horror, her boyfriend was running after him. 'Otto, don't!'

For one eerie moment Leia was nowhere to be found. Then Shawna rolled away the garbage can and saw the figure lying in the shadows. She knelt next to it and listened for signs of life, taking the woman's hand in hers.

'Leia?'

A guttural groan.

'Are you all right?'

'Who the fuck are you?'

'Never mind. Just a friend. Can you sit up?' She slid her hand under Leia's back only to hit something syrupy and warm and yank it away again.

'Owww,' screamed Leia.

'I'm sorry, I'm sorry!' The carrion stench of the woman was going straight to the pit of Shawna's stomach. 'Just lie still, sweetheart. We're gonna take care of you.'

Shawna dug her phone out of her coat and dialed 911.

'I have a woman here,' she told the operator. 'She's been stabbed, I think.'

'You *think*?' growled Leia.

'And what's the location?'

'Oh . . . shit . . . I don't know. It's an alley in the Tenderloin. It's off of Hyde Street. Please hurry.'

'I'll need a name, ma'am. Is there someone there who can—?'

'Cocksuck,' said Leia.

'Hang on, Leia . . . Operator, maybe I could meet them out at—'

'Cocksuck Alley!'

Shawna looked down at Leia. 'Seriously? That's the name?'

The woman grunted in the affirmative. 'The cops call it that, too.'

'Okay . . . great. Operator, apparently it's known on the street as Cocksuck Alley.'

Silence.

'Please don't hang up. This isn't a prank, I swear.' Desperate, still holding Leia's hand, Shawna looked toward the end of the alley where Otto had just re-appeared, breathing heavily. 'What does that sign say?' she yelled.

'What sign?'

'On the wall there. Where are we?'

Otto looked. 'Cossack,' he hollered back.

'Like . . . Russian?'

'Yeah.'

Shawna clarified things for the operator, spelling the word for her. 'We need an ambulance quick. She's bleeding a lot.'

Otto joined them, stroking Shawna's hair while she held Leia's hand.

'Did he take my knife?' asked Leia.

139

Down the alley the guy under the polyester blanket continued intoning his evening prayer: 'Shut up, shut up, shut up.'

Even the sirens, when they came, didn't silence him.

13

A Nibble On The Line

'I have the perfect person,' said DeDe Halcyon-Wilson as she topped off Mary Ann's wine glass like the gracious hostess she'd been raised to be. 'Her office is just a couple of miles away. You could recuperate here, if you like.'

Here was Halcyon Hill, the mock-Tudor manor house in Hillsborough that had been DeDe's home since childhood. She and D'orothea had recently re-chintzed the furniture and installed pretty green-silk Roman shades, but the house was still very much the way Mary Ann remembered it. Only DeDe herself had changed significantly; the prodigal debutante who'd returned from Guyana so sinewy and serious was now this pleasant little partridge of a woman.

Her patrician, finely furred jawline evoked the previous mistress of this house, DeDe's long-dead mother, Frannie Halcyon. And Mary Ann could well imagine what Frannie would have said about the fountain on the wall of the sunroom: a stylized vagina with water sluicing through petals of smooth pink marble.

'Too much?' asked DeDe, seeing where Mary Ann's eyes had landed.

'No . . . it's very subtle, actually. It's like a Bufano.'

'That's what it is.'

'You're kidding?' Mary Ann had prided herself on spotting the sculptor's distinctive work when she'd lived here – all those faceless penguins and slope-shouldered mama bears embracing their young. 'I didn't know he did . . . people.'

DeDe chuckled. 'He didn't. D'or bought it in a spiritual shop in Gualala. I told her it was a horrid idea, but she'd just taken a Lorezepam and could not be contained.'

'It's not a Bufano, you mean?'

'God, no. I feel so insensitive, Mary Ann. I should have taken it down before you got here.'

'Why?' Mary Ann gave her a spunky smile. 'I get to keep *that* part.'

Clearly relieved by this offhanded absolution, DeDe managed a laugh. 'Leaving in the playpen, as they say.'

'What?' said Mary Ann.

'Our friend Barb had a hysterectomy last summer. She told us: "They may be taking out the baby carriage, but at least they're leaving in the playpen."'

Cute, thought Mary Ann, if not especially comforting, since these days her playpen saw about as much action as her baby carriage. 'So your friend is okay?'

'She's great. Just fine. I asked her to join us today, but she had a meeting of her sustainable-gardening group. You know, it's the most fixable form of cancer there is.'

'So they tell me.'

'Are you scared?'

'Oh, yeah.'

'Of what exactly?'

Mary Ann's gaze drifted through the diamond-paned window into the green-and-gold blur of the garden. 'That I'll be different when it's over . . . or dead. I alternate.'

DeDe, thank God, didn't try to be a Pollyanna about it. 'You'll really like Ginny, I think. She's a good egg.'

'The oncologist?'

'Mmm. She's a serious advocate for women.'

'She's gay, I take it.'

'Is that an issue for you?'

'Of course not. Please. I was just curious.'

'I can drive you there this afternoon, if you like. I've already told her we might stop by.'

Mary Ann felt a rush of unalloyed affection for her

old friend. 'Oh, DeDe, would you? That would be such a load off my mind.' It soothed her considerably to have someone she trusted take matters in hand like this. She felt so much less alone.

'Ginny says it's a simple matter to have your records transferred. There are no hard feelings, are there? With your oncologist in Darien, I mean?'

Mary Ann shook her head. 'Not yet. I haven't said a word to him.'

'Guess you'd better, then.'

Mary Ann hesitated, imagining that awkward scenario as she took another sip of her Sauvignon Blanc.

'What's the matter?' asked DeDe.

'It's a little too close for comfort. He plays racquetball with Bob at our club.'

'Oh, shit.'

'Of course I didn't find that out until I was in the stirrups and he asked how good ol' Bob was doing in Europe.'

DeDe groaned. 'No wonder you wanted a new doctor! Jesus, do you think he knew about . . . you know . . . Bob and your life coach?'

Mary Ann shrugged. 'I wouldn't put it past Bob to brag about it.'

DeDe absorbed that for a moment. 'Let Ginny handle it, then. That's just the sort of challenge she enjoys. Does Bob know yet, by the way?'

'About what?'

'That you caught him in the act . . . or where you are, for that matter.'

Mary Ann shook her head grimly. 'I don't have the energy for that.'

'I hear you,' said DeDe.

What they *both* could hear in the weighty silence that followed was the gurgle and purr of the vagina fountain.

'Listen to that infernal thing,' DeDe muttered. 'I could just kill D'or. The pump got clogged one week last month, and it started spitting at people.'

'No.'

DeDe smirked like a wicked teenager. 'It happened during D'or's Buddhist study group.'

And they laughed, wearily, for a good little while.

The oncologist's office was in a rambling shingled L tucked in a grove of gnarled oaks. It reminded Mary Ann of a small but elegant shopping complex in Darien where she had sometimes bought wine-and-cheese baskets as last-minute birthday presents. Dr. Ginny herself was equally reassuring: fortyish and clear-eyed, authoritative without being bossy. 'I want you to know,' she said, 'I've done this over eleven hundred times.'

Mary Ann's response was a softspoken 'Wow,' as if this handsome woman had just announced an impressive golf score.

'I'm good at it, in other words. I consider it my calling.' The doctor's honeyed earnestness was a

145

perfect fit with her neutral-toned office and its Zen-spa furnishings.

'How long will it take?' Mary Ann asked.

'We'll have you out in a day.'

Mary Ann heard herself exhale. 'Great.'

'Have you had your appendix out yet?'

Mary Ann was thrown. 'No . . . actually.'

'I can do that at the same time, if you like.'

Mary Ann was beginning to feel like a dusty attic from which useless items were being systemically discarded. 'Do you think my appendix might be . . . cancerous?'

Dr. Ginny shook her head with an indulgent smile. 'Here's how it'll play out, Mary Ann. Once I'm in there, I'll lift out your uterus very gently' – she cupped her hands as if holding a small, helpless animal – 'and then I'll slip it into a plastic bag and hand it to the pathologist, who will proceed to slice it finely to determine the extent of the cancer. Which means that you and I will have some time on our hands. Well, *you'll* be asleep, of course, but I might as well make myself useful . . . hence the appendix.'

'But it's never given me any trouble,' Mary Ann offered feebly.

'Yes, but next year you'll be scuba diving in Palau and it *will* give you trouble, and they'll airlift you to Guam, where they have a 1984 MRI machine, and so one of my well-intended colleagues will give you a big ugly scar that I can avoid completely with laparoscopic surgery. I plan on leaving you with a nice smooth tummy.'

'Oh . . . okay, then . . . I guess.'

'No extra charge, of course.'

'Thanks.' It was the same tone Mary Ann would have used with a saleslady at Bergdorf Goodman who'd just offered to throw in free alterations. It occurred to her that this was Dr. Ginny's gift: the ability to make something casual out of the cataclysmic.

'So here's the deal. From now on, I'll do all the fretting, because I intend to do this as perfectly as possible. I'm funny that way.'

Under other circumstances, such cavalier boasting might have annoyed the hell out of Mary Ann, but certainly not here, not now; she craved the steel-reinforced tenderness that Dr. Ginny was offering, and that made her a believer on the spot.

'I'll warn you,' the doctor continued, 'you may feel a little depressed afterwards, but that's just part of the healing process.'

Mary Ann figured that couldn't possibly be worse than the suffocating gloom she was feeling now.

'Are you staying with DeDe and D'or?' asked the doctor.

'No. Friends in the city.'

'Would you like a hospital there?'

'If possible.'

'Of course.' Another smile. 'We're in this together, Mary Ann.'

147

* * *

That night, while Michael and Ben were visiting friends on Potrero Hill, Mary Ann brewed a pot of peppermint tea and took it out to her cottage in the garden. There was finally a nip in the air, a pungent dampness that suggested the onset of winter. She found herself grateful for the jokey gift the guys had bought her several days earlier: a ridiculous blanket with sleeves they had all seen on television and laughed about.

Sitting in her only chair with her laptop on her lap, the lights of the hillside winking through her window, she logged onto Facebook and posted her status report:

Mary Ann Singleton is drinking peppermint tea in her Snuggie, wondering if life is going to get better.

Then she waited, like a fisherman, for a nibble on the line.

As usual, she'd been careful not to betray her location. She didn't want Bob – or any of her friends in Darien – to start making inquiries. She was savoring the sensation of floating free in cyberspace, tethered only to a growing number of capital-F Friends who, with half a dozen exceptions, were not her friends at all. In the beginning most of these people had some connection to Michael or Ben, but now she was engulfed in an everwidening vortex of friend requests, and she was recklessly accepting them all.

Most of them, as Ben had predicted, recognized her name from the old days in San Francisco:

i watched yr show when I stayed home sick from school,
*   freeze-dried pets, lol*
My dad thought you were way hot
I am soooooo honored to be your friend
I love that dress you wore when the Queen of England ate
at Trader Vic's
Are you really THAT Mary Ann Singleton?

Using her maiden name had not only severed her from all things Bob but also unearthed people who actually predated her celebrity in San Francisco. There were three high school classmates, all looking *ancient* and only one of whom she remembered, because of her weird-looking close-set eyes. There was a lumpy old Irish guy who had worked on 'the floor' – as he had called it – when she was still a secretary at Lassiter Fertilizer in Cleveland. This wasn't so much her youth as a previous incarnation.

From her San Francisco days she had found people who'd been featured on her show: a white witch she had interviewed one Halloween, a beefy Samoan guy who had made scrapwood sculptures on the Emeryville flats. She had never really *known* these people; their value at the moment lay in the fact that they had passed through her life without lingering. This enabled her to create a manageable version of the past, an epic drama with a cast composed entirely of walk-ons. These nearstrangers with whom she bantered so breezily could hold a mirror to her life without ever reflecting the pain.

A week earlier she'd imagined scaling down her life to the size of this cottage, but, in reality, she'd shrunk it smaller still. Tonight, as DeDe had driven her home from Hillsborough, uttering sweet reassurances, Mary Ann's mind had already been racing ahead to the cozy hearth-glow of her laptop. She assured herself that this was *not* addictive behavior, since there was really nothing else for her to do right now. Social networking was just a salve for her troubles, a harmless diversion to fill the hours until she went under the knife – or the laparoscope – and knew where she was heading.

While waiting for a response to her post, she accepted three more friend requests and blocked an application for something called 'Farmville' – another imbecilic game, no doubt. She'd already rejected a glut of offers to participate in 'Mafia Wars' or to suck on someone's 'Lollipop,' whatever *that* meant. She preferred the kind of Friends who just talked about the weather, or showed off their vacation snaps of Fiji, or wondered aloud whether to eat that bar of 70% dark chocolate *right now*. There was a terse sewing-circle flavor to this discourse, a genial brevity, that she found appealing.

The first person to react to her post was someone called Fogbound One. There was no photo on the profile, just the little silhouette of a cowlicked head that Facebook provided as a placeholder. 'Happiness is a choice,' wrote Fogbound One, displaying his/her usual weakness for bumper-sticker wisdom. Mary Ann had hidden this person from her News Feed as soon as she'd learned it was possible, but he/she was technically Mary Ann's Friend, so, when the chat box pinged onto her screen, she felt obliged to respond.

Still feeling blue?
Little better, thanks.
What color is your Snuggie?
Red.
Mine's blue.
Lol. Silly aren't they?
Their warm.
Yeah they are.
I loved your show.
Thanks so much.
Didn't you use to live on Barbary Lane?
Yes.I was not far from there.
Somewhere in the fog, I take it.
ROFLMAO
Sorry. What's that? New to this.
Rolling on the floor laughing my ass off.
Ah.

Your quick.

Thank you.

Do you still live on Russian Hill?

No. I miss it.

Me too. I used to be friends with somebody who lived in your building.

Who?

Norman Neal Williams. Remember him?

Sorry. Doesn't ring a bell.

I thought you dated him.

No. Sorry. Long time ago. Nice talking to you.

She clicked the little x to make this awful thing go away. She'd wanted to stay for another comment or two, just to look natural about it, but she could already feel the coppery sting of vomit in the back of her throat. Shoving the laptop aside, she flung off the Snuggie and lunged for the bathroom, but made it only as far as the shower stall.

Dwelling On Things

'Watch it!' yelped Michael, 'that guy is totally shitfaced!'

Ben winced, tightening his grip on the steering wheel. 'I see him.'

'Didn't look like it.'

'Michae—'

'Okay. Fine. He was staggering into the street, that's all. You could barely see him in the dark.'

'I saw him.'

'I was trying to be helpful.'

'It doesn't help when you do that. Believe me.'

Michael maintained a moody silence as they passed Dolores Park on their way down 18th Street to the Mission. When he spoke again, his hand was on Ben's thigh.

'Is it backseat driving when you're both in the front seat?'

Ben smiled but said nothing. In the five years they'd been a couple, he'd always been the one to drive when they traveled together. They both preferred it that way, since Michael was a dangerously nervous driver, though that hadn't stopped him from being 'helpful' to the point of obnoxiousness. Ben let it go most of the time, since he knew it had far less to do with control issues than with Michael's morbid preoccupations.

Tonight they were on their way to see their friends Mark and Ray at their flat on Fair Oaks Street. Mark was sixty; Ray was eighty-two. The difference in their ages was almost the same as Ben and Michael's, making the older couple both an intergenerational role model and, for better or worse, a possible bellwether of things to come.

Ray had Alzheimer's these days ('a fairly mild form,' as Mark had gamely put it), which rendered him foggy but jolly, a nicer person by far than his former ornery self. It was Mark, poor guy, who'd been shafted in the bargain. The lupine young man in drawstring pants, whom Ray had fallen for one balmy night at Short Mountain, had been forced, after thirty years of contented man-on-man love, to open their relationship to another person.

This made for some interesting dinner parties.

'Gentlemen, gentlemen,' Ray crooned from the top of the stairs, as soon as he had buzzed them in. 'Did you find a place to park?'

'No problem,' yelled Ben, peering up that alpine slope at the lower half of Ray's skinny legs. It amazed Ben that the old man could still negotiate this climb, though it was saddening to have such demonstrable proof that Ray's body had outlasted his mind. He was wearing sneakers tonight, Ben noticed – fluorescent green ones, polka-dotted with peace signs – which an outsider might have taken as another sign of dementia. Ben saw them as an echo of Ray's Radical Faerie days, and therefore found them reassuring.

'Cool shoes,' he said.

'Who? Me?'

'Who else?' He kissed Ray's parchment cheek, joining him on the landing. 'Don't let my husband see them. He'll want some.'

Ray seized Ben's hand and held on to it. 'Where *is* he?'

'Down here with the Sherpas.' Michael was halfway down the stairs, exaggerating his breathlessness as he held tight to the iron banister. It was the game he always played, a pose to make Ray feel younger and stronger. Ben loved him for it.

'C'mon,' said Ray, beckoning Michael with a skinny arm. 'There's hot buttered rum at the summit.'

They followed Ray into what Ben always thought of as the great room, a long, warmly lit space on which this couple had left their vaguely hippiefied mark since the early eighties. There was nothing special about the flat, decoratively speaking – Bohemia by way of Pottery Barn – but Ben loved the sheer *archaeology* of the place, the history buried under magnets on the refrigerator door. These guys had lived a life here, and it showed.

Ray hollered into the kitchen for Mark, who appeared seconds later carrying a tray of mismatched ceramic mugs. 'What is it, you cuntface?'

The old man hooted with laughter. Ben shot a glance at Michael and saw that he had been every bit as jolted by the greeting as Ben himself.

'It's from *The Sound of Music*,' Mark explained, holding the tray out to his guests. 'You know the scene where—'

'I was going to do that,' Ray said, interrupting.

'Do what?'

'Bring out the rum.'

'That's sweet, my darling, but it's hot. Not to mention buttered.' Mark shot a knowing look at Ben and Michael. Ben could remember a time, only a few years earlier, when Ray could be entrusted with a tray of cocktails without danger of losing a drop.

No longer, apparently.

Michael took one of the mugs. 'I don't get it. What's from *The Sound of Music*?'

Ray grinned impishly. 'The Mother Superior says it to . . . whatshername . . . the star.'

'Julie Andrews,' Michael offered.

' "What is it, you cuntface?" ' This time it was Ray who said it, giggling.

Ben was still lost. 'Is this in a drag version or something?'

'It's in the movie,' said Mark. 'Julie doesn't want to be a nun anymore and tells the Mother Superior she just can't face it anymore, so the Mother Superior says, 'What is it you cahnt face?' You know . . . with a broad European *a*. Hence . . .'

' "What is it, you cuntface?" ' Ray crowed the line one more time before pressing his fingers to his mouth. 'Hope Arlene didn't hear. She hates that kinda talk.'

Ben's eyes darted nervously toward Michael, who, in turn, glanced at Mark, who connected with them both in a cat's cradle of wordless mortification.

'Shall we get comfortable?' said Mark.

'Arlene should be down soon,' said Ray. 'She's putting her face on.'

Mark sighed and took Michael's arm, leading the way to the sofa.

Ben sidled up next to Ray, placing his hand on the small of Ray's back as he did his level best to shift the focus. 'I hear you guys went out to Cavallo Point last week.'

'Mmm.'

'What did you think of the new restaurant?'

'It used to be a military base, you know.'

'I did . . . yes. Did you like it?'

Ray eased himself into a big armchair upholstered in paisley wool. 'I thought it was completely stark and charmless, to tell you the truth. And way too expensive.'

'I agree with you completely.'

'Arlene adored it, though. She's always been partial to fancy places.'

Arlene had once been Ray's wife. They had divorced several months before the life-changing Faerie Gathering where he met Mark. Arlene had stayed in Fort Wayne for a few more years before moving to South Dakota with a widower she'd met on a bus tour of the Holy Land. After that, by mutual consent, Ray and Arlene lost touch. Ray, in fact, hadn't learned of Arlene's death until eight months after her funeral, when a former neighbor from Fort Wayne was visiting San Francisco. Mark, who was almost forty by then and had never even met Arlene, had confessed, shamefully, to a certain relief. With Arlene gone, the slate would finally be clean; Ray would be his and his alone.

Or so he'd thought. Arlene had come back with a vengeance after Ray came down with Alzheimer's. It wasn't that his failing mind had resurrected the strained decade he'd spent with Arlene; it had simply imported her into his life. Anything Ray had shared with Mark inevitably became a fond, fuzzy memory of life with Arlene. She was gobbling up Mark's marriage like a fungus – even recent events like Cavallo Point, where, if Ben recalled correctly, the two men had celebrated their thirtieth anniversary.

After dinner, while Michael and Ray were having coffee in the great room, Ben helped Mark with the dishes.

'It's getting worse, isn't it?'

Mark nodded grimly. 'Last week he told the cleaning lady that him and Arlene had just gone to the nude beach in Sitges.'

'Ouch.'

'It wasn't like he ever loved her. He didn't even *like* her that much. He barely talked about her at all for thirty years.'

Ben towel-dried a plate and handed it to Mark. 'Do you ever correct him?'

'They tell you not to. They say it just confuses them and makes them feel bad.' He put the plate on the shelf above the sink. 'I really hate that dead bitch.'

Ben smiled faintly.

'At least he still remembers me,' said Mark. 'I shouldn't complain.'

'Go ahead. You're entitled.'

'No . . . really . . . we still have the moment. That's all anybody has. And he's always a lot of fun.'

As if on cue, Ray bellowed from the great room: 'Arlene! We need a fill-her-up out here. You still there, Arlene?'

Mark sighed and grabbed the carafe off the coffee maker.

'Hate her,' he muttered, as he leaned into the swinging door.

On the way home, neither of them said anything for a long time. Michael was the first to break the silence: 'I would never mistake you for anybody else.'

'Oh, yeah?'

'I mean it. I might be a cranky old fool some day, but I'll never forget who you are. Or what we've done together.'

Ben took Michael's hand and kissed the back of it. 'We don't come with that kind of warranty.'

'Well, *I* do. Just take me to Pinyon City or . . . make me something vegan . . . or flop your balls in my face. I'll remember.'

Ben chuckled. 'He spooked you?'

'Oh, yeah.'

'Me, too. A little.'

'You know, they say that marijuana actually helps prevent Alzheimer's.'

'Who said that? Woody Harrelson?'

Michael mugged at him.

'Speaking of Pinyon City,' said Ben, 'why don't we head up there in a few days? Are you locked into anything workwise?'

'Not that I can think of. Is there snow on the way or something?'

'Yep. You think Mary Ann would like to hang with you while I go boarding?'

'I dunno. She's having the surgery next week.'

'Maybe she could use a change of scenery.'

'We could always ask,' said Michael.

There was still a light on in the cottage when they got home, so Michael went out to talk to Mary Ann. When he finally returned, well over half an hour later, Ben was already in bed with Roman, giving him his obligatory nightly belly rub.

'Watch out,' Ben warned. 'He's been farting.'

Michael rolled his eyes. 'Great.'

Ben gingerly shifted the dog to the end of the bed while Michael shed his clothes. 'What did she say?'

'About what?'

'Pinyon City.'

Michael seemed distracted. 'Oh . . . she's up for it.'

'But?'

'Nothing. She wants to go.'

'So why did that take half an hour?'

Michael climbed into bed and snuggled into Ben's side. 'I had to hold her hand for a while. Somebody on Facebook mentioned somebody she used to date, and she was weirded out about it. It was no big deal.'

'What did they say?'

'Nothing, really. Just brought up his name.'

'Why would that weird her out?'

'She's in a really dark place right now. Who can blame her? I think Pinyon City will do her a world of good. We can go to the hot springs, or maybe snow-shoe across the meadow. Do we have a ski jacket she can wear?'

'Michael, who was this guy? What is it you're not telling me?'

'She really hates talking about it, sweetie. I'm the only one she's ever shared it with.'

'Fine. I won't ask her about it. And I won't tell her you told me.' He held up his hand, pointing to his wedding band. 'Full disclosure.'

Michael took a while to compose his answer. 'He was this creep . . . this pedophile who lived on the roof.'

'That she dated.' Ben gave him a heavy-lidded look.

'She didn't know that when she dated him. He was just a shy guy who had a crush on her, and she felt sorry for him. They had dinner a few times, that's all.'

'How did she find out, then?'

'Find out what?'

'That he was a pedophile.'

'Oh . . . she found kiddie porn in his room. Norman was in some of the pictures. He had one of those black bars over his eyes, but she could tell who it was. Plus, she recognized the little girl. They'd gone trick-or-treating together.'

Ben frowned. '*Who'd* gone trick-or-treating?'

'Mary Ann and Norman and this kid.'

'And she didn't wonder what he was doing with this child?'

162

'He was supposedly babysitting for some friends in the East Bay.'

'Jesus. Did she call the police?'

'Of course. But he was gone by the time they showed up.'

'Gone from where?'

'Barbary Lane. He didn't even leave his room key with

Anna. He just left on Christmas Eve and never came back.'

'So he must've known that they knew about him, right?'

'Oh, yeah . . . I'm sure.'

For some reason, Michael didn't sound entirely convinced about this, but Ben decided not to badger him about it further. 'So when did this happen?

'Thirty-two years ago. The first year Mary Ann was in town. You were barely on the planet at that point.'

Ben squeezed Michael's arm in rebuke. 'That doesn't mean I'm not supposed to know about it.'

'I know you think she's a drama queen,' said Michael, 'but she's had some actual drama.'

'Apparently,' said Ben.

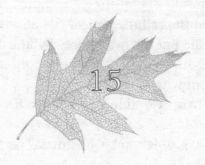

15

To Save Some Guy

With the weekend came rain – or at least a drizzly mist – so Jake proposed they blow off the new science museum and stay home. Anna was chipper about it, insisting that all she needed on a day like this was to snuggle up in the new gazebo with a pot of Earl Grey tea and a box of ginger snaps. Jake would have much preferred the albino alligator and the living roof and the four-story rainforest, but he knew that Anna's energy was lower than usual, so there was no point in braving the park in this shitty weather.

He dragged a space heater into the gazebo and rolled down the plastic curtains before settling Anna in her chair with her Hudson Bay blanket. He was glad to see that the gazebo wasn't leaking, since he'd built it himself a few months earlier. Anna was making a methodical show of appreciation, surveying the space like an astronaut checking her capsule before a flight. 'Perfect,' she said. 'I couldn't ask for more.'

Jake pulled up a chair next to her. 'Warm enough?'

'Oh . . . dear . . . before I forget . . . a young man came by yesterday when you were at work.'

Jake felt tightening in his gut. 'Oh, yeah?'

'His name was Snow, I believe.'

'Flake,' Jake muttered.

'What, dear?'

'His name was Jonah Flake, right?'

'Yes! That's it.' She rapped her knuckles comically against the side of her head, so as to reprimand her brain for its silly mistake. 'He thought he had the wrong place until I told him I was your roommate. I hope I didn't frighten him.'

'Who cares?'

'What, dear?'

'He's a Mormon. He's trying to save me.'

'How interesting.'

'Correction: he's trying to save some guy I haven't even *become* yet.'

Anna studied him for a moment, blinking her bleary blue eyes. 'He thinks you're gay, you mean? A gay man?'

Jake grunted in the affirmative.

'Well . . . isn't that sort of encouraging?'

'C'mon. If he wants to fix a gay man, what the hell's he gonna think about a trans man? I haven't got time for that kind of shit.'

'Was this the boy from the floating island?'

'Yeah. Why?'

'Well, he seems to like you. He said to tell you he was sorry.'

Jake said nothing; there was nothing to say.

'He looked like he meant it. He looked bereft, in fact.'

He shouldn't have snapped at her, but he did. 'Anna, did you hear what I said? He's trying to save me.'

Taking her time about it, Anna tucked a wisp of hair behind her ear. 'Or trying to be saved. Most of us are doing one or the other.'

'What does that mean?'

'I have no idea, and you won't either unless you call him back.'

It was typical of Anna to toss out something mysterious like that, then run away before she was forced to explain herself.

Jake folded his arms with a sigh. 'Would you like your cocoa now, Your Majesty?'

Anna ignored the question. 'You know, dear, I know exactly how that feels.'

'How what feels?'

'To know who you are inside when other people don't.'

Of course he knew that she knew that, but he didn't feel like a pep talk right now, even from his tran mother. He didn't feel like anything. He felt dead inside, a total nonbeing whose feelings didn't matter one way or another.

'The thing is,' Anna went on, 'you can't stay open to love if you're always afraid of being hurt.'

'I wasn't looking for love. He's not even gay. I thought we could be friends.'

'Then how can you know if that's possible if you don't—'

'What? Come out to a Mormon? A guy who came here to stop gay marriage? He even calls himself a missionary!'

'Then you should be one, too.'

'That's not me, Anna. I'm a private person.'

Anna rearranged her long, pale fingers in her lap. 'I used to think the same thing about myself. But I was only postponing the chance to be loved as myself.'

'C'mon. He would freak out.'

'Maybe.'

'*Maybe?*'

'Probably, then. But this is about *you*, dear. You would be claiming who you are, whatever happens. There's something to be said for that. Believe me.'

The rain was coming down harder now, clattering like a handful of gravel against the roof of the gazebo. Rather than argue with Anna, Jake made a dash for the kitchen, where he microwaved two mugs of tea and shook half a dozen ginger snaps into a wooden salad bowl. When he returned, he discovered that Notch had taken refuge in Anna's lap.

'Poor old girl,' said Anna, stroking the little cat's raggedy black fur. 'The rain caught her off guard.'

'I wondered where she was,' said Jake. He set the bowl down on Anna's flat-topped ceramic elephant, then handed her a mug of tea. She sipped it wordlessly, solemnly, gazing into the distance, letting the silence speak for itself.

'I get what you're saying,' Jake said at last.

'But?'

He shrugged. 'It'll be easier to do when I'm finished.'

She nodded slowly. 'The surgery.'

'Yeah.'

'You still want it, then?'

'Oh, yeah.' The issue, of course, was not whether Jake wanted the surgery but whether he could ever afford it. The nest egg he'd brought with him from Tulsa had been spent on his double mastectomy, and he'd been scrambling ever since just to keep his head above water financially. Michael paid him as well as he could, but – almost overnight, it seemed – the recession had turned gardeners into a disposable luxury.

'You know,' said Anna, 'there have been people who regret having the change. Whatever direction they're heading. I'm sure they told you that at your meetings.'

'Did *you* regret it?'

'No.' She shook her head. 'Not for a minute.'

'Okay, then.'

'I'm not you, dear.'

Jake shrugged. 'Close enough.'

Anna smiled, taking Jake's hand in hers and nestling it in her lap where he could feel the warmth of Notch's percolating body. 'I had a daughter once,' she told him. 'It agreed with me tremendously. I think I could use a son.'

Jake retracted his hand. 'You might have to wait a little.'

She shook her head. 'No time for that, dear.'

'Maybe not but—'

'I'm paying for it, Jake, and that's that. I don't want an argument. I've spoken to Selina and Marguerite and they're making all the arrangements.'

Jake's face reddened with embarrassment. 'It's a lot more expensive than you think. I don't even have health insurance.'

'Hush,' she said. 'I'm about to shuffle off this mortal coil. The money might as well do somebody some good.'

Jake didn't get the 'mortal coil' part, but he caught her drift just the same.

Like a Dog Before an Earthquake

*N*ecrotizing fasciitis.

Shawna had heard the paramedics use that term the night the ambulance rushed Leia to San Francisco General. A day later, on Shawna's second visit to the hospital, she heard it again as she passed the nurses' station. It stalked her all the way down the hall to Leia's ward, droning in her head like some creepy, demonic incantation.

Necrotizing fasciitis, necrotizing fasciitis, necrotizing fasciitis . . .

The common term for it was 'the flesh-eating disease.' It was extremely rare in the general population, but not so much among street people who used heroin. Leia had an advanced case. The doctors in the emergency room had been far less concerned with the surface knife wound on her back than with the gruesome stew of rotting flesh on her left leg. The knife attack had actually been something of a blessing, in fact, since it brought immediate medical attention. Without it, they said, she'd already be dead.

Shawna strode into the ward, her eyes fixed straight ahead so as not to invade the tenuous privacy of the other patients. The salmon-and-green curtains on Leia's cubicle were closed, so Shawna paused and read the sign that identified the occupant:

LEMKE, Leia

The last name was news to Shawna, since Leia had been too fucked up and frightened to reveal anything on the night of her admission to the hospital.

Shawna cleared her throat. 'Leia?'

A growl from behind the curtain.

'It's Shawna. May I visit?'

Another growl, apparently signifying yes.

Shawna pulled open the curtain and closed it behind her. Leia was sitting up in bed with an IV line sprouting grotesquely from a hole beneath her collarbone. As a nurse had explained on Shawna's previous visit, there was no other spot on the patient's over-perforated body that could accept the antibiotic. A tented sheet over Leia's legs spared visitors – and presumably the patient herself – the sight of a body eating itself alive.

Shawna pulled up a chair. 'They're treating you okay?'

Leia grunted. 'Methadone sucks.'

That may be, thought Shawna, *but you're not screaming anymore. You're not clawing at your skin. You seem almost human now.*

'You cut your hair,' Leia remarked. 'It looks better.'

Shawna was touched by the observation, coming as it had from someone who'd long ago abandoned control over her own appearance. 'I wanted something simpler,' she said, reflexively touching the tips of her new pixie cut. She had banished the Bettie Page look an hour earlier; she knew for sure now that it didn't suit this new chapter in her life.

'Why are you doing this?' asked Leia.

'Doing what?'

'This. Hangin' out with me.'

Shawna tried to answer truthfully. 'I don't know exactly.'

'You with an agency or something? Rehab?'

'No. Nothing like that. I just saw you under the freeway and . . . I really enjoyed what little I saw of you, so . . . I decided to come looking for you.'

'*Lookin' for me?* You came there on purpose?'

Shawna nodded. 'You think I normally go strolling down Cocksuck Alley at that time of night?'

A quick flash of ruined teeth as Leia laughed.

'Give me a little credit, lady.'

Leia regarded her soberly for a moment. 'They wanna cut off my leg.'

Shawna nodded. 'I know.'

'I can't do that.'

'I hear you. I'd feel that way too.'

'Well . . . tell 'em I won't, then.'

'No, Leia. I can't.'

'Why not?'

'Because . . . the infection will spread if they don't amputate.'

'Fuck it, then.'

'It'll kill you. It *is* killing you. You can start to get better once the leg is gone. That's what these antibiotics are for . . . to get you stronger before they . . . do it.'

'Please don't . . . please.' Leia was sobbing now.

Shawna took her hand. 'Would you like me to stay?'

'Stay?'

'Yeah. Be with you when you go in, and be there when you wake up.'

'FUCK THAT SHIT. THEY'RE NOT CUTTIN' OFF MY LEG.'

'Okay,' Shawna replied feebly. 'Whatever.'

'Get the fuck out of here, you pesky cunt. Who the fuck do you think you are?'

Shawna backed toward the door, then fled without another word.

*　*　*

She called Otto as she left the hospital. Hearing the alarm in her voice, he offered to meet her for lunch at the Café Gratitude on Harrison Street. Otto was no more a vegan than she was, but the restaurant was an easy walk from the hospital, and they both liked the cheery neo-Aquarian vibe of the place. On previous visits, she had cut them slack about the pretentious-sounding menu items, but she was in no mood for that today.

'I'll have the large café salad,' she told the pony-tailed girl server.

'You mean "I Am Fulfilled"?'

'Okay.'

'You want that, then?'

'Yeah. Are you gonna make me say it?'

The server gave her a curdled smile and turned to Otto. 'How about you?'

' "I Am Elated", please.'

'Would you like that with sour cream?'

'Yeah. "I Am Elated" with sour cream.'

'Excellent.'

'And for dessert we'll both have "I Am Awakening." '

Seeing that Otto was enjoying himself, Shawna found herself smirking. When the server had left, she said: ' "I Am So Over This." '

'C'mon. They have to say it. It's part of the gig.'

Shawna heaved a sigh. 'What am I gonna do, Otto?'

He didn't have to ask what she meant. 'You'll go back, is my guess.'

'Then what?'

He shrugged. 'You'll be with her.'

'They say she's dying. With or without the amputation.'

'Want me to go with you?'

'Would you? You don't have to see her. I just need you there.'

'Should I bring Sammy?'

Her first instinct was to roll her eyes, but Otto had such a goofy, hopeful look on his face. 'I don't think that's her kinda thing, honey.'

He cocked his big head of lion hair. 'Really?'

'Yeah . . . really. Let's don't do that.'

Otto shrugged, looking a little hurt.

An hour later, while Otto lost himself in a curling paperback of *Infinite Jest*, Shawna spoke to the nurse on duty, a gaunt white guy with a blurry tat on his neck.

'We gave her something,' he said. 'I think she'd like the company.'

'Promise?'

He smiled. 'She's feeling pretty good now.'

She headed straight for the cubicle, fearful of losing her nerve. Leia's bed was tilted a little higher this time, but her eyes were closed.

'It's me again,' said Shawna.

'Who's me?'

'The pesky cunt.'

Leia's eyes fluttered open. 'What do you want?'

'Just to talk for a while. If you like.'

'Oh, shit. You're a priest.'

Shawna shook her head, smiling. 'Nowhere close. Just another fan of your sign.' This was incredibly lame, she realized, but it was the easiest way in.

'My *sign*? That horseshit about mamas?'

'Yeah. "Your mama would give a damn" I thought that was clever.'

'Because everybody loves their mama.'

This was neither a question nor a statement, just something vaguely, sorrowfully, in between. Shawna didn't know where to go with it, and she was already feeling stupid and cowardly. 'I was having dreams about you,' she confessed. 'About the two of us.'

Leia scowled.

'Not like that. We were hanging out. Talking about ordinary things. Like old friends. People who'd known each other for years.'

Leia absorbed this for a moment, fiddling with her IV line as if it were a string of pearls languishing on her chest. 'Did I look good?'

Shawna laughed. 'Yeah. You did. We both did.'

A long silence while Leia's eyes stayed glued on Shawna's. 'You're one of those spooky people, huh?'

Shawna felt strangely sheepish. 'I am. A little. Hope that's okay.'

Leia shrugged. 'Maurice was spooky. He felt shit all the time . . . shit that hadn't happened yet. It would wake him up. Like a dog before an earthquake.'

'Maurice was—?'

'Just this guy on the island. He made that mama sign you love so much. I inherited it when he died. He had the same nasty shit I got.' She gazed down grimly at the tented atrocity, then, just as quickly, looked up again. 'You always been that way?'

'What? Spooky?'

'Yeah.'

'Not always . . . but it started fairly early, yeah.'

'How'd you know you weren't crazy?'

Shawna smiled at the memory. 'I had a grown-up who recognized it in me. She was that way herself sometimes, so she taught me to go with it and not make a big deal of it.' She was picturing herself at ten or eleven in Mrs. Madrigal's kitchen at 28 Barbary Lane. *You'll be tempted to talk about it, dear, but don't. Just let it be your secret friend.*

'I don't really believe in it,' said Shawna. 'I just notice it sometimes.'

'Maurice was just flat-out crazy.'

Shawna chuckled. 'Maybe I am, too. Or maybe you and I just met somewhere. Once upon a time.'

'Ever shop at the Foot Locker in West Portal?'

'No.'

'The Fabric Barn in El Cerrito?'

177

Shawna shook her head. 'You worked in those places?'

'Long time ago. Before I started chasing the dragon. I got one of those faces, I guess. People always say I look familiar.'

'Maybe that's it.'

'What's your name, honey? You never told me.'

Shawna had introduced herself to Leia in the ambulance, but wasn't surprised that she had forgotten. 'Sorry . . . I'm Shawna Hawkins.'

'Alexandra Lemke.'

Such a noble-sounding name was extremely hard to attach to this ruin of a woman. 'I knew Leia was just a nickname, but . . . that's lovely.'

'What about Shawna? Where did they get that?'

'I never knew, actually. The woman who gave birth to me picked it out, and she died just after I was born. She just passed it on to my adoptive mom.'

'She raised you, then? Your mom?'

Shawna shook her head. 'She left when I was little. My dad raised me. I can't say I've ever had a mother.'

Leia nodded. 'That's some bad shit.'

'Hey . . . we deal.'

'Musta been hard when you were little.'

'Well, I always tried to—'

'My mom rented me out to perverts when I was little.'

Shawna flinched. 'What do you mean?'

'Sent me on dates with grown men. They messed

with me and took pictures of it for paying customers. Split the profits with my folks.'

'Your father was in on it, too?'

Shawna's reaction drew a phlegmy chortle from Leia. 'Got you beat, huh?'

'Guess so.'

'Parents ain't always a *good* thing, ya know.'

Shawna gave her a sardonic smile, feeling shamefully self-indulgent. She retreated to more practical matters. 'Is there somebody I should notify, Alexandra?'

The woman frowned suspiciously. 'About what?'

'About you. About your being here.' *In the event of your death* were the words she couldn't bring herself to speak.

'Oh . . . no . . . nobody. Well, you could tell Maurice.'

'The guy who made the sign?'

'Yeah.'

'I thought you said he was dead.'

'Oh, yeah . . . right.' Leia nodded slowly, tears streaming down her face.

'I'm so sorry,' said Shawna.

'Ain't your fault,' said Leia.

A Thing About Cliffs

Mary Ann had considered defriending the Facebooker who asked her about Norman, but decided against it. Such a move would only make her look as if she had something to hide. Instead, she just deactivated the chat function. Her fear, of course, was that Fogbound One was someone who had known Norman well – or well enough to know that he'd been with Mary Ann that long-ago Christmas Eve.

Worse yet, what if this guy was a homicide cop investigating a new development in the long-cold case of Norman's disappearance?

This was paranoia, she told herself. Ben had warned her that social networking could unearth all sorts of stuff, so it wasn't *that* surprising, really, that

Norman's name had surfaced. She had dated this man, after all, so lots of people could have seen them together. She and Norman had eaten at Sam Wo's in Chinatown and gone to an old movie at the Castro Theater. They had even gone treat-or-treating on Russian Hill with that poor little girl, though Mary Ann had still been clueless at the time. She'd found it endearing that this shambling sasquatch of a man would babysit for his friends. She took it as a sign of Norman's basic decency, his obvious yearning for home and family.

She had never been serious about him. He'd been forty-four, for one thing – almost twenty years older – and not all that handsome. She had seen him more as a project, a humanitarian effort. After only a year in the city, she had already had her fill of beautiful, unavailable men, so Norman, with his low self-esteem and adoring gaze, had struck her as an easy, risk-free object of her affection. Since she'd never slept with him, she'd been caught off-guard the night he'd all but proposed to her at the Beach Chalet.

She had sometimes wondered if Norman had seen her as a cure for his pedophilia, his last serious shot at a normal life. Whatever his motives, his anguish had seemed real enough when she turned him down. And it was still in his eyes on Christmas Eve when they were walking along the cliffs at the Legion of Honor and she confronted him about the disgusting magazines she'd found in his apartment. Even then, he still wanted her, still believed he could win her over, if only she would listen to his side of the story.

She'd been over this so many times in her head. Things might have been different if he hadn't been so drunk that day, if they hadn't chosen that particular path, if he hadn't stumbled and lost his footing, if he'd just *held still* when he began to slide on his back toward the precipice, if he'd worn the goddamn tie she'd bought him instead of his usual tacky clip-on, which came loose in her hand when she reached down to rescue him.

There'd been nothing to like about Norman, but she hadn't wanted him to die. She had never seen herself as someone who could flee such a terrible scene, but fate or karma or *something* had offered her a clean break, and she'd chosen to take it. There had been no witnesses, and even if Norman's body *did* wash ashore, an autopsy would reveal the huge amounts of alcohol in his blood, and the police would assume (correctly, of course) that a drunk had fallen off a cliff. So she'd taken a bus back to Barbary Lane and gone to Mrs. Madrigal's Christmas party. She'd never told anyone about it except Michael.

In the intervening years (including the dozen or so more years she'd remained in San Francisco) Mary Ann had never spoken of Norman again, and – even more damning to the memory of a dead man – not a single living soul had ever asked about him.

Norman's ugly little life had left him seemingly devoid of all human connection.

Until Fogbound One.

Now Mary Ann was wondering if Norman had had a friend she'd never known about, someone who'd grown curious about his old buddy once her name had shown up on Facebook. What if he (or she) was trying to torment her about Norman's disappearance?

Or what if the police had simply found new evidence?

What if a human jawbone with an easily identifiable filling had turned up in the rocks below those cliffs?

Stop it, you ridiculous woman. Just stop it.

'See if this fits.'

Mary Ann looked up with a start from her Facebook page. Ben was holding out a puffy powder-blue ski jacket. 'For Pinyon City,' he explained.

'You sure I'll need that?'

'Oh, yeah. It gets into the twenties at night.' He smiled, revealing that delectable gap. 'Didn't you ever go to the Sierra when you lived here?'

'Not really. Well . . . once or twice, but usually in the summer. I've never been a skier.'

Ben guided her arms into the cushiony sleeves. 'It's a little roomy, but the color's really good on you.'

He was right about both things. She admired

herself in the mirror next to the bed, mostly to show him her appreciation. 'You sure you can spare this?'

'We've got tons of 'em.' Ben gestured toward her laptop. 'You won't be needing that, by the way. There's no Wi-Fi in Pinyon City.'

Her face must have betrayed her chagrin.

'Are you addicted already?'

She knew he was talking about Facebook. 'Not really,' she said, lying just a little bit. 'But I do wanna stay in touch with my doctor.'

Six days to go, she thought. *Is this really a wise idea? Will a radical change of scenery in the middle of nowhere make the time pass slower or faster?*

'No worries,' said Ben. 'We usually have breakfast over in the next valley. They've got Wi-Fi in the café there. And we're only gone for two nights.'

'Right . . . okay.' She folded her laptop and swaddled it in a pair of slacks before tucking it into her suitcase.

'I'll see you in a bit,' said Ben, backing out the door. 'I've gotta get Roman's stuff together.'

Oh, shit. The dog.

'You knew we were bringing him, right?'

'Oh, well . . . yeah . . . I figured.'

'He lives for these trips,' said Ben. 'He's so much fun in the snow.'

'And he's good in the car?'

'Oh yeah. He's great.'

*   *   *

He was not great. He whimpered, for one thing – not loudly but steadily – for the first two hours of the trip, supposedly in anticipation of the natural wonders awaiting him. When he finally settled down, he sprawled on the seat with all the entitlement of a temple lion, his wet, black nose planted squarely on Mary Ann's lap. She wondered if he could actually sense something, smell something – *feel her disease*, as that cryptic old Beatles song went. *How did that go? He got . . . something, something. He got feet down below his knees, hold you in his arms so you can feel his disease, come together right now . . .*

'You okay?' Michael was peering at her from the front seat.

'We're fine.' She had answered for the dog as well, since they were a couple for the purposes of this trip, whether she liked it or not.

'I can switch with you when we stop for lunch.'

'No. I'm good.' She might have agreed had she not noticed how often Michael and Ben had reached across the coffee holders to touch each other. It was part of their road ritual. Her first husband, Brian, had been like that. Bob, of course, not so much.

Feeling a shiver of isolation, she found herself stroking the wooly head in her lap. The dog was a pretty mottled color, like an Irish cable-knit sweater, a flurry of grays and browns. She spotted a grain of crud in the corner of his eye, so she picked it out with delicate care, only to have the creature turn and lunge at her hand.

'Shit . . . sorry.'

'What happened?' Ben found her in the mirror.

'I was picking something out of his eye.'

Michael chuckled. 'He wasn't trying to hurt you. He just wanted the booger.'

'What?'

'He loves to eat eye boogers. It's his favorite thing.'

She saw Ben shoot a peevish glance at his husband. 'Michael . . . TMI.'

'And you feed them to him? Ew . . . Mouse . . . that's disgusting. And who calls them eye boogers, anyway?'

'Who says "ew" anymore?'

'Plenty of people.'

'At *our* age, I mean.'

'Our age,' she echoed flatly, shooting him a look. He had tried this several times already: invoking their common decrepitude in front of Ben, so that he, Michael, could strike the pose of the wise old sage. She wasn't ready to claim that crown yet.

'All dogs like to do that,' Michael insisted. 'It's a natural thing. Besides, it's neater. What did you do with it?'

'What do you mean? I flicked it away.'

'On the *floor*?'

She reached out to swat him, but he intercepted her hand and held it for a while, almost tenderly, against the snowy bristles on the back of his neck.

'You're bad,' she said, embarrassed by the intimacy.

They stopped for lunch, as custom seemed to demand, at an In-N-Out Burger just off the freeway. It was perched on a small, barbered knoll that offered a surprisingly unspoiled view of the foothills. The air was much colder here, and the sky was as dingy as an old hankie, but there was no evidence of snow beyond a few ski-racked Outbacks in the parking lot. Some of these patrons had to be locals, she figured, given the patriotic frenzy of their bumper stickers and the sheer height of their vehicles.

For ten minutes, they went their separate ways, two- and four-legged creatures alike. While Ben was at the counter placing their orders, Michael led Roman around a plaza of asphalt-framed grass, and the lone female finally relieved herself in a restroom that was much cleaner than she'd expected. When she was done, she pushed the paper horseshoe into the toilet with the tip of her Pumas and flushed without looking. She would *not* dwell morbidly on her cancer. Dr. Ginny had laid down the law about that in their last phone conversation. *Stop horriblizing, Mary Ann. It will do you no good.*

She studied her face in a streaky mirror as she washed her hands. She'd been accused of horriblizing before – that very term, in fact – by someone else looking out for her welfare. Calliope, of course, had not been a doctor; her certification had been from a place called Coach U. *That should have been a fucking clue*, thought Mary Ann. *That should have given me the tiniest inkling that this oh-so-earnest shaman with trout pout and cone-shaped breasts might not be the most trustworthy keeper of my heart's secrets.*

'Don't be such a horriblizer,' Calliope used to say whenever Mary Ann began to fret about the world. 'You're just worrying about stuff that hasn't happened yet.'

Right, thought Mary Ann, drying her hands on a paper towel, *like the sight of my life coach sucking off my husband in a fancy Italian hotel. Good thing I didn't horriblize about that before it happened. Who knows where I would have gone with it.* She flung the towel into the trash and charged out of the restroom in a blind fury, nearly colliding with a balding, pink-haired old woman toting an infant in a Baby Bjorn. Outside, where a gust of cold air slapped her into a semblance of sanity, she saw that Ben had already returned to the car, so she collected herself as believably as possible before climbing into the backseat. She was instantly enveloped in a warm fog of cheeseburger smells.

'Yum,' she said.

'Eat yours now,' Ben told her with a wink. 'It's a lot easier without the doodle in here.'

'I guess I shouldn't ask,' she said, unwrapping one of the burgers.

He grinned knowingly as he wiped cheese from the

corner of his mouth. 'It's hard to be vegetarian on the road. We let ourselves transgress when we're out of town.'

'No complaints here.'

'Good, aren't they?'

'Mmm.'

'It's the soda cups that bother Michael.'

'What's wrong with them?'

'They've got Bible verses printed on the bottom.'

'Really?' Mary Ann tilted a cup to see what he meant, and proceeded, of course, to spill diet soda on her leg. 'Shit,' she murmured. 'Shit, shit, shit.'

Ben sprang from the car and opened the hatchback, returning seconds later with a ragged terrycloth towel. 'It's Roman's, but it should be clean.'

She thanked him and dabbed at her sodden leg, infuriated by her own stupidity, her own mindless panic.

'Do you need to change?' he asked. 'I can leave for a bit.'

His sweetness made her want to cry, but she held it back.

'It's okay,' she said. 'No big deal.'

Ben smiled sleepily. 'It's the one about living forever.'

'What?'

'The Bible verse. John something. "All who believe in Him shall not perish but have everlasting" . . . et cetera.'

'All that's written on the bottom?'

He shook his head. 'Just the chapter and verse numbers.'

'But you *knew* them?'

'I Googled them.'

She laughed. If Ben had been a closet believer, it would have been a revelation, since Michael had indicated that the two of them had given up on organized religion. She felt curiously let down. She wasn't all that religious herself, so it might have been useful – or comforting, anyway – if someone she knew had Wi-Fi to the Almighty.

The highway wound into the mountains so gently that she barely noticed the climb. It was not until the trees had become pointy and a boulder-strewn river was racing them through a gorge that the change was undeniable. Then, out of nowhere, filaments of snow began to lash the windshield from every direction, making even the dog take notice. Roman was sitting by the window now, enraptured by the gradual whitening of things.

'Is this the Sierras?' she asked.

'Sierra,' said Michael, correcting her. 'Singular. Sierra Nevada means "snowy range" It's plural already.

'Oh . . . pardon me.'

'He does that to everyone,' Ben told her.

She changed the subject. 'We have chains, I take it?'

'Yeah,' answered Ben, 'but the snow isn't sticking

yet, and we passed the checkpoint a few miles back. We should be fine.'

Ben was a snowboarder, of course, so his definition of 'fine' could very well differ from hers. Already she'd been horriblizing about the narrow shoulder of the road, the ominous rake of the slopes leading down to the river. She had always been a confident driver and a nervous passenger, and her not-so-latent acrophobia wasn't helping matters.

'So Pinyon City is . . . up here somewhere?'

'Well, up and then down,' said Michael.

'What do you mean?'

'It's on the eastern side of the range. Almost in Nevada.'

'So . . . what's the descent like?'

Smelling her distress, Michael gave her a cagey look over the seat, like a spiteful little brother. 'A lot quicker, for one thing.'

She would *not* let him torment her, however playfully he'd meant it. She distracted herself with the scrolling scenery: a neon beer sign in a tavern window, a bright yellow snowplow, an archipelago of snow from an earlier snowfall, gleaming under the dark pines. But it was no use. She couldn't stop clocking the relentless climb or the weave of the road or the ominous blossoming of caution signs.

'I take it we're reaching the crest,' she said, as casually as possible.

'Yes, ma'am,' said Michael brightly, with barely a

hint of sadism this time. 'You'll be able to see the lake. Or half of it, at least.'

She didn't want to see half the lake. She wanted down from there as soon as possible. She hated to sound hysterical in front of Ben, but she had no choice.

'Ben . . . could you slow it down a bit?' He was going forty-five around a bend where thirty-five had been suggested, and she'd just caught a glimpse of the gaping chasm beyond the road, the instant oblivion that some people liked to call a View.

The trouble with Views was where you had to see them from.

Ben said, 'No problem,' but didn't seem to slow down much. He was a good driver, she reminded herself, and extremely careful most of the time, but knowing that did little to relieve the abject panic that was already gripping her.

'Thanks,' she said. 'I'm sorry. It's not you, it's me.'

The road leveled out, giving her a chance to breathe and loosen her viselike grip on the arm support. It didn't last for long. Another yellow sign was screaming at her:

EXTREME CAUTION.
DANGEROUS CLIFFS AHEAD.

'Jesus,' she muttered. 'What cliffs? Where?'

Her answer came as soon as they rounded the

bend. They were hugging the side of the mountain now. There were sheer granite cliffs above and below them, and only a stone wall – two feet high at the most – separated the right-hand lane from certain death. On the serpentine descent she saw places in the wall where the stones were missing or the mortar had been crudely patched, obviously because some poor soul hadn't heeded the warning sign, or was too drunk to notice. Her leg stiffened against phantom brakes as a warbling groan escaped from the back of her throat through clenched teeth.

'For God's sake,' said Michael. 'Stop with the Indian war chant.' He pointed out the window. 'Look! There's Tahoe.'

Ben, to her horror, actually turned his head to admire the view, and she was certain she could feel the car veer in the same direction. 'Ben . . . please don't do that.'

'Then *you* look,' said Michael. 'You're missing it.'

'I see it. It's beautiful.'

'You're not even looking.'

'I am, Mouse! Mountains, lake, snow . . . oh Jesus Fucking Christ!'

A huge, sooty Safeway truck was thundering toward them around the bend. As it passed with a ghastly whoosh, she closed her eyes and stopped breathing altogether.

'You're being silly,' Michael told her like a scolding parent. 'And you're not making it any easier for Ben.'

'I know.' She was completely mortified now. She'd always had a thing about cliffs – even before that horrific day with Norman – but she had never before exposed to it so blatantly. Maybe that was because her acrophobia had offered an acceptable outlet for the panic that had been brewing in her for days. The terror in the pit of her belly was less about the altitude than, well, the terror in the pit of her belly.

'It's almost over,' Ben assured her. 'It's always a little creepy the first time.'

Tell me about it, she thought.

As Michael had promised, they reached the valley floor in a matter of minutes. Mary Ann was relieved to be done with her vertigo, but she'd expected more for her suffering than the free-range commerce that had suddenly blossomed along the highway: hot tubs displayed in parking lots, spangly billboards for nightclub acts, 'cyber chalets' strung with icicle lights. Not exactly honky-tonk, but not that far from the outskirts.

'Are we there yet?' she asked, hoping the answer was no.

Michael parried her query with one of his own. 'Don't you wanna stop and buy a chainsaw sculpture?'

He was enjoying this, she realized. As long as she'd known him he'd made a game out of toying with her expectations, building suspense for what lay ahead. He was like an annoying little kid leading a blind-folded friend to his secret fort in the woods.

'You're not going to tell me a thing, are you?'

'Just soak it in, babycakes.'

'I feel like I'm being abducted.'

'Great. That's what we're going for.'

A green highway sign pointed the way to Pinyon City, but neither Ben nor Michael remarked upon it. This smaller road led them through a cluster of houses with suburban-looking street signs and seasonal flags flying over the garages. Within minutes, however, the houses had disappeared and they were cruising through a broad, seemingly unpopulated valley. The meadows on both sides of the road were vast and already dusted with snow; the mountains in the distance imposing but somehow incapable of menace. They embraced her, in fact, made her feel safer than she'd felt in weeks.

She remembered a magazine called *Christmas Ideals* that her grandmother had sent her every year when she was a little girl back in Cleveland. It was sturdier than most magazines, and glossy, and inside there were poems printed on scenes from nature. If she were to see one today, she would probably find it corny, but back then her easy childish heart had soared at the sight of those snow-laden pines and starlit valleys.

Ideals had been the ideal name, she realized, since

what the magazine had offered was the sweet re-assurance that life could not be improved upon. A pristine landscape was perfection itself; it was only when you added people that everything changed.

Maybe that's why she was feeling so peaceful.

There was no one around. Anywhere. And the world was fading to white.

'Where did everybody go?' she asked.

'Exactly,' said Ben.

18

Unclean Urges

Jake was surprised when Anna told him of her plans for the afternoon. These days she rarely left the house without him, and then only for brief strolls around the neighborhood. He might have caught on to her scheme had he thought about it for a while, but he was glad to have the flat to himself, and Anna seemed excited about seeing Michael Tilson Thomas conducting something or other at Davies Hall. When she left with the upstairs neighbors, Selina and Marguerite, she was dolled up in her fanciest floral kimono and the little velvet cap that Michael had given her for her birthday.

'If you're feeling inspired,' she told Jake, holding on to Marguerite's arm, 'Notch's litter box could use a little freshening. Otherwise, enjoy yourself, dear. We won't be home until after dinner.'

He watched from the door as the three of them – all moving at Anna's speed – headed down the street toward the Muni Metro station. When they were out of sight, Notch approached and did her little leg-rubbing dance, so he took it as his cue to grab a bag of Feline Pine from its usual spot beside the washer. The ammonia smell stung his nostrils as he twist-tied the heavy bag of dirty litter and moved it, gingerly, to the trash. As he replaced the litter, Notch sat perfectly still on the kitchen counter, watching the operation with the air of a rich lady keeping an eye on her housekeeper.

So now what? With Anna at the symphony and Michael in the mountains for two days, Jake's major responsibilities were gone. He considered raking the soggy bamboo leaves from the terrace, but that would feel too much like his day job, so he settled on watching television. Anna had never cared for television ('except in times of national emergency'), so, despite the fact that the set was in his bedroom, he tried not to watch it when she was around. You could hear it all the way down the hall, so it would have been disrespectful to invade her space like that, considering the preciousness of her days. But sometimes, thanks to TiVo, when Anna was visiting her acupuncturist, or camped out on a bench in the art museum, he could steal a few guiltless moments in bed with ESPN.

He had already watched two satisfying hours of soccer when the doorbell rang. By the time he'd pulled on his sweats and considered the usual suspects – Jehovah's Witnesses, delivery dykes, neighbors with flyers for poetry jams – another possibility had presented itself. A glimpse through the window confirmed the worst.

The Mormon kid. Jonah Flake.

Jake sighed and opened the door. He waited for the intruder to speak.

'Your grandmother said you'd be home today.'

'My grandmother.'

'The elderly lady. Whatever. She called herself your roommate. I figured she was kidding.' A crooked smile split the soft, round peach of Jonah's face.

Jake just stood there.

'Dude . . . can I come in?'

'Not if you're packing a Bible.'

Jonah grinned and held up his hands as proof. 'I'm totally clean.' He cocked an ear toward the hallway. 'Is that soccer?'

'Yeah.'

'AC Milan?'

This is what they do, thought Jake. *Find something they have in common with you and use it to get their foot in the door.*

'Listen, man, I hafta tell you, you're wasting your time if—'

'It's not that, dude. I need your help.'

Jake was thrown by the urgency in the kid's eyes. '*My* help?'

'I'd rather tell you inside, if that's okay.'

'Well . . . we gotta make it quick . . . I don't wanna miss this match.' This was bullshit, of course, since Jake could watch the match whenever he wanted, but he needed an easy way out if Jonah tried to get all churchy on him again. 'You can sit over there,' he told Jonah, gesturing to Anna's armchair.

The kid sat down, but only on the edge of the chair, and his back remained unnaturally straight. He might as well have had a Bible on his knee.

'So wassup, Elder Flake?'

Jonah flinched as if he'd been slapped.

'That's what you call yourself, right? When you're a missionary?'

'That's not what I am today.'

'Okay . . . whatever.'

The kid was quiet for a moment. 'The thing is, Jake, I have the same urges you did. Toward men, I mean.'

This wasn't exactly news. The kid had practically said as much on Forbes Island. 'But you don't act on them. You've got . . . whatshername now.'

'Becky. Yeah, I love her . . . for sure. She's a wonderful girl. But I still have these feelings. I pray for them to go away, but it's a struggle. It's the biggest struggle of my whole life, but I'm making it for Heavenly Father.' The kid's big gray eyes were damp now. 'But sometimes it's like . . . there's nothing I can do about it.'

Oh shit, thought Jake. *So that's where this is going.*

'It's not like I wasn't prepared. I was. I knew that a place like San Francisco would put me in the path of temptation. But sometimes when I meet somebody new, the urges get too much for me and . . .'

The kid didn't finish the sentence, so Jake tried to spare them both the embarrassment. 'Jonah . . . dude . . . I'm really flattered, but I don't think that sexually you and me would be—'

'No! I don't mean you!'

The response was so fierce that Jake couldn't help but feel stung by it. 'Okay, man . . . cool . . . whatever.'

'No offense . . . you're handsome and all, but you're more like a friend. I just meant . . . I met this dude at Starbucks today, and he asked me to go home with him.'

Jake took that in. 'I thought you guys couldn't drink coffee.'

'What guys?'

'Mormons.'

'I was having a brownie.'

'So . . . what? . . . You had sex with this dude, and you're feeling guilty now.'

'No. I told him no. I said it was against my faith.'

'Well . . . there you go. Nothing to be worried about. Your sacred purity is intact.'

'But . . . I'm still feeling the urges. I haven't stopped feeling them for the past two hours.'

'Then go back and fuck him. Get over yourself,

dude. Get over your damn faith. It's gonna kill you.'

The kid looked devastated. 'Haven't you ever had something you wanted to change . . . and you couldn't . . . and it made you feel like a crazy person?'

Oh, one little thing, thought Jake.

'If you don't wanna help—'

'I just tried to, Jonah. I gave you my best advice. What else could I possibly do?'

Jonah hesitated, his fingertips fidgeting at his temple, where a sprinkling of acne betrayed his idling adolescence. He seemed to be weighing something.

'It's gonna sound wack,' he said.

'Try me.'

'I need you to hold me.'

Jake just blinked at him.

'It's part of my therapy. Back in Snowflake my therapist does it, but I don't know anybody here besides the other elders, and I don't . . . they don't know about my, you know . . . You don't have to, dude, if you don't—'

'Your therapist *holds* you?'

'It's called touch therapy. I'm supposed to do it when I feel unclean urges. He says the urges come to me because my dad was so distant, so . . . if I can find a man to hold me, I'll be getting what I want, and sex won't have to be part of it. He says gay men really just want strong masculine love.'

Jake remembered now. He'd seen this on a CNN report about ex-gays: one grown man holding another on his lap, rocking him like a baby, stroking his head.

'Is this guy like . . . a therapist therapist?'

'What do you mean?'

'Like . . . a psychiatrist or something?'

Jonah shrugged. 'He's a reparative therapist . . . a highly respected LDS leader. He went through this himself. Personally.'

'He's gay, you mean.'

'*Was*. He's married and has kids now. Listen, dude . . . it was wrong of me to ask. You've made your own choices. You've got your life worked out.'

Right, thought Jake.

The kid stood up, stumbling a little, obviously embarrassed. He headed for the door, looking much more rejected than Jake had felt moments earlier.

'What the hell,' said Jake.

Jonah turned. 'What?'

'What do I have to do? Do I have to talk?'

'You'll do it?'

'I'll give it a shot.'

The kid's peachy face went red with relief. Or gratitude. Or something.

He blushes like I do, thought Jake.

'You don't have to say anything at all,' Jonah assured him. 'You can watch the match, if you want.'

'The TV's in the bedroom, dude.'

'That's okay. I trust you.'

'We keep our clothes on, right?'

'Totally.'

Jake led the way to the bedroom – and the bed – where he propped pillows against the headboard and let Jonah lie against his chest. Jake wondered what to do with his hands, until Jonah guided him, placing one of them behind his own head and the other on his waist. He did this with such practiced authority that Jake was reminded of a ballroom dance class he had endured one summer as a kid in Oklahoma. Only then he had been the one with a hand on his waist.

'So this is it?' he asked.

'Yep.'

'How long do we do it?'

'Ten or fifteen minutes . . . usually. As long as it takes for the urges to pass.'

Jake felt another twinge of resentment toward this unforgettable stud from Starbucks, then made himself let it go. 'Just lemme know, dude.'

'You can rock me, if you don't mind. That's part of it.'

So that's what happened. Jonah lay there in Jake's arms, his body pulsing with warmth, his thick, wheat-colored hair smelling of coconut gel, while Jake watched AC Milan lay waste to Livorno. Since Jonah couldn't see the TV screen, the undulating roar of the crowd and Jake's own yelps of support sometimes stirred his curiosity.

'Was that Ronaldinho?'

'Yeah. Fucking brilliant block.'

'Ronaldinho rules,' said Jonah.

'Word,' said Jake, rocking away.

Time passed, but Jake could not have said how much. He was lost in the easy communion of bodies breathing in unison, like those sea lions hauling out at Pier 39. This experience could have made him crave sex, but it didn't; it just calmed him, released him from the usual expectations, the usual guilt. He had never lied to Jonah, and Jonah was getting the cure he'd been prescribed: tenderness from a masculine heart without the danger of lust. Hell, there wasn't even the danger of dick. Jonah was getting a deal.

The doorbell rang.

'Shit,' he said, throwing Jonah off his chest.

The kid, naturally, looked rattled. 'You expecting somebody?'

'No.'

'What about your grandmother?'

Jake didn't bother to correct him again. 'She's not coming back until dark.' He left the bed, heading for the door.

'Wait,' cried Jonah. 'It could be one of the elders.'

'How the fuck could it be one of the elders?'

The kid looked sheepish. 'I gave the address to a buddy of mine.'

'Why?'

'Just . . . you know . . . in case of emergency. They

like to know where we are.'

It was ridiculous how guilty the two of them were acting, so Jake tried to be the voice of reason. 'Just stay put. I'll take care of it.'

Closing the bedroom door behind him, he headed for the front door. Through the peephole he saw Shawna Hawkins, the daughter of Michael's old business partner, Brian Hawkins. Shawna was another of Anna's chosen 'grandchildren' – a lively, dark-eyed girl a few years younger than Jake and more than a few inches taller. She had changed her hair; her shiny retro bangs had given way to a shorter, simpler cut.

He opened the door. 'Hey there.'

She seemed unusually subdued. There were dark circles under her eyes. 'Sorry to show up un-announced, Jake. I really need to talk to Anna.'

'She's at the Symphony,' he told her. 'She won't be back till dinnertime.'

'Shit.'

She looked so disappointed that Jake couldn't leave it at that. 'Is there something I can do?'

'No . . . I just, you know . . . need me some Anna.'

'Right. Well, maybe this evening . . .'

His nervousness wasn't lost on Shawna. 'You've got someone with you.'

'No . . . not really.'

'Yeah, you do.' She smiled conspiratorially. 'That's great. Don't let me intrude.' Shawna, like Anna, took more than a passing interest in Jake's love life – such as it was. Shawna could handle this situation better than anyone Jake knew – she wrote a sex blog, after all – but her assumptions were already making him uncomfortable. He wondered exactly what sort of Olympian fuck-fest she'd been picturing.

'I'll check back later,' she said. 'I've got some errands to run anyway, so . . . oh . . . sorry to barge in like this.'

This second apology puzzled Jake until he turned to find Jonah standing behind him.

'No sweat,' Jonah told Shawna, before turning to Jake. 'Talk to you later, dude.'

'Please don't leave on my account,' Shawna said, as Jonah made his escape down the passageway to the street.

When he was out of earshot, Shawna widened her eyes. 'Adorable. Now I *really* feel bad.'

'Don't,' said Jake. 'It was nothing.'

But it hadn't been, he realized; it had definitely not been nothing.

Refuge Once Removed

Pinyon City, she realized, had never been anything like a city. The highway and the main street were one and the same, and downtown, if you could call it that, consisted of a general store, a real estate office, a restaurant/saloon, and a derelict mini-mall that, according to a flaking sign, had been the 'Sierra Meadow Wellness Center' in an earlier incarnation. The village was tiny, and virtually free of traffic, since two of the highpass roads leading into it were closed during the winter. The one road in use – the one they'd just come down – was already velvety with snow. The whole effect was otherworldly.

Ben pulled the car off the road across from the general store.

'How's that for parking karma?' he asked, grinning over the seat at Mary Ann.

She wasn't sure what he meant until Michael climbed from the car and began unloading their bags from the hatchback. They had apparently parked directly in front of their accommodations – a matchbox of a bungalow, probably from the forties, encircled by a charmless aluminum fence. The sight of it sent Roman into fits of ecstasy.

'Just head on in,' Michael told her. 'We'll bring your stuff.'

'Won't I need a key?'

'It should be open. They leave the key inside.'

So she led the way into the house, passing first through an unheated mudroom with a four-foot patchwork unicorn standing sentry at another door. Beyond that, she found the main room: a relentlessly plain but serviceable space painted a serviceable shade of cream. There was a battered upright piano, a large refectory table, and a cluster of kitschy but comfortable-looking eighties furniture. Someone had clearly anticipated their arrival, because an electric wall-heater was already droning away in the corner.

Roman shot past her into the room, touching base with other doors leading to other rooms – the bedrooms, presumably – as if systematically checking items off his arrival list. Mary Ann was charmed by his excitement, even found it a little contagious, until the dog stopped cold, hunched his back, and began heaving on the carpet.

'Oh, baby,' she said. 'Did you get carsick?'

The dog had coughed up a few blades of grass (from his pit stop at the In-N-Out Burger, no doubt), so Mary Ann hurried off to the kitchen for a wad of paper towels. When she returned, Roman was standing uncharacteristically still in the middle of the room. A thick rope of slime, viscous as an egg white, was dangling from his shiny black lips. Hearing Mary Ann approach, he turned his head slowly and regarded her with blank-eyed bafflement, as if seeing a human being for the first time.

Then, suddenly, he dropped to the floor, his legs stiffening grotesquely in a series of spasms, his mouth foaming, his black marble eyes showing crescents of white.

'Oh, fuck . . . oh shit . . .' Mary Ann cried, just as the guys came staggering in with the luggage. 'Something's happened to him, Ben.'

Ben dropped his bags and rushed to kneel by the quivering dog. 'It's okay, Roman, we're here. That's a good boy. That's a very good boy.' He looked up at Michael with the sober calm of a paramedic. 'Is there anything in the fridge?'

'I doubt it. Unless maybe the last people . . . wait!' Michael scrambled out the front door and came back, seconds later, holding a clump of compacted snow in both hands. He dropped to the floor and pressed the snow against the base of the dog's spine.

Roman was still shaking violently. 'Hang on, Mr. Doodle, we're almost there.'

Feeling useless, Mary Ann stayed out of the way as Ben and Michael cooed to the dog. When the spasms finally stopped, Roman just lay there panting. The dry air was spiked with the smells of bile and urine: the melting snow had formed a dark green continent on the light green carpet. Michael gazed up at her. 'You should go to the bedroom. Close the door behind you.'

'If there's anything I can do . . .' Roman began to snarl through clenched teeth.

'Go, Mary Ann! It's Cujo time!'

This was all the shorthand she needed. She bolted for the nearest door and slammed it behind her, only to watch it spring open again as Ben and Michael joined her. The dog was barking like a fiend now, just beyond the door, knocking over lamps and end tables as it thrashed about the room in a seeming fury. 'He's blind right now,' Ben explained. 'He knows that he lost it somehow, but he doesn't know what's happened.'

Neither did Mary Ann, of course.

'A grand mal seizure,' Michael explained. 'He's epileptic. This is called the postictal period. We have to stay away from him until it passes.'

She asked how long that might be.

Michael shrugged. 'Hard to call. Whenever he calms down.'

Mary Ann felt wobbly, so she sank to the edge of the bed and tried to soothe herself with the thrift-shop art over the dresser: an incongruous tropical beach scene.

Seeing her rattled state, Ben sat next to her and took her hand.

'Welcome to Pinyon City, Mary Ann.'

Ten minutes later, the guys left on an exploratory mission, closing the bedroom door behind them. She heard them speak softly to the dog for several minutes before Ben summoned her to join them. Roman was stretched out on the sofa now; Ben and Michael were sitting on the floor next to him. 'It's okay,' said Michael. 'It's over.'

The dog looked up as she approached, flapping his plumy tail against the sofa cushions in weary recognition. 'Yeah,' said Ben. 'There's Mary Ann. She's back.' He smiled at Mary Ann. 'He always does that afterwards. He takes a head count.'

She was touched, somehow, to be one of the heads that Roman would count.

'Poor little boy,' she said, sitting on the floor next to Michael. She reached out and held one of the dog's paws. The pads were enormous, the size of pennies, as dark as charcoal and almost as rough. His breath was foul, but she didn't mind.

Michael stroked Roman's side methodically, as if grooming a horse. 'Look at him checking things out. He's like Dorothy after the tornado. "I had the strangest dream, Auntie Em. And you were there . . . and you . . . and you."'

Mary Ann smiled at her old friend. Was there still nothing in Michael's life that couldn't evoke a reference to *The Wizard of Oz*?

'How often does this happen?' she asked him.

'Only twice before. The last one was four months ago. We've got him on meds, but . . . maybe we'll have to increase the dosage.' He cast a questioning glance at Ben.

'What causes it?' she asked.

'His is hereditary,' Ben answered. 'His mother had an epileptic pup in an earlier litter.'

'Did you know that when you bought him?'

'No, but . . . really . . . what are you gonna do? He belonged to us the moment we picked him up. Didn't you, Mr. Dood?' Ben looked down tenderly at the exhausted dog. Mary Ann thought she saw him get misty-eyed, but he shifted almost immediately to a breezier tone. 'So what do you think, you gnarly beast? Is it time for a bath?'

Roman scrambled to his feet with the ungainly zeal of a newborn colt, that gross string of saliva still swinging from his lips, though this time it verged on the comical.

'I take it he likes baths,' she said.

'Oh, hell, yeah,' said Michael. 'Anything to do with water. Wait'll you see him in the snow. He's a total fiend.'

As the guys led Roman to the bathtub, Mary Ann found herself envying the dog his blithe amnesia, the apparent ease with which he'd let go of something awful. He had endured a grand mal seizure – the perfectly named Big Bad – but the only thing on his mind now was the prospect of a warm bath and, maybe later, the pleasures of snow.

I used to be that, she thought.

She was offered her choice of bedrooms, so she took the smaller one at the back of the house. It overlooked a meandering creek lined with chalet-style cabins. There was gray smoke curling from one of the chimneys and, somewhere farther down the valley, a dog barking erratically, but few other signs of habitation. She unzipped the duffel bag the guys had given her for the trip and arranged her things methodically on white plastic hangers in an otherwise empty closet. There wasn't much to unpack; she was traveling even lighter now for this escape from her escape, this refuge once removed.

When she joined the guys again, they were in the kitchen loading groceries into a rusty old Buick of a refrigerator. (Ben had brought along several tote bags of leafy green vegetables, primordial-looking and streaked with red cartilage, like pterodactyl wings.) Roman was lapping water from a stainless steel bowl they'd also imported from the city.

'I'm making coffee,' said Ben. 'Do you take cream?'

'If you have it,' she said.

'We don't, actually. And we could use some mustard. Do you think you could make a run to the general store?'

It was such quaint thing to be asked – so absurdly *Little House on the Prairie* – that she smiled. 'Across the road, you mean?'

'Do it,' said Michael. 'It's a trip.'

So she put on her borrowed ski jacket and headed through the swirling snow to the store. The few cars that were parked along the road, their own included – were already morphing into giant white tortoises; the only color remaining in the landscape was the blue-and-red glow of a Pepsi machine on the porch of the store.

She tugged open the door and entered a fetchingly decrepit scene: slanting floors, pegboards hung with fishing lures, a dormant potbellied stove serving as a perch for the resident cat. It might have been something out of Norman Rockwell if not for the glass-fronted freezers full of packaged pizzas and, mounted above the checkout counter, a flat-screen TV set on mute, with subtitled carnage from a car bombing in Iran. *Why would you want that here?* she wondered, until she saw the look of leaden boredom on the face of the young cashier. He was like some heartsick captive creature in a roadside zoo.

And apparently he'd been alone until her arrival.

'Wow,' she said, brushing the snow off her jacket. 'It's really starting to come down.'

'Don't worry, lady. You'll be able to get out. The plow comes through this evening.'

'Oh, I didn't mean that. I like the snow, actually.'

He grunted noncommittally.

'We're staying across the road,' she added with growing discomfort. 'That little rental house? It's very sweet. This is such a charming town.'

Another grunt. 'Anything in particular you're lookin' for?'

She shook her head. 'I'd just like to browse, thanks.' She didn't like this kid's energy, and she didn't like to be called 'lady,' so she chose not to squander another moment in conversation. Still, to keep from looking like a fraud, she had to make a show of 'browsing,' so she began meandering through that tilty-floored room, stopping to admire things that would never normally attract her attention. A box of jackknives, for example, and a creaky carousel of Day-Glo postcards emblazoned with flaming skulls.

Michael had been right; the place was a trip, a head-on collision of country funk and city demands. There was an alcove to one side, an obvious add-on to the original building, that did its best to im-personate a wine cellar, complete with an arbor of dusty plastic grapes. There was even an 'antique nook' – a sad collection of cobalt medicine bottles and horseshoes – but she could smell mold from the door, so she didn't go in.

She found the condiments on a scantily stocked shelf near the back of the store. There were two squeeze bottles of Grey Poupon, amazingly enough, so she took one, then headed toward the freezers for the half-and-half. The cashier was dealing with someone else now, laconically ringing up an order, so she lurked out of sight to avoid further awkward transactions. The funny thing was: she'd heard no one else enter the store. She had to assume this other customer had been shopping in the antique nook.

She waited for proof of the customer's exit – the telltale jingle of the cowbells on the back of the front door – before bringing her items to the desk. She wondered how she'd become like this: afraid of everything and everyone, even herself. Cancer and infidelity were two good answers, except for the fact that her failure of nerve had come to her long before those particular calamities. Once, when she was younger, she would have stopped at nothing to charm this cashier – even *after* he'd been so rude to her – just to prove that, deep down, people were decent, and, even more important, that she was.

She no longer had the energy for that tiresome dance.

She paid for the items in cash without saying a word, mostly to see if the guy could complete the transaction in total silence. He did, and she wasn't surprised. She stuffed the mustard and the half-and-half carton into the pockets of her jacket and left the building. It was already dusk, so she stopped on the porch to study the nondescript house across the street, her harbor for the next two nights. She could see someone moving about in the living room – Michael, it looked like – and there was light spilling from the windows onto the new-fallen snow. It felt like spying on someone else's life.

It took her a while to notice the footprints leading from the store to the end of the block. There, next to the restaurant, she finally saw the other shopper, a slow-moving figure in a dark overcoat and a brimmed hat, hunching into the snow on his way home to somewhere. She could feel the bite of the wind now, so she tugged tight the hood of her jacket and proceeded to trudge toward the house. She was almost across the road when the all-but-soundless landscape was pierced by the hideous howl of an animal – a dog, she supposed, though, in these parts, according to Michael, it could just as easily be a coyote. They howled out of loneliness, apparently, and sometimes to celebrate a kill.

She turned in the direction of the howl, but there were no four-legged creatures in sight, only the anonymous person from the store. She stopped long enough to see that he had also been stopped in his tracks by the sound and was facing in her direction now. He was featureless at that distance, a solitary exclamation mark against the blank white page of the road, but she felt a certain primal kinship with him, this fellow traveler pricking his ears to an ominous call from the wild. Instinctively, she raised a gloved hand to mark their shared moment, as if to say: *Yes, stranger, I heard it, too.*

But he didn't return the salute; he just stood there looking at her, perfectly still for the longest time. Then he arched his neck to the darkening sky and released a second, even more sinister howl.

When he walked away, she began to run.

'You must've heard him,' she said. 'It was almost triumphant.' She was standing in the kitchen with the guys now, still panting a little, the snow still melting on her jacket. Ben was sautéing onions in a battered wok, while Michael, under Ben's occasional instruction, was dicing a Japanese eggplant at the kitchen table.

'*Triumphant?*' asked Michael.

'You know. Like a coyote celebrating a kill.'

Michael rolled his eyes. 'I should never have told you that.'

'You're stoned,' she said dismissively, having noticed his vaporizer on the refectory table. It must have been the very first thing he'd unpacked. She turned to Ben instead. 'You heard it, right?'

'Sorry.' Ben tapped the scalloped yellow vent over the electric stove. 'This thing roars like a blast furnace. Are you sure he was howling *at* you?'

'He was looking at me, and he was howling like a werewolf. He did it the second time, I think, just so I could see that he was doing it.'

Michael looked up from his dicing. 'You should probably take it as a compliment.'

'Really,' she said with murder in her eyes. 'A compliment.'

'Sure.'

'Remind me not to hire you at a rape crisis center.'

'When have you *ever* worked at a rape crisis center?'

'Hang on.' Ben held up his hand like a crossing guard, silencing Michael, before turning to Mary Ann with an appeasing smile. 'You should know . . . howling is fairly common around here.'

'What do you mean?'

He shrugged. 'A lot of bikers stop at the saloon. They're just tourists like the rest of us, but they can get a little . . . piggy sometimes about women. Some of them. Up until a few years ago, they were stapling bras to the ceiling of the saloon.'

'Lovely,' she said.

'To be fair,' said Michael, 'it was the *women* who did the stapling. It wasn't like a gang rape or something. They were totally in on the gig.'

'Who told you that?' asked Ben.

'Bernice.'

'Bernice?'

'From the county office. The one who makes that ugly shit with yarn.'

'Oh, God, yeah.'

Mary Ann was annoyed by this diversion, since it was clear now that her scary episode had yet to be taken seriously. 'This guy seemed way too old for a biker.'

'You haven't seen our bikers,' said Michael.

'*Your* bikers?'

'He thinks he lives here already.' Ben had turned to wink at her as he stirred the onions. 'We humor him as much as possible.'

'Anyway,' she went on, 'he wasn't coming out of the saloon. He was coming out of the store.'

'Right,' said Michael. 'Where he'd just bought a couple of Sara Lee chocolate pies because he'd already gotten hammered at the saloon.'

'Okay, smart-ass, then what?'

'What do you mean?'

'Gimme the scenario, Mouse. He spots me crossing the street in a fucking snowstorm . . . this silver-haired fifty-seven-year-old woman—'

'C'mon,' grinned Ben. 'You know that men still notice you.'

'No . . . I don't . . . I don't know that at all.'

'Well,' said Michael, 'you still have your teeth. That counts for a whole lot around here.'

She laughed in spite of herself. Then, because Michael had never once looked up from his chopping during this exchange, she yanked a glove from her pocket and hurled it at him. It fell short of his smirking face, which was what she'd been aiming for.

'She's thrown down the gauntlet,' said Michael.

'That's right, you little turd.'

'Look who's picked it up.' Ben was now pointing to Roman, who was prancing triumphantly out of the room with the five-fingered treat in his jaws.

Michael went after him, laughing. When he was out of the room, Ben shoehorned in a moment for just the two of them. 'Don't take it personally, Mary Ann.'

'Oh, I don't. I've known him too long for that.'

'No. I mean . . . the howler. It probably wasn't about you at all.' Ben cast his eyes toward the window, toward somewhere-out-yonder, then lowered his voice as if somewhere-out-yonder might be listening. 'There's meth in them thar hills.'

She nodded soberly. 'So tell me again why you love this place.'

He smiled just enough to reveal that beguiling gap between his teeth, the gap she'd explored vicariously when she'd first imagined Ben and Michael in the throes of sex. The thought of that made her squirm, knowing them as she did now, but she had definitely gone there, semi-incestuously, in her head.

'We'll get an early start in the morning,' he said. 'You can see for yourself.'

Look Again

It was twilight when Shawna returned to Anna's flat. Jake met her in front and led the way down the passageway past the furred antlers of the air plants on the wall of the house next door. This sliver of green offered only a dim echo of the garden Anna had presided over on Barbary Lane. Shawna remembered that paradise well – and how wildly her heart would race as she ran across the courtyard to show Anna her latest treasure: a rock, a seashell, an ivory elephant her dad had bought her in Chinatown.

Her heart was racing now, for entirely different reasons.

And the 'treasure' in her knapsack was anything but.

223

'She's expecting you,' Jake told her. 'She's been looking forward to it.'

Shawna almost apologized for disrupting Jake's afternoon tryst, until it occurred to her that he might not want to discuss it, whatever the outcome had been. How easy could it be to be him? If Jake was shy, it was mostly because he'd been burned in his search for a man who would love (and desire!) the man he wanted to be. Shawna's own appetites were catholic – as she liked to put it in her blog – but her body and her gender had never warred with each other. Even when wearing a strap-on and pounding her sweet hippie boo into his futon, she'd never felt like anything but a girl.

Maybe that was why she loved coming here. Not just because of Anna, though Anna's loving counsel had certainly been part of it, but because both these singular souls, by their very existence, challenged Shawna's comfortable assumptions about what it meant to be male or female. They compelled her, if only temporarily, to live in the genderless neutrality of the human heart.

Jake was leading her to the backyard, she realized.

'What's happening here?' She had just spotted a whimsical wooden structure she didn't recognize, an enclosed gazebo with a pointed roof.

'I guess you haven't been here for a while.'

'Well . . . a month or so, I guess.' She knew Jake hadn't meant to make her feel guilty, but she had gone there anyway, all on her own. A month was too long to risk at this stage of Anna's life. Anna deserved better from a member of her 'logical family' – Anna's pet term for her chosen brood – logical, that is, as opposed to biological.

But Anna was still there, bundled up in a black fur blanket, looking like a dowager empress trying out a brand-new throne. Shawna leaned down and kissed her cool, dry cheek. 'So soft and cozy,' she said, caressing the blanket.

'It's not real,' said Anna. 'Don't fret.'

'I did wonder.'

'Don't be silly. Jake got it for me at the Pottery Shed.'

'Barn,' said Jake, winking at Shawna.

'Did you do this all yourself?' asked Shawna, perusing the gazebo with genuine admiration.

Jake shrugged sheepishly. 'Don't look too close at it.'

'No, Jake. It's a total work of art.'

He was actually blushing, she realized. 'I'll leave you two to talk,' he mumbled, before tromping back to the house.

Shawna pulled off her backpack and set it on the floor with unnatural care, as if it contained a nest of sleeping rattlesnakes. She perched on the edge of the chair and took Anna's hand as she cut to the chase: 'I just lost someone,' she said, as unhysterically as possible. 'It hit me kind of hard. I need to talk to you about it.'

Anna winced in sympathy. 'Not the young man on the unicycle?'

This made Shawna smile. Anna had referred to Otto as 'the young man on the unicycle' ever since she'd seen him perform one sunny afternoon at the Now and Zen Fest in the park. 'No, he's perfectly fine,' Shawna assured her. 'I just left his place.' She wondered if Anna had remained benignly ignorant of Otto's name because she'd somehow divined that Shawna wasn't serious about him – at least not *serious* serious.

'This was someone I didn't know well,' Shawna explained. 'She was homeless. We saved her life, I think, for a little while . . . so it was hard to see her go.'

Anna nodded. 'Of course.'

Shawna told the story from the beginning: that first day under the freeway, the eye-catching MAMA sign, Shawna's inexplicable bond with Leia, the obsessive search that led to Cossack Alley, the knife attack, the ambulance ride to the hospital, the flesh-eating disease, the monstrous strangers who had rented Alexandra as a child.

'Unthinkable,' said Anna.

'That's the word,' said Shawna.

'So they never . . . took off the leg?'

Shawna shook her head. 'She was adamant about it . . . and it was too late, anyway. She was too far gone.'

'When did she die?'

'Last night. Late. I should have been there.'

'No, dear. You did well. You were the angel who took her home.'

Briskly, with a lopsided smile, Shawna brushed away a tear. 'They asked me if I wanted her things. I didn't even know she *had* things.' She picked up her knapsack and removed the revelatory item she'd brought with her: a *Star Wars* lunch box so rusty and battered that Princess Leia's face was all but obliterated. 'She kept her cash strapped to her leg – and the knife, of course – but this is where she kept her memories. The guy who was guarding her cardboard box brought it to the hospital this morning.'

Shawna opened the lunch box and removed one of the photos, holding it out for Anna to examine. 'She worked in the East Bay for a while. That's the Fabric Barn, I guess, judging from those bolts of cloth.'

'Lovely,' said Anna, and she wasn't just being gracious. The young woman behind the counter was a stunning brunette with a sparkling smile. When Shawna first saw the photo, it had taken her a while to connect this Alexandra with the wretch she'd met under the freeway, but there had been no denying that it was the same person. It pleased Shawna that Anna would never know anything but this version of the woman, that Alexandra's beauty was still intact in the eyes of someone who had never known her.

'And here she is as a little girl,' said Shawna, trying to sound matter-of-fact, because this image, the one with 'me' inscribed crudely on the back, was the one that was flooding her mind with nameless dread. The photo had lost all its colors except orange and green. Little Alexandra was wearing a dirndl and standing alone at a window. She wasn't smiling in this picture; she looked completely miserable, in fact.

'She looks like Heidi,' said Anna, choosing to focus on the dress.

'Look again.'

Anna pulled a pair of reading glasses from the depths of the fur-free blanket and maneuvered them, shakily, onto her face. 'She doesn't seem happy, does she?'

'Look at the background. That's Alcatraz, right? And look at that railing outside the window. And that little plywood terrace.'

Anna nodded but said nothing.

'It's the pentshack, isn't it?' This was their common term for the studio on the roof of 28 Barbary Lane. Anna had rented it out to tenants, but Shawna had been allowed to play there whenever the place was empty. It had been her secret castle in the sky.

'Well, it's certainly Russian Hill,' Anna conceded. 'But it can't be the pentshack.'

'Why not?'

Anna shrugged. 'Because there were never children living there.'

Shawna looked at her. 'Maybe not *living* there.'

It didn't take long for this darkness to find its way onto Anna's face. '*Oh*,' she murmured.

'Didn't my father live there?'

Silence.

'He was seeing Mary Ann, right? She used to sleep over there sometimes. Before they got married and adopted me. He told me so himself.'

'Well . . . yes, but it was also the TV room for a long time, so . . . dear, I hope you're not suggesting—'

'No, of course not!' Shawna snapped. 'I'm just trying to figure this out!' She was starting to sound like a waterboarder at Guantanamo, so she returned the snapshot to the lunch box and softened her tone considerably. 'Sorry. My nerves are kinda frayed.'

Anna's wheels seemed already to be turning. 'When was that taken?'

'I'm guessing late seventies. Maybe a little earlier.'

'Why are you guessing that?'

'Because she looks to be about seven or eight, and the coroner said she was barely past forty when she died. If that.' Shawna was trying hard to absorb this fact herself, reckoning with the bitter truth that Alexandra had only recently achieved middle age. 'Plus,' she added, 'the photo has that orangey seventies look.'

Anna was no longer listening, just blinking into the distance, engrossed in some flickering old movie of her life. After a moment she said: 'Mr. Williams.'

'What?'

'He lived in the pentshack for about six months. He

was a private detective. My wife – my ex-wife – hired him to track me down and spy on me.'

'Did you ever see him—?'

'—with a child? No. Never. He was a mean, conniving little man . . . he tried to blackmail some-one . . . that I was seeing at the time and had grown very close to, but I never saw any evidence that . . .' Anna's words trailed off feebly.

'But he might have been capable, right?'

Anna nervously rearranged the folds of her throw. 'I can't imagine *anyone* being capable of that. Much less under my roof.'

'What happened to him?'

'I don't know. He got very drunk one Christmas Eve, and he never came back.'

'*Ever?*'

Anna shook her head slowly. 'We called the police after a week or so, but nothing came of it. I always assumed he skipped town once his cover was blown.'

Anna's crime-fiction lingo made Shawna grin.

'What?' asked Anna. 'That's what they say, isn't it?'

'That's what they say.'

Anna regarded her with grandmotherly concern. 'I hope you're feeling better, dear. You had me worried.'

'I just don't understand, that's all.'

'Understand what?'

'Why the universe hands me such random shit.'

Anna's smile was inscrutable. 'Sometimes the universe has a slow day.'

* * *

Not long after dark, back at Otto's cramped studio in the Crocker Amazon, Shawna provided her own coda to the saga that had consumed her for weeks.

'I've asked them to give us the ashes,' she said. She was lying naked on Otto's futon, her head resting on the warm slab of his chest, trying to find her way back to the ordinary and the beautiful.

'Cool,' he said. 'What do you wanna do with 'em?'

'I thought we could take them to the headlands when the weather gets better. Or maybe the park. Stow Lake or something.'

'Totally.'

They were both silent for a while as she rode the rhythm of Otto's heart, drugged by his ripe, cedary essence. It was raining now, so hard she could hear it, and there were fat droplets, like beads of mercury, rolling down the security bars in the window.

Otto said: 'I have to tell you something.'

She thought she'd heard guilt in his voice. 'Oh, yeah?' she said, bracing herself for another unpleasant surprise, another shitstorm out of nowhere.

He pulled her closer until she was straddling his leg like a koala on a tall, skinny tree. Finally he said: 'I went to see Alexandra last night.'

She was infinitely relieved. 'That's it?' She had planned to stop by the hospital herself, but she'd already committed to a reading at 'Writers with Drinks' and hadn't wanted to disappoint her friend

231

Charlie, who hosted the event. 'Why is that something you have to tell me? That's wonderful, Otto. She had company before she died.'

'I dunno . . . you were sort of funny about it before.'

'Funny about it? I asked you to be part of it.'

'Yeah, but . . . just me.'

It took her a moment to get it. 'You took Sammy, you mean?'

'Yeah.'

Of course he'd taken the monkey. Sammy was Otto's envoy, the purest and deepest expression of his heart. It shamed her to think that she'd denied him the use of that silent language. She scooched her hand up his leg and cupped his junk, loving its silken familiarity, the reassurance of her own puppet pal. 'Was she aware of you?'

'I don't know. Maybe.'

'She wasn't when I was there.'

'I think she may have smiled once.'

'Well, that's good.'

'Whatever.'

'No. It's good, baby.'

'It was good for me,' he said.

An Old Familiar Impatience

'Why is the water yellow?' Mary Ann asked, wrinkling her nose.

It was barely nine a.m., and the three of them were standing on the edge of the hot springs that Ben had been raving about since breakfast. It was not what she'd imagined. It looked like a smallish suburban swimming pool, complete with a blue-painted bottom. Only it didn't look blue in the least, it looked green, because of that disgusting water.

'It's not really yellow,' Michael asserted.

'Right.'

'Seriously. That's just the light refracting off the minerals.' He sat down on the edge of the pool and dangled his feet in the steaming saffron broth. He was wearing baggy surfer shorts with washed-out purple swirls that worked nicely with his white hair. Ben was wearing a dark blue Speedo that worked nicely with pretty much everything. She did her best not to stare as he eased himself into the water.

'C'mon, Esther,' said Michael. 'You'll love it once you're in.'

This was a reference to her own swimsuit, a modest granny model with overlapping ruffles of brown polyester that looked, in fact, much worse than anything Esther Williams ever wore. The guys had found it that morning, all by itself on a rack at the general store, and brought it back to her bedroom with great merriment. Once she hit that water, of course, her suit took on a sickly orange hue, and its ruffles began quivering like the diaphanous folds of a jellyfish.

'Eat shit,' she said, seeing the grin on Michael's face.

'I have to have a picture of this.'

'Only if you wanna lose the camera.'

'At least there aren't that many witnesses,' said Ben.

There were half a dozen other people steeping solemnly at the other side of the pool. They seemed to be Eastern Europeans, communally bathing the way they would in their homeland. Mary Ann had already overheard two of the women, both of them large and fish-belly white, chattering away in the changing room. Their grim, guttural tongue had been as foreign to her as Brazilian waxing obviously was to them.

'This is nice,' she told the guys, trying to be a good sport.

'You're looking the wrong way.' Ben took her head in his hands and turned her gaze to the right, then upward, above the redwood perimeter fence. Half a mile away was a canyon wall roofed with unrelenting blue and flanked by a meadow so white it was almost blinding. Wisps of steam were wriggling from its surface like frisky phantoms.

'My God,' she said.

Ben smiled and, without fanfare, began to massage her shoulders. 'This is why there's a Pinyon City. People have been coming here a hundred and fifty years. White people, that is. The natives have been here for eons, of course.'

'They would migrate from Tahoe in the winter,' Michael added. 'It's warmer on this side of the mountains, and the pinyons provided pine nuts for them to eat.'

This National Geographic Special was not typical of Michael, so Mary Ann figured he was aping Ben, playing faithful assistant tour guide. She might have ribbed him about it, considering his glee over the swimsuit, but she was too blissed out to bother. Ben was working her flesh like a wizard, seemingly unafraid of her aging body, somehow making her at one with the earth in a pool of pee-colored water.

Then self-consciousness took over. Those gloomy Borat people across the way were deadpan as ever, but it wasn't hard to imagine what they were thinking. Who were these weird Americans anyway? This silver-haired old couple traveling with their grown son? Why was the son touching his mother's body with such intimacy? And why was her husband watching them? And what was up with that swimsuit, anyway?

'That was heaven,' she said, straightening her neck, discreetly signaling an end to the massage. 'Thank you so much, Ben.'

'You want me to stop?'

'Let him do it,' Michael told her. 'He enjoys it.'

She glanced briefly toward the other bathers, prompting Michael to roll his eyes skyward with an old familiar impatience. *Get over it*, he was telling her, as he so often had when they were young. *Why do you care what* anyone *thinks, when you could be dead or dying in six months? Nobody's watching but you.*

'Okay. Fine. Thank you. Have at it.'

So Ben dug into her neck while Michael leaned on his elbows at the edge of the pool, reminding her very much of a self-satisfied old walrus.

'You're lucky we didn't take you to Harbin,' he said.

'What's Harbin?'

'Another hot springs.' Ben was moving on to her shoulders now. 'North of the city. Clothing optional.'

'No thanks.'

'She's a priss,' said Michael.

'I'm not a priss. I've been to clothing-optional places.'

'Yeah. The ladies' spa at Canyon Ranch.'

She shot him a withering look. 'No . . . smart-ass . . . I went to Lands End with you and Brian once.' She flashed briefly on her now-nomadic first husband, wondering, as she sometimes did, where on this continent his beloved Winnebago had landed.

'You went,' said Michael, 'but you didn't get naked.'

'Yes, I did.'

'Trust me. I would've remembered.'

What was *that* supposed to mean? 'I just don't think,' she added as pleasantly as possible, 'that people my age should be inflicting their naked selves on the landscape. It's not generally appreciated. It's the same reason I don't litter.'

Ben chuckled but didn't comment.

'Lots of people at Harbin are older than us,' Michael said.

'Oh, well . . . yum! Why didn't you tell me? Can't wait.'

Michael chortled. 'Hopeless.'

'It's all good,' Ben offered noncommittally, ending the discussion as he finished off her shoulders with an amiable whack. 'Wanna see our property now? It's on the way back to town. I'd like to try to get to the slopes by noon.'

She wondered if she and Michael were starting to get on Ben's nerves.

* * *

Their land was only a mile or two down the road, but, just before they reached the turn-off, the guys decided they shouldn't go there without the dog.

'Why?' she asked. 'Are there wild animals or something?'

Michael chortled. 'Lotta help the doodle would be. It's the critters that eat the dogs around here. We just take him with us for ceremonial purposes. It feels more like home every time he pees on the property. For that matter, every time *we* do.'

'You don't plan on *living* here, do you?'

'Just for a few weeks at a time,' said Ben, looking over the seat at her. 'A month or two at the most, maybe. It'll be our getaway.'

'It's already your getaway. That's the wonderful part.' She knew they were nowhere near being able to afford to build something.

The dog went berserk when he saw them again, though they'd been gone only for a couple of hours. They loaded him into the car and headed back to the turn-off. The road, which had recently been plowed, ascended in a leisurely switchback fashion that didn't bother Mary Ann in the slightest until Michael ordered her not to look back.

'Oh, fuck,' she said. 'Not another cliff.'

'No. I just wanna save it until we get there.'

What he was saving she finally saw after trudging up a roadside bank to the promontory where their land lay. There was nothing precipitous here to work her nerves, just the gentle falling away of the pines to the long, narrow valley that contained Pinyon City. She couldn't see the town, though, or even a single house. There was a range of saw-toothed mountains in the distance, but no evidence of the highway that had brought them here. The hum she had mistaken for traffic had turned out to be wind in the trees.

'The living room will go here,' Michael told her, pointing to a flagged stake in the snow. 'The big window will face that way, so we can look directly at Pinyon Peak.'

She asked, perhaps indelicately, how they planned to get up here from the road, and what they would do about water and sewage.

'We'll have to dig a well,' said Ben. 'And put in a septic tank and a driveway. It's no biggie.'

It seemed like a huge biggie to her, but she didn't say so. Michael now had his arm around Ben, who'd just thrown a pine-cone for Roman, and the two of them were watching the dog bound through the snow like a four-legged Muppet. She had the sense that it wouldn't matter to either of them if they were never able to build here. This was just the canvas on which they could paint their modest dreams, and, as such, it could always be the beginning of something, not the imperfect, inevitable end.

Once Ben had left for the slopes at Kirkwood, Mary Ann and Michael camped out on opposing sofas in the living room. Michael had told her that he was 'jonesing' for hot chocolate, so he'd already made a run to the general store for the necessary ingredients, including a bag of mini-marshmallows so ancient and crusty they might have been geological specimens.

'They're okay,' he said, after sipping from his mug. 'They soften up a lot once they get hot.'

She half-expected him to make a bawdy joke about that, but, for once, he didn't strain for a double entendre. He did worse; he asked her about Bob.

'Do we have to talk about him?'

He shrugged. 'Just wondering if you've heard anything.'

'He left a message on my cell.'

'And?'

'I deleted it.'

'Well, fine, but—'

'I'm divorcing him, Mouse. I have nothing to talk to him about.'

'Then . . . how will he know you want one?'

Why was he doing this? Couldn't he see that she might not want to talk to Bob about *anything* – especially the smoking wreckage of the marriage – when she was on the verge of having her woman-hood extracted? She wouldn't have put it that way to Mouse, of course, since she didn't want to be smothered with platitudes about femininity not being an organ but something in the heart and the mind, and blah, blah, blah . . .

'He'll find out soon enough,' she told him. 'I texted Robbie.'

Michael's forehead furrowed in bald-faced disapproval. 'You really think he should hear that from his son?'

'Why not?'

'It's not fair to Robbie, for one thing. He shouldn't have to deal with that. He's just barely got his toes into college.'

'You don't know what's fair to Robbie. You've never even met him. He and I are very close. We talk about a lot of things.'

'Did you talk to him about the tennis pro?'

'What tennis pro?'

'At the country club. Last year.'

'He was a scuba diver, Mouse. I was getting certified.'

'You certainly were.' If he'd had a big cigar in his hand, he would have waggled it at her, Groucho-style. 'So, did you?'

'Did I what?'

'Tell your stepson about the redheaded scuba diver. With the crooked dick.'

Mary Ann sighed. Interesting, the details Michael chose to remember. 'I love Robbie too much to tell him about something like that.'

'But not enough to keep quiet about his father screwing your life coach.'

'It's not the same thing, Mouse. It's entirely different.'

'How?'

'Why are you picking on me?'

'I'm not. I just wanna know how it's different.'

'Okay, then, think about it for a while . . . these were my two closest confidantes. Well, *she* was, anyway. I told her *everything*, Mouse.'

Michael's mouth slowly went slack. 'You told her about Crooked Dick.'

It wasn't a question, exactly, so she didn't reply.

'Tell me you didn't tell her about Crooked Dick.'

'Stop calling him that. Of course I told her. That's what you do with a life coach.'

'No. That's what you do with a shrink. A life coach teaches you how to keep a gratitude journal and sleep with potpourri under your pillow.'

She almost smiled, but repressed it. 'This *hurts*, Mouse. You don't seem to be getting that at all. I told Calliope the most intimate details of my . . . issues with Bob, and she just took them and ran with them. She used them to lure him.'

'What sort of issues?'

'Oh, no. Not on cocoa.'

'You'll tell Calliope but you won't tell me?'

'That's right.'

'Well, thanks a whole heap. That's nice to know.'

'It's not that big a deal. You're making too much of it.' She leaned forward and set her mug on the coffee table in slow motion, buying time so she could compose her thoughts. 'I just got tired of doing certain things, that's all.'

'Like . . . ?'

'Like blowing his wrinkly old cock.'

Michael's expression betrayed nothing, so she went on:

'Calliope agreed with me, too. That's what pisses me off. She'd just gotten a divorce and we had a big laugh over it. It was a real bonding moment for us.'

Michael was frowning now. 'Cocks don't wrinkle, for the record. They're pretty much the only thing that doesn't, thank God. If you mean plain ol' bed death—'

'No, Mouse. I didn't want it in my mouth anymore. It's no more complicated than that. It was okay for a while, but I got tired of it. I wanted to sit by the fire and go on trips with my husband and look at sunsets. I didn't want Cirque du Fellatio!'

'And you told Calliope this?'

'Lots of women are like this, Mouse, especially when they get to my age. You don't know. Viagra is *not* our friend.' She curled her feet under her butt, turning defensive in the face of this interrogation. 'Yes, I told Calliope.'

'Shit.'

'I *know*. I should've guessed she'd do anything for money.'

Michael nodded. Mary Ann thought he was finally grasping the heinousness of what had happened, but, typically, he had drifted in a different direction entirely.

'You know,' he said, leaning back, as if sweetly ruminating on the shape of a cloud. 'I've never heard a man complain about having to suck dick . . . a *gay* man, I mean. I've heard women complain about it a fair amount, but never men. Men don't say: 'Damn, do I have to do *that* again?' It just doesn't happen.'

She could hardly believe what she was hearing. 'Am I on trial here, Mouse? Are you telling me this is *my* fault?'

'No . . . I'm just sayin''.'

'Well, stop sayin''.'

'It was an observation, Mary Ann. Not a criticism.'

'Why are you defending him?'

'Who? Bob? I don't think I'd even *like* him. All I know about him is what I hear from you.'

'And stop making it sound like I'm off sex.'

'Isn't that what you just said?'

'No! Every now and then is fine.'

''I have always preferred an occasional orgy to a nightly routine.' '

'What?'

'Aunt Augusta said that. In *Travels with My Aunt*.'

She didn't have the energy to ask him what the hell he was talking about. 'Whatever.'

'I'm *agreeing* with you, Mary Ann. I think it's a lot better if it's an event. Ben and I plan our week around it sometimes. We make a date for Sunday morning.

Or whenever, depending on our schedules. If Bob was getting tedious about it—'

'God, you guys are all the same.'

Michael raised an eyebrow. '*We guys?*'

'Men.' He'd obviously thought she meant gay men and was already set to pounce on her homophobia. '*All* men. Sex is all you ever think about.'

'Not always. But it's a good thing.' He smiled. 'As Martha says.'

'Aren't you just getting *tired* of it? How can you even do it anymore on a regular basis? You're the same age I am.'

He shrugged. 'I have help.'

'Viagra, you mean.'

He shook his head. 'That stuff's not good for your heart. And it hasn't been working that great lately, to tell you the truth.'

'Then what?'

He took a sip of his cocoa. 'Sure you wanna hear this?'

'No, but tell me anyway.'

He set the mug down again. 'I have a shot.'

It didn't register right away. 'A shot of what?'

'A *shot* shot.' He mimed using a syringe – and aimed it in the direction of his crotch. 'My doctor prescribed it.'

She was sure he was kidding. 'Right.'

'Well . . . you asked.'

'*You give yourself a shot in your penis?*' She winced as if she had one of her own and was already feeling the pinch of the syringe.

'Oh, God, no,' said Michael. 'I could *never* give myself a shot. Ben does it.'

She had a concrete image to work with now, and she wished like hell that she didn't. 'And he doesn't mind?' she asked incredulously.

'*Mind*? It turns me into a dildo for two hours. Why should he mind?'

'Mouse!'

'Sorry. You asked . . . I told.'

'Doesn't it hurt?'

'Oh, no . . . Ben does yoga, you know. He's amazingly—'

'The needle, Mouse! Does the needle hurt?'

He shook his head. 'It's just a little prick.'

This whole exchange could have been a setup for that stupid joke, but she knew that it hadn't been. She did her best not to register her instant revulsion, moving away from the specifics as quickly as possible 'Isn't that a little . . . unromantic?'

'You'd think so, wouldn't you? It's not, though. It's the most romantic sex I've ever had. I mean, most of that has to do with Ben, but . . . the shot adds a whole other dimension. It leaves room for tenderness. It gives you that . . . leisure. You're thinking about the other person, not your dick . . . well, not *your* dick—'

'Shut up,' she said in the friendliest way possible. It was hard enough to picture Ben and Michael, but now, perversely, she was wondering if Bob and Calliope had heard about this stuff, and if it was figuring prominently in their Italian idyll.

'Am I oversharing?' he asked.

'When aren't you?'

'Well . . . when *you're* talking, for one thing.'

She gave him a withering look that even the dog seemed to notice.

'On the *phone*,' Michael hastened to add, apparently thinking he was making things better. 'It's much better being face-to-face. You should come out more often.'

That last remark, delivered with a crooked smile, was tinged with both tenderness and resentment. He seemed to be asking: *Why does it take a calamity to get you here?* His neediness came as a complete surprise to her, but it made her feel, well, needed.

'Do you wanna take Roman for a walk?' she asked.

They followed the river road out of town. They walked down the centerline, in fact, since traffic was non-existent, and it was difficult to navigate the mounds of plowed snow on the shoulders. The landscape was different here, more desert than forest, really. The taller pines had vanished in a matter of minutes, leaving only the squatty pinyons on the hills and the silvery skeletons of aspens along the riverbank.

'I'd be more than happy to go with you,' Michael said out of nowhere.

It took her a while to realize that he was talking about her surgery.

'You haven't said anything,' he added, 'but the offer is there.'

'Thanks, Mouse. That's really sweet, but . . . I think DeDe has pretty much got me covered. It's sort of a girl thing, anyway, you know.'

He gave her a heavy-lidded scowl.

'It's just an overnighter, Mouse. I'd rather have you guys waiting for me when I get out.'

'As you wish, madam. Whatever gender role you require.'

She socked him on his shoulder with a gloved hand. It would have been nice to have taken his arm and simply strolled for a while through this bleakly beautiful place, but the dog was trotting between them on his leash, keeping apace. She'd noticed that Roman wasn't good at heeling for one person, but he had to be in the middle if two were traveling as one. He had his own insecurities, this dog, and wasn't letting go of them.

After a long silence, she asked: 'Have you seen Anna lately?'

The name didn't come naturally to her. First-name familiarity seemed almost disrespectful to the kind, stately presence Mary Ann had known as Mrs. Madrigal. But Michael had apparently been calling their former landlady 'Anna' ever since he'd reached middle age, so Mary Ann had taught herself to follow his custom.

'We had her over for dinner last month,' Michael replied. 'I see her a fair amount, of course, when I have to pick up Jake . . . or drop something off.'

She had met Michael's assistant only once, when she had flown back to San Francisco in Bob's jet after Mrs. Madrigal had suffered her stroke. He had struck Mary Ann as extremely shy but conscientious. She hadn't had a clue that Jake was transgendered until Michael told her after her return to Connecticut.

'It's wonderful that she has him, isn't it?'

'And vice versa,' said Michael.

A big black bird – a raven, she supposed, or maybe a crow – flew from the riverbank and landed just ahead of them on a yellow-and-black highway sign reading ICY CONDITIONS AHEAD. The bird cackled for a moment, as if punctuating the message, then flew away again, a harbinger out of Poe lost in the twenty-first century.

It all goes so fast, she thought. We dole out our lives in dinner parties and plane flights, and it's over before we know it. We lose everyone we love, if they don't lose us first, and every single thing we do is intended to distract us from that reality.

'Will you take me to see her?' she asked.

Michael had lost track of the conversation. 'Sorry . . . what?'

'Will you take me to see Anna?'

'Of course.' He seemed almost relieved. 'As soon as we get back, if you like.'

'Let's wait until after the surgery,' she said. 'It'll be better then.'

She was always putting things off, she realized, always assuming she'd have at least one more chance. Sooner or later, she would probably have to pay for that.

Sacred Garments

Jake was wearing one of Michael's old coveralls that day. They were too tight around the waist for Michael, but they were still in good shape, so Michael had been happy to pass them along – tickled about it, in fact. Jake liked the retro eighties lettering of the name on the back – PLANT PARENTHOOD – and liked explaining its history, though the nursery hadn't been Michael's for years, and had since been renamed.

There had been a break in the rain, so Jake was on a ladder at a client's house in Presidio Heights, cleaning leaves out of the fancy bronze gutters before the next downpour arrived. When his phone vibrated, he looked to see who it was – then took the call.

'Dude.'

Jonah didn't say anything right away. Jake hadn't talked to him since their soccer-and-cuddling session, so he wasn't sure whether to expect regret or righteousness or what. In his mind, though, he was already watching TV with Jonah again (Manchester United, this time) and playing by the same uncomplicated rules of love.

'I need your help,' Jonah said at last.

'What's goin' on, man?'

'I've been lustful again.'

'Okay.' Jake's face was aflame with unmanly blushes. *Nice, dillweed. Good thing you're just on the phone.*

'Where are you?' asked Jonah.

'At work.'

'You get lunch off? Can we meet at your gramma's place?'

'She's not my gramma, dude. And she's got company.' The upstairs neighbors, Selina and Marguerite, were probably hanging out with Anna now, since they'd all gone to the four-story rainforest that morning and had planned on coming home for lunch. 'You've gotta give me some warning,' Jake said with a rapidly sinking heart.

'You could come here,' Jonah suggested.

'Where are you?'

'At the condo.'

'What condo?'

'The one they rented for the elders.'

'Dude.'

'It's cool. I'm by myself. The others have gone back to Salt Lake.'

That's right. They won. Their job is done.

'Gimme the address,' said Jake.

'You don't mind?'

'Nah. I can get off. I'm my own boss.' That was *almost* true, since Michael was still in the mountains and lunch hour was always Jake's to call.

'Praise God,' said Jonah.

'Whatever,' said Jake, already feeling like a fool.

The condo was on the fourth floor of a modern building near the Moscone Center. Jake had been expecting the chaos of a dorm room, but there was very little evidence that four other young guys had recently been camping out there. It wasn't until they passed an empty room on their way to Jonah's room that he spotted, stacked against a wall, signs of recent activity. That's exactly what they were – signs – printed political posters that bore messages like YES ON 8 AND MARRIAGE = ONE MAN + ONE WOMAN. There were also some obviously homemade efforts: cardboard crosses nailed to wooden stakes with Bible verses rendered in Magic Marker.

Jonah closed the door as they passed.

So that's what the left-handed scissors were for.

'We don't have to do it in the bedroom,' Jonah told him. 'I just thought it might be easier on the bed.'

'Whatever,' said Jake.

In the bedroom, Jonah waited solemnly, word-lessly, for Jake to assume the position before crawling into his arms. There wasn't a TV in the room this time, so they wouldn't have soccer to talk about. Jonah was wearing a starched white shirt and creased trousers, which made Jake self-conscious as soon as the kid had settled against his chest.

'Sorry about the grody coveralls.'

'That's okay.'

'I can take 'em off. I've got clean clothes under-neath.'

'No . . . it's more masculine this way.'

'Okay.'

'I need that energy, you know.'

Jake began to rock him, as the so-called therapy demanded, instinctively adopting a gruff tone. 'I know, son. I know.' The 'son' part might have been overdoing it, but Jake had seen enough daddy porn to know how easily he could pull off the slow-talking country contractor thing. He was from Tulsa, after all. If Jonah needed the sexless affection of a man's man to escape the fires of damnation, Jake was willing to oblige.

'What was it this time?'

'The same,' Jonah replied dolefully.

'The same guy?'

'The same *thing*. Lust.'

Jake could feel the heat of the kid's breath on his

chest. It felt pleasurable all by itself, so he found himself grateful that the doctor who had done his top surgery had done such a good job of keeping his sensitivity intact.

'Where were you?' asked Jake.

'A bus shelter out on Market Street.'

'What happened?'

'There were two guys. One was black, and one was white. And they were both naked and had their arms around each other.'

'Dude . . . I mean, son . . . in the bus shelter?'

'Behind the glass.'

'You saw them through the glass, you mean?'

'On a poster, dude. It was like . . . an ad for some AIDS thing. Ginormous. As tall as me.'

'Okay.'

'I'm like standing next to them. And they're both smiling like everything is cool. It was the sin and the punishment, all in the same picture, and they're smiling about it.'

'And you were turned on?'

'Yeah.'

Jonah's despair hung heavy in the air, and Jake didn't know what to say, so he just kept rocking for a while. 'Am I doing okay, son?'

'Yeah. This is good.'

'Cool.'

'I just have to talk it out. Put it all out there, so I can banish it. That's what my therapist says.'

Jake stroked the kid's hair a few times. Jonah snuggled closer, like a big yellow cat getting comfortable. 'I think Heavenly Father sent me here to test me.'

'And distribute flyers,' said Jake.

The crack carved out another silence between them. 'You know, dude,' Jonah said. 'I don't judge you for your lifestyle. That's your choice. I just don't choose that myself.'

'Gotcha.'

'Then who is she, if she's not your gramma?'

The sudden change of subject threw Jake. 'Oh . . . she's just a friend. She's my boss's . . . my business partner's old landlady. I keep an eye on her and cook and stuff, help out with things.'

'She was nice to me,' said Jonah.

'That's how she is.'

'Are you worried about losing her?'

No one had ever asked Jake that question. He'd heard Shawna and Michael talk about Anna's mortality on several occasions, once even in front of Anna, but he'd never been asked how he personally would feel about her passing.

'I think about it,' he said.

'She's way old, I guess.'

Jake nodded. 'And she seems like she's kinda ready.'

'Like . . . how?'

'I dunno. She fusses over her clothes in the morning like it's the last thing she's ever gonna wear. Scarves and little hats and shit like that. Then she goes out and just sits there for hours, all dressed up, like she's just waiting for a bus or something.'

'Sits where?'

'You know what a gazebo is?'

'My sister got married in one. At the Radisson in Phoenix.'

'Right . . . I built one of those for Anna out back, and that's where she hangs out. Sometimes it looks like she's expecting a mother ship to arrive.'

'Or the Lord.'

Jake wasn't going to argue about who or what Anna might be expecting, but the constant intrusion of the divine made him begin to wonder about something.

'So . . . are you wearing your sacred underwear now?'

Silence, and then: 'They're called temple garments, dude.'

'Whatever.'

'People mock 'em, but it's no different from any other religious garb. Like nuns with the habits . . . or Jewish people with those little beanie things.'

'C'mon, dude, it's underwear. Underwear is funny.'

Jonah held his ground. 'Not to us. We wear them to remind ourselves of the covenants we made in the temple. And to gird against temptation. They give them to us at the Endowment Ceremony.'

They have an underwear endowment ceremony. 'So now that you're a man, Jake, here is the endowment for your underwear . . . your sacred packer.'

He smiled to himself and continued to rock Jonah. 'How much of you does it, like, cover up?'

'We're not supposed to talk about the garments.'

'Dude, I can Google it.'

Jonah sighed. He'd obviously been asked this one too many times. 'The pants go down to the top of my knees. The top is like a regular T-shirt, only longer. You're not supposed to see skin if you put your hands over your head.'

'Can I just . . . feel?' Jake slipped a finger between two of the buttons on Jonah's shirtfront.

'Whoa . . . dude!'

Jonah's squirming overreaction annoyed Jake. 'This is supposed to be a nonsexual thing, right? Just man-to-man affection with our clothes on.'

'Yes.'

'So why are you acting like it's something else? I'm down with the program, Jonah. You're the one who's actin' like a teenage girl.'

'I just don't—'

'If I'm gonna cure you from being a homo, the least you can do is let me touch your magical garments.'

Jonah smiled, rolling his eyes in a way that struck Jake as totally gay. 'They're not magical,' he said, undoing a single button on his shirtfront.

'Obviously.' Jake rubbed the cotton fabric briefly, chastely, before buttoning up Jonah's shirt again. 'When you headin' back to Snowflake?'

'Day after tomorrow. Another elder is takin' the

bus in from Bakersfield, and we're flying out together.'

'He was . . . what? . . . going door to door?'

'Yeah.'

'I guess it's easier in Bakersfield. Than here, I mean.'

'Word,' said Jonah. 'Prop 8 passed in Bakersfield.'

'Sorry we've been so hard on you.' Jake's lip curled just enough for Jonah to catch his meaning. 'Listen, Jonah, you're gonna hafta take cold showers from now on.'

'What do you mean?'

'Just . . . I won't be available for therapy tomorrow. I've got a big gardening job, and I won't be home until late.'

'Oh.'

'So don't plan on any emergency boners.'

The kid sighed. 'I never plan on it, dude.'

'Funny how that works.' Jake rocked him for a while. 'Almost like it's natural, huh? Like it's who you are, and there's nothing you can do about it. And it's not just about your dick, either. It's about who you are inside, and what you need to be happy.'

Twisting his head to look at Jake, Jonah frowned.

'You know what I think?' He coaxed the kid's head back into his hands. 'I think you're gonna go back to Snowflake and have a nice reunion with Becky, and the next day you're gonna go to your therapist and climb on his lap, and tell him all about me.'

Jonah wrenched himself free from Jake's embrace, rising to his knees on the bed.

His face was contorted and completely aflame, like he was some other person entirely. Jake braced himself for the jolt of a fist across his jaw.

'You fucker,' Jonah murmured, before leaning down to kiss Jake on the mouth.

They stayed that way for a while, Jonah's soft lips nestling in Jake's beard while his tongue foraged for something he seemed to have wanted for a long time. Jake gave it to him, too – not because he required anything more, but because he wouldn't settle for anything less. It was a turning point for both of them, and it deserved recognition.

Afterward, as Jonah lay in his arms, Jake asked: 'Was that your first kiss with a guy?'

'Oh, yeah.'

He tousled the kid's hair. 'It's been an honor, then.'

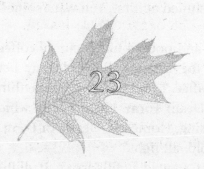

Beauty Sleep

Otto, still panting from the bike ride through the Mission, set the box on Shawna's kitchen table. He had ended up taking his two-wheeler, though he'd argued compellingly for the unicycle, claiming it would lend an air of whimsy to the proceedings and make the whole thing more of a celebration. The idea had actually appealed to her, for a moment or two, until she made herself picture a unicycle arriving at a crematorium, or – worse yet – leaving. It might have seemed a tad indecorous.

Otto used both his hands to rake his unruly hair. 'Did you know they call them cremains?' he said, sitting down at the table. 'Whatever happened to "ashes"? 'Ashes' is poetic. "Cremains" sounds like some sorta powdered shit you put in your coffee.'

Shawna smiled at him. 'You want some?'

'Sure.'

She rose and poured him a cup of coffee, bringing it back to the table. 'I didn't do any better at the coroner's office. I had to fill out something called a Homeless Death Form. I'm not sure which word is less depressing: Homeless, Death, or Form.'

'That's cold, all right.'

'They just wanted it filled out. It didn't seem to matter much if it was the truth. They told me to write "unknown" when I didn't know the answer, and I must've written it a dozen times. It felt like I was erasing her life.'

Otto held the coffee cup under his nose and sniffed it. This was one of his funny rituals around food, something he called Active Appreciation. 'Any luck with that?' he asked, meaning Alexandra's lunch box, which was next to her ashes on the table.

Shawna shook her head. 'Too bad a picture isn't *really* worth a thousand words.' She'd hoped to find something in the photos that might lead her to one of Alexandra's survivors, if such a person existed. There had been those parents, of course, the ones who'd rented their child to strangers, and that creepy Mr. Williams, who may or may not have been a client, but Shawna had no illusions about bringing them to justice thirty years after the fact. All she was hoping was that someone, at some point in Alexandra's short, miserable life, had loved her enough to wonder what had happened to her.

'How many pictures are there?' asked Otto.

'Not many. The young one at Barbary Lane and maybe a dozen others that were obviously taken before she started using. The other people in the pictures seem friendly enough. Coworkers, maybe. Or friends, even. But who the fuck *are* they?'

Otto opened the lunch box and riffled through the photos.

'Damn, she was fine.'

'Tell me about it.'

He held up one of the photos. 'What about this fabric store?'

'I called them already. Nobody's heard of her. It was at least fifteen years ago.'

'You said she worked at a Foot Locker, too. West Portal, right?'

'Same thing. Those places have a huge turnover.'

'And you Googled Lemke.'

'Of course. They're all over the place, believe it or not. There are even some other Alexandra Lemkes. The Web tells you *too* much sometimes.'

Otto took the lunch box and dumped the contents on the table. Amid the photos was a pathetic tangle of costume jewelry and condom wrappers, glinting with sooty shards of aluminum foil that Alexandra must have used for smoking crack. Otto seemed fascinated by the inside of the lunch box itself, where Obi-Wan

Kenobi was gazing up from the bottom with melancholy wisdom. He began to pick at the corner of the image.

'What are you doing?'

'It's cardboard. I think it comes out.' He fiddled with it until the bottom pulled away completely, revealing the raw tin innards of the lunchbox. '*Et voilà!* Princess Leia's secret hiding place.'

There was a letter there, still in its envelope, though it had already been opened. It was stuck to the tin, so Otto pried it away and handed it to Shawna. 'Would you like to do the honors?'

There was a major revelation even before she removed the letter. The envelope was addressed to Alexandra Lemke at 437 Tandy Street, San Francisco, California.

'She had an address! She lived somewhere!'

'What's the postmark say? What year?'

She squinted at the faded numbers. '1995. So she was . . . what? . . . in her late twenties?'

Otto was enjoying her excitement. 'Open it.'

Her hands were actually shaking as she read aloud to him.

Dear Lexy,
Only 2 or 3 more days in Coos Bay and then I'm coming home to you. My aunt is very sick and they say she doesn't have much longer. Please don't do any more of the bad stuff. You know what I mean. I

know its hard when I'm not their, but I will help
you get better. I know you had it bad when you
were little, but I truely believe that our love will
make it better. Your my angel and you always will
be. You are safe now. I will always be grateful to
God that you married me – and that I went to buy
those shoes. Ha ha.
See you soon!
Love always,
C

Shawna set the letter down and gaped at Otto.
'Jesus. She was married.'

'Yep.'

'And it sounds like she was already using.' She
pondered that for a moment. 'Why do you think
she kept this so long? Because he never came home
again?'

'Why would you say that?'

*Good question, Shawna. Why are you projecting your own
half-assed desertion issues onto a dead homeless woman?*

'What . . . then?' she asked. 'You think she was too
fucked-up to stick around? That she left *him*?'

'Maybe. Or they could've had a few more years
together before she hit the skids. Who knows? It's a
nice letter. She probably saved it for sentimental
reasons.'

'She must've met him at the Shoe Locker.'

'Yeah.' Otto tilted his chair back and rocked on it,

his long, denimed legs extended, as if he were trying out a new prop for his act.

'Ever heard of Tandy Street?' she asked.

'It's behind the Mint, I think. Up there on the hill.'

'Wanna go for a ride?'

Otto winced. 'Aw . . . jeez.'

'What?'

'I thought we were gonna take her to Stow Lake.'

'We can do that later,' she told him. 'If that's what we wanna do.'

'This woman is dead, Shawna. It's over. Do you really wanna make a pilgrimage to some place she lived thirteen years ago?'

'What if her husband still lives there? That's possible, isn't it?'

'Pretty remote, I'd say.'

'Yeah, but if he *is* still there, wouldn't he like to know what happened to her?'

'Right. That she ended up turning tricks in Cocksuck Alley.'

'*I* would like to know,' she said. 'If it were you, for instance. If you ended up, say, disappearing into the sordid underbelly of Pier 39.'

He smiled at her like a sleepy forest cat. He was used to her jokes about that venue. 'We have to leave the ashes in the car. We can't just show up with his wife in a box.'

'Please. Gimme some credit.'

'And what do we do if the current Mrs. Lemke answers the door?'

That threw her for a moment. 'Then . . . we'll deal.'
'*You'll* deal.'

'Fine. Whatever.' It hadn't occurred to her, actually, that Lemke might have been Alexandra's married name. This opened a whole new range of possibilities.

'Are you down with this?' she asked. 'I can do it on my own.'

Otto brought his chair down with a thud, clapping his hand around the box of ashes.

'Why don't we ask *her*?' He held the box out as if he were Hamlet addressing the skull of Yorick. 'Alexandra, are you down with this? Do you wanna go to Tandy Street?'

'Fuck no,' he said, assuming a high-pitched voice that was nothing at all like Alexandra's gravelly growl. 'Tell that pesky cunt to leave me the fuck alone. I'm over this shit. I need my beauty sleep.'

Shawna laughed. 'Stick with the monkey, kid.'

'And tell me, Alexandra, do you think Shawna will go to Tandy Street anyway, no matter *what* we think?'

'Fuckin'-A! She needs an end to her motherfuckin' story.'

'Very funny.'

'And she'll probably wanna scatter my cremains all over some stranger's motherfuckin' yard.'

His intuition amazed her sometimes.

Personal Effects

There was a rosy dawn on the day of Mary Ann's hysterectomy, so she took that as a good omen. DeDe was arriving at six a.m. to drive her to St. Sebastian's Hospital; the surgery would be at eight. She'd asked Ben and Michael – ordered them, in fact – not to get up early on her account and to go about their usual workdays. She didn't want a fuss made unless (or until) she actually needed one. It had been a stupid instruction, driven largely by superstition, so she was glad to see the guys had ignored it. She was locking up the garden house when she found the floral-patterned gift bag on the doorstep.

Inside, bundled with a curly pink ribbon, was a T-shirt that read PINYON CITY: THE MIDDLE OF NOWHERE.

She'd seen these shirts at the general store, so Ben must have bought it when he came back from snowboarding at Kirkwood. Unless, of course, Michael had grabbed it on a whim when he went to get those Neolithic marshmallows for their hot chocolate. Either way, the subtext of the gift made her smile. The guys weren't taking no for an answer. They were marking this passage in her life – her *womb voyage*, as Dr. Ginny had once called it – whether she liked it or not.

She opened the door again, and left the T-shirt on the bed, since she'd have no use for it at the hospital. It was nice to think of it waiting there upon her return. They really were her angels, those two. She'd been dead right about coming here. Darien, with its treacherous crosscurrents of pity and gossip, would have been intolerable.

Locking up again, she crossed the garden with her overnight bag and stood on the sidewalk in the clarifying light, waiting for DeDe to whisk her away to whatever came next. She felt almost buoyant, hanging in the balance like this, since she'd lost the weight of her usual distractions; everything she needed for this journey had to come from inside of her now. It was that simple. She wasn't even bringing her laptop to the hospital, and, even more tellingly, hadn't laid eyes on her Facebook page since they got home from Pinyon City. She was her own woman now, for better or worse.

*   *   *

DeDe's well-bred little Audi was new, and Mary Ann found comfort in the virginal smell of it. *If we could just keep driving*, she thought, concocting her own pushing-sixty version of *Thelma and Louise*. Let's just stay here forever in this clean, well-cushioned place, listening to John Mayer on the Blaupunkt, while we gab about our favorite hill towns in Italy and all the silly things we've ordered online. DeDe had been fastidiously avoiding the topic of the hour, and Mary Ann had so appreciated that.

'Do you see much of Shawna in New York?'

'Once. Once I saw her.'

'Oops.'

'It's not bad. It's just . . . . nothing. I don't blame her. I'd feel the same way myself. I don't have any claim on her.' She gazed out the window, marveling at the girth of the passing street trees; it wasn't the buildings here that told her how long she'd been away but the forests that had grown up around them. 'It's funny,' she added, 'her dad doesn't hold a grudge anymore. He sees how wrong we were for each other. But to her I'm still the bad guy. You can't break a five-year-old's heart and not expect to pay for it sooner or later.'

'C'mon now.'

'It's true, though. Actions have consequences. *In*actions have them. We set things in motion by what we *don't* do. I'm not saying I would have done things any different. Brian was born to raise children, and I wasn't. Anyway, she was always

Daddy's little girl. She ended up in the right place.'

'Well, now that you're on the same coast . . .'

'No, she's back again. And I'm not sure *what* coast *I'm* on.'

DeDe glanced at her. 'She's back *here*, you mean?'

'Yeah. Michael keeps up with her. She lives in the Mission somewhere.'

DeDe was silent for a moment, so John Mayer's lyrics filled the gap: *No, it won't all go the way it should, but I know the heart of life is good.*

'I love that song,' said Mary Ann.

'Me too.'

'I made it my ringtone, actually.' She smiled at her taciturn old friend. 'That's hopelessly unhip of me, right?'

'Who cares?'

'I'm sure it is. It's gotta be. I never like anything hip. I used to like John Denver, for heaven's sake.'

DeDe chuckled. 'D'or gave me shit about that last month. We were driving out to Skylonda to get her *dosha* balanced, and I was singing along to "Country Roads." '

'To get her *what* balanced?'

'Her *dosha?*'

'What on earth is that?'

'Who knows? I get my nails done while she's doing it.'

Mary Ann laughed, and it felt really good.

'She loves Shawna's blog, by the way. She's been

writing about some homeless woman, and D'or can't get enough of it.'

'Well . . . D'or is hip. Always has been.'

DeDe caught her drift and smirked. 'Too much for ya, huh?'

'I don't read it. Well, once. Once I read it.'

DeDe chuckled. 'Not my cup of tea either, I have to admit.'

This was what Mary Ann loved about her. DeDe never claimed to be hip, and really didn't care who knew it. 'I love that we can talk like this,' she said. 'We have such a great bond after all these years.'

DeDe gave her a sly smile. 'We know where the bodies are buried.'

When they arrived at St. Sebastian's, she was disconcerted by the number of times she was asked the purpose of her visit to the hospital. She hadn't expected a welcoming committee, but it was bothersome and, yes, faintly demeaning to have to keep repeating herself at a time like this. It was DeDe who explained they were just making sure they didn't remove a uterus from someone who had come there, say, for a heart transplant, though that wasn't especially reassuring. The sense that she was losing her identity in the clanking machinery of this pastel place was only heightened when they gave her a locker key with a wristband and a plastic bag for her 'personal effects.'

'What next?' she whispered. 'Delousing and leg irons?'

DeDe chuckled, handing her the final humiliation, her backless hospital gown. 'The ladies' room is over there. I'll guard the door while you change.' Mary Ann had a quick, amusing image of that: DeDe standing like a lone sentinel with her arms firmly folded across her matronly bosom. Mother Goose in a Chanel suit.

In the women's room she slipped out of her skirt and blouse and put her cocktail rings and tennis bracelet in the plastic bag. She was glad she'd left her wedding ring back in Darien, since she didn't have to confront the symbolism of removing it now. She had put on makeup that morning, out of old habit and something to do with pride, but she refrained from checking it in the mirror. She didn't want to see herself in this moment.

DeDe followed her down the hall to anesthesia. 'Don't worry,' she said drily, 'I've got your back,' by which she meant she was doing her best to block the public view of Mary Ann's flagrantly exposed ass. 'And, by the way, missy, if that were *my* booty, I'd do all these sick people a favor and let 'em see it.'

Mary Ann laughed. 'You're a shameless liar.' *But such a lovely friend*, she thought, since lately most of her female comforters had been paid professionals. First Calliope – well, that harridan hadn't been professional, but she had certainly been paid – and now, of course, Dr. Ginny, whose strong, calm presence had been wonderful, but all in the line of duty. DeDe, however, was not being reimbursed for her support. Mary Ann had almost forgotten how good it felt to have a woman like that in her life.

The anesthesiologist was a blotchy-faced bald guy with a German accent, who wasted no time smiling as he inserted the needle into her arm. 'I think you are nervous,' he said sternly, almost as if he were scolding her. It struck her as odd and inappropriate. She was about to lose a smorgasbord of organs: uterus, cervix, ovaries, even her goddamn appendix; all things considered, she thought she was holding up pretty well.

'No,' she said evenly. 'I'm okay.'

He shook his head. 'I think you are nervous.'

'Of course she's nervous,' snapped DeDe. 'She has cancer. What the hell do you expect her to be?' This was exactly why DeDe had worn Chanel, Mary Ann realized, so she could say things like that and not be thrown out of the room.

But it dawned on Mary Ann that what had seemed like callousness on this man's part may have been something else entirely. 'I think,' she said, casting a quick glance at DeDe, 'he's asking that because he needs to determine . . . what he needs to give me in the way of . . . mood elevators.'

'Oh,' said DeDe, looking instantly humbled. 'She's nervous, then. She's really, really nervous.'

The anesthesiologist permitted himself a smile. 'Is that your opinion, too?'

'Yes,' Mary Ann said, grinning back at him. 'It is.'

Once he had made his final adjustments and they were alone again, DeDe leaned closer to Mary Ann. 'That's what you get for bringing a pushy old lesbian.'

Mary Ann smiled. 'Will you stay until I'm out?'

'You bet. And I'll be here when you wake up. They're putting a bed in your room for me. We can have a slumber party tonight.'

'Forty-fives,' said Mary Ann.

'What?'

'You know, those little record cases we brought to slumber parties.'

'Oh, yeah.'

'Tell me you did that in Hillsborough. It wasn't just Cleveland, was it?'

''Course not. I had slumber parties all the time. D'or and I still sleep in that room, in fact.'

'Sweet.' Mary Ann looked at the tube sending sleep into her arm. 'Anesthesia is such a beautiful word, isn't it? A-nes-thesia. It's like a little town in Mendocino. 'Let's go up to that wonderful B&B in Anesthesia.' '

'Sounds like a plan.'

'No . . . I didn't mean that liberally.'

'Literally.'

'Right, I didn't mean it . . what?'

'Nothing, Mary Ann. Sweet dreams.'

25

Resident Darkness

Three or four times a week, usually in the afternoon, Ben would leave his workshop on Norfolk Street to swim laps at the Embarcadero Y. This stolid old brick building (according to Michael, at least) had been a sort of seedy flophouse/orgy palace back in the days before the Village People told the world that it was fun to play at the YMCA. Now – inside, at least – it was a modern health club whose indoor pool and StairMasters had dramatic close-up views of the Bay Bridge. The locker room could be cruisy from time to time, but only in a subtle, subterranean way, since there were plenty of straight guys and kids who went there. The members were wildly diverse, in fact. Some of them looked like

CEOs, others like homeless men on a day pass.

The showers were semiprivate. There were dividers between them, but they were open on the end, so you could see the person showering across from you. At the moment, that was a beefy, hook-nosed Mediterranean – Italian or Greek, Ben guessed, and probably in his mid-fifties – with a dense doormat of a chest and a hefty provolone between his legs. He was doing the familiar mating dance of the shower, lathering longer than necessary, making extravagant white slaloms of soap through his fur.

He glanced at Ben enough to make his interest clear, so Ben shortened the ritual with a welcoming smile before heading to his locker. Three minutes later, as Ben was climbing into his jeans, the guy appeared in his boxer shorts, presenting his business card.

'My cell is on the bottom there. If you wanna call.'

'Cool,' said Ben, putting the card in his back pocket.

'Unless you got time now. My place is in South Beach. Walking distance.' The guy smiled at him; his teeth were good, and he seemed straightforward enough, trustworthy. His hair was dyed – unnecessarily and not very well – but some things could be forgiven, if the other elements were right. And, man, *were* they.

He had planned on going back to the studio to finish an end table for a client in Seattle, but early-afternoon hookups worked well for him, since

Michael raised a fuss when Ben's play cut into their evening time. On the other hand, Michael expected full disclosure after the event, and this was not the day for that: they'd be waiting for the results of Mary Ann's surgery, and there would be other things to talk about before dinner. 'Sorry,' he told the guy. 'I'll give you a call, though.'

The guy nodded but looked rejected, so Ben showed his sincerity by fishing a business card from his wallet. 'That's my cell,' he said. 'Or you can call me at my studio. I'm usually there during the day.'

The guy studied the card. 'Master craftsman, huh?'

'I work wood.'

'Oh, yeah? Sure hope so.' The guy winked and squeezed Ben's arm as if no one had ever made that joke before, then sauntered back to his own locker.

Too bad, thought Ben, as he watched him round the corner out of sight.

Then, as he tugged his T-shirt over his head, someone came up behind him and asked: 'How was Pinyon City?' He pulled the T-shirt into place and turned to find a face so jarringly out of context that it took him a while to identify it.

Cliff from the dog park. Cliff of Blossom and Cliff. The old man was shirtless and wearing baggy brown trousers that were shiny-thin with age.

'Oh . . . hey, Cliff . . . it was fun.' Ben had mentioned their upcoming trip to Pinyon City on his last visit to the dog park. In fact, he'd probably bored the old man on the subject, since Ben tended to babble around Cliff just to keep the conversation afloat. For someone who seemed to crave company, Cliff wasn't especially gregarious.

'And your friend from the East?'

'Oh . . . Mary Ann? Yeah, she went with us.'

'She liked it?'

'Yeah. She loved it. It snowed while we were there.'

'That's nice.'

'Yeah . . . it was.'

Long, awkward silence.

'I didn't realize you were a member here,' Ben said, filling the void. 'I mean, I've never seen you.'

'I come on a day pass sometimes.'

'Right.'

'I like the pool.'

'Yeah, me too. Especially when it's nasty outside.'

'Yep. Nice today, though. The weather.'

'How's Blossom?'

'She's good.'

'That's great. Cool name, by the way. Perfect for a little dog.'

The old man nodded, then sighed with unexpected intensity. 'The wife named her. After Blossom Dearie. The jazz singer. She was one of our favorites.'

The wife, thought Ben. Such a straight-guy thing to say. But Ben liked knowing that this melancholy codger had company at home. Assuming he wasn't a widower.

'Is she . . . still with us?' he asked.

'Think so. Don't know if she's still singing, but—'

'I meant your wife.'

'Oh . . . yeah . . . she's alive.' Cliff looked flustered. 'But she's not . . . with me anymore.'

'Sorry to hear that.'

'She had problems. I tried to make it better, but . . .' His voice trailed off as his eyes filled with weariness and despair. 'I have to get home . . . speaking of Blossom.'

'Nice seeing you,' said Ben. 'Say hi to her for me.'

'Will do.' Cliff stood there a moment longer, avoiding intimacy by keeping his eyes fixed on the tile floor. 'Thanks for being so nice to me.'

It was heartbreaking to hear him lay out his loneliness in such a blatant way. 'Oh . . . hey . . . it's easy, Cliff. You're good company.'

'No, I'm not. You don't have to say that.'

Ben would have protested, but the old man turned and walked away.

'Catch you at the dog park,' Ben called, trying to end this on an upbeat note.

Cliff lifted his hand in mute reply and just kept walking. It was then that Ben noticed the scar on his back: an ugly puckered line, smoothed somewhat by the passage of years, running all the way from his shoulder blade to his waist.

Surgery? For a tumor or something? It seemed too irregular for that.

A war wound, then? Ben remembered Cliff's story about the mascot dog that had to be shot when he was serving in Vietnam.

Whatever its cause, the scar only deepened the sense that Cliff's gloom was the product of a lifetime of troubles. There were layers to that resident darkness, Ben thought, and no one outside of the old man himself would ever know what they were.

26

A Grace Period

Tandy Street was a bitch to find. It wasn't on the hill behind the Mint, as Otto had remembered, but closer to the Lower Haight, and its only street sign had been all but obscured by graffiti and antiwar stickers. What's more, the address they were looking for – 437 – was not displayed on any of the houses. They located 429 and 445, so they had to assume it was the house between them, a Victorian cottage made Spanish in the twenties by a flat stucco facade. The Band-Aid-colored plaster was falling away like so many scabs, exposing the laths beneath. The window's colorless curtains were drawn.

'Alexandra's love nest,' Otto said sardonically.

'Well,' said Shawna, 'it could have been heaven on

earth, considering her shitty childhood. Maybe it was nice when she lived here. Maybe there's a garden in back.'

'Maybe Jeffrey Dahmer has a workshop in the basement.'

It irritated her that Otto was trying to fuck up Alexandra's happy ending – or, at least, her happy middle. Who was Otto to point fingers? His own little alley studio was way depressing, but it could still be incredibly sweet on a rainy evening when they were snuggling after sex. She needed to know that such pleasures had come to Alexandra, however briefly, that somewhere between the child rape and that flesh-eating disease someone had made her feel safe and loved and at home. Shawna was beginning to think she couldn't scatter Alexandra's ashes *anywhere* without some reassurance of that. There would be nothing to celebrate but her death.

'It looks deserted,' said Otto.

'Why? Because it's rundown?'

'Well . . . yeah.'

'So let's ring the bell and see.'

'Why not just look through the curtains?'

She rolled her eyes impatiently. 'Like that's any less invasive than ringing the bell?'

'I didn't say that. I just think it might be advisable, under the circumstances. Wouldn't you like to see how they live before we see who comes to the door?'

This did make a certain sense, so she looked both

ways down the sidewalk to make sure they were alone before sidling over to the window, a featureless rectangle of aged aluminum, speckled with corrosion. She peered through the footwide opening in the curtains to what she could see of the living room, then reported back to Otto.

'It's not the tidiest place, but it's not Grey Gardens either. It's kind of homey, actually. They've got a Snuggie.'

'A what?'

'You know. Those ridiculous blanket things with sleeves. As seen on TV?' She grinned at him. 'That soul-sucking corporate appliance you want no part of?'

He gave it right back to her. 'It's a good thing *you've* got one, then, or I never would've known what a Snuggie is.'

'I'm gonna ring the bell.'

'Go right ahead.'

'If somebody's here, we can show them the picture. If not, we can go home and fuck.'

Otto held up crossed fingers, smiling.

She pressed the dark Bakelite nipple of the doorbell. It made no sound at all, so she pressed it again. 'Do you think they can hear it inside?'

He shook his head. 'It's dead.'

She rapped on the door, and, almost immediately, a dog began to bark.

'Hey there, little buddy,' Otto crooned, when the apoplectic dog appeared in the window to confront the intruders. It was tiny, though, and its tail was wagging.

'I guess *he's* the doorbell,' said Shawna.

They waited for someone to show up. No one did.

'C'mon,' said Otto.

'Just a little longer.'

'The neighbors are noticing, Shawna.'

Across the street an old woman with garish red hair was eyeing them as she poured water from a saucepan onto a potted plant on her doorstep.

Shawna strode over to talk to her, with Otto close behind. 'We're looking for the people who live here.'

The woman regarded her dubiously. 'Are you here for the environment?'

'No, no.' Shawna grinned. 'Not at all. I mean . . . we're totally *for* the environment, but . . . we've just got something we'd like to show them.'

'Them?'

'Well . . . whoever lives there.' Realizing how shady this was sounding, Shawna got specific. 'We have some information about someone who used to live there back in the nineties. Alexandra Lemke?' She pulled one of the photos from her shoulder bag (the gorgeous grown-up shot taken at the fabric store) and showed it to the neighbor. 'This is probably ten or fifteen years old, but . . . maybe you recognize her?'

The woman said nothing.

'That may have been before you lived here, of course.'

Shawna's effort at a smile was not returned. 'You social workers, then?'

'No. Just . . . private citizens.'

Seeing how badly she was bungling this, Otto stepped forward and tried to establish their credentials. 'She was a friend of Alexandra's. We both were.'

'Are,' said Shawna, correcting him. She didn't want to relay news of Alexandra's death until she was able to do so in a respectful fashion, explaining things in her own words. For all she knew, this woman would call her neighbor as soon as they left.

'Can't help you,' the woman said, returning the photo. 'You'll have to come back when he's home.'

He, thought Shawna. *It's a man, and he lives there alone.*

'Would that be Mr. Lemke?' she asked. 'Is that who we're looking for?'

'Come along,' said Otto, slipping his arm around Shawna as if she were a benign lunatic who had strayed too far from the asylum. He was lighthearted about this, but she still found it annoying. She kept her eyes fixed on the neighbor lady. 'But you recognize her, right? She used to live here? They were married, weren't they?'

The woman went back into her house and closed the door.

Otto was smirking. 'Nice work, Sherlock.'

'Fuck you.'

'I believe that was the plan, yes.'

She began walking across the street. 'You can forget that shit.'

'Aw . . . dude.'

'You saw her expression, didn't you? She recognized Alexandra.'

'Yeah. The fucked-up junkie who used to live across the street. Wonder why she wasn't more helpful?'

'How do you know Alexandra was already fucked up? She could've had a grace period. She and her husband could've still been . . . you know . . .'

'Honeymooning.'

'Yeah . . . in a manner of speaking.' She studied his face for a moment, wondering where he planned to go with that.

'You're funny,' he said.

'Am I?'

'Yeah. For a "grrrl on the loose" who doesn't believe in marriage.'

She gaped at him. 'By which you mean . . . ?'

'Just that you seem determined for her to have been married. You've got one letter . . . a nice letter, granted . . . and now you've got this whole chick-flick message-in-a-bottle thing going on, and I find it a little strange that you're doing that, that's all.'

'Strange,' she repeated in the most neutral tone she could muster.

'Not strange. Just . . . it doesn't seem like you at all. Is it for your blog or what?'

287

She didn't defend herself, since she had just figured out what he meant: *Why can't you be that way about us? If you can make all this fuss over a dead woman's romance, why not ours?* His big, wounded, monkeyloving heart was fully exposed.

She picked her words with care. 'I want her to have been happy. It's not about marriage. Yes, it's partially for the blog . . . but it's also about . . . I dunno. Wouldn't you like to know that someone had at least been kind to her before the drugs took over?'

He didn't answer right away. He seemed to be considering the perils of pursuing this discussion. 'Fine. Sure. Why not leave a note, then?'

'Funny you should say that.' Perhaps a little too jocular now, she reached into her shoulder bag and removed the note she'd composed that morning.

He asked her what it said.

'Just that I'm a friend of Alexandra Lemke . . . who used to live here . . . and that she died this week at SF General . . . and to call me if they knew her and want to talk.'

'That should do it,' he said.

She slipped the note under the door.

'It's certainly worth a shot,' she said.

'It always is,' he said vaguely.

She was pretty sure he was talking about them.

Waiting for Word

The worst thing about trimming dead fronds from tree ferns was the itchy brown dust that clung to Jake's skin every time he tackled the job. If the ferns were tall, like the ones in this particular garden, the nasty shit would fall into his eyes whenever he looked up, or creep down his collar onto his neck, like the needling remnants of a haircut. As pleased as he was about his newly forested forearms, all that hair was a magnet for fern dust, and he would find himself – as he did now – scratching like an addict in withdrawal.

'You okay?' Michael was stacking the fronds for removal to the truck. 'I could spell you for a while.'

'Nah. I'm good.'

'You sure?'

'Yeah.'

Jake was trying hard to make an extra effort, since he planned, any minute now, to ask a favor of Michael that probably couldn't come at a worse time. Business was lousy, and Michael's shoulder was giving him more trouble than usual. If that weren't enough, Michael seemed weirdly distracted and distant today. Jake was even starting to wonder if Michael had guessed what was coming and wasn't happy about it.

Still, there was no way to do this but to do it.

'Feel like some coffee?' Jake asked.

Michael didn't answer right away, as if this were a really difficult question. 'Sure,' he said, finally. 'That would be good.'

The garden they were tending was only a block from the Marina Green, so they hosed off their faces and arms and took their thermoses down to a bench by the bay. The sky was clear; there were more sail-boats than usual for a late-autumn day.

Jake pulled a Clif Bar from his shirt pocket and offered it to Michael.

'No, thanks.'

'You sure? I got two.'

'Yeah . . . thanks.'

Jake hesitated, then took the leap: 'Is something goin' on, boss?' Technically, of course, Michael was his business partner, not his boss, but Jake was still using the b-word and wasn't sure if he would ever stop. It was a term of respect, more than anything.

Michael gave him a hangdog look. 'How could you tell?'

Jake shrugged. 'Well . . . for one thing, you're not humming.'

'Humming?'

'You know . . . while you work.'

'I thought that annoyed you.'

'It does, but . . . I figure it would take something pretty big to make you stop.' Jake tore open the Clif Bar and bit off a chunk. 'You wanna talk about it?'

Michael gazed morosely at the water. 'Mary Ann is in the hospital. She has cancer. I'm waiting for word right now.'

This relief that Jake felt, if only briefly, turned into shame as soon as he saw the tears on Michael's cheeks. At least he thought that's what they were. Michael's eyes were always leaky, especially in the open air, so it was hard to say for sure.

'Why didn't you say something before?' he asked.

'She asked us not to. She didn't want a lot of drama around it. Please don't mention it to Anna. Or Shawna, for that matter. Not for a while, anyway. We'll know a lot more by this afternoon.'

'What are they doing, exactly?'

'She has cancer. She's having a hysterectomy.'

Jake just stared at him silently. At first he thought Michael was making a twisted joke, until he remembered that people didn't joke about that.

'I know,' said Michael. 'I know.'

It took Jake a while to say anything. 'You coulda told me. I woulda kept quiet about it. I coulda been really helpful. I've been reading up on it.'

'I know. I just thought . . . I dunno.'

'You just thought what?'

'That it might somehow . . . rain on your parade.'

Jake nodded slowly, absorbing that. 'My hysterectomy parade.'

Michael smiled sheepishly. 'You know what I mean. It's a whole different thing for you. Yours will be cause for celebration. Hers . . . not so much.'

'It will be if they get the cancer out.'

'You're right. Of course.' He laid his hand on Jake's knee and shook it, as if he were shaking off that terrible word. 'So . . . it's all you want for Christmas, huh?'

Jake felt his face go hot. *Anna must have spilled the beans already.*

'If it's the wrong time, boss . . .'

'It might be exactly the right time. Ben and I have been talking about going to Maui for Christmas.'

'Really? But . . . then we'd both be off work.'

Michael shrugged. 'And neither one of us would have to feel guilty.'

This was something of a revelation to Jake. 'You feel guilty about that?'

'Of course. Every time you're working and I'm not. We're in this together, buddy.'

Now there were tears in Jake's eyes, but they had nothing to do with the bite of wind off the bay. He had simply realized that he'd just cleared the last obstacle to his dream.

'You sure about this, boss?'

'Absolutely. I'll go with you to the hospital, of course. We'll just be recuperating in different places.'

Swiping at his eyes, Jake told him that Selina and Marguerite had already offered to help during the surgery, but that he appreciated the offer just the same.

'Well . . . that sucks. This is the second hyster-ectomy I've been barred from this month.'

Jake grinned. 'You're not barred, boss.'

'Mary Ann told me it was a "girl thing."'

'Well . . . you won't get that from me.'

'No . . . guess not.' Michael smiled faintly. 'I'd just rather have a buddy waiting for me on the other side.'

'That's pretty much what *she* said.'

There was a long, peaceful silence as they both gazed out at the bay, where a square-nosed freighter was sailing out toward the Golden Gate.

Finally, Michael said: 'Anna tells me you're seeing someone.'

Jake shook his head. 'Not really. Not in the usual way.'

'Is there a "usual way" around here?'

'He was only here for a few weeks.' Jake decided on

the spot not to mention the reason for Jonah's visit, since it would only endanger the fragile beauty of what had happened before he left. 'He lives in a place called Snowflake.'

'Where's that?'

'Arizona.'

Michael widened his eyes optimistically. 'That's not all that far away.'

'Oh, yeah it is.'

Michael chuckled.

'He wasn't the right one, anyway. We were on different journeys.'

'Well,' said Michael, 'if you were good for each other ... even for a while ... sometimes that's enough.'

For Jake, it was enough to know that another man had desired him enough to risk everything – even the promise of everlasting life – for a kiss.

28

The Last Thing She Needed

At first there was only a face, floating free in a borderless nimbus.

'Welcome back, Mrs. Caruthers.'

It was such a sweet face, too, so full of kindness that it might have belonged to an angel at the gates of heaven, and she actually entertained that possibility for a moment or two. But it made no sense at all. How could you be welcomed *back* to heaven? And since when did angels have blue titanium lip studs and fauxhawks?

The nimbus melted, like frost in sunlight, and the whole person appeared.

'I'm Seth,' he said. 'The nurse.'

'Hey, Seth.'

He was fiddling with a tube – a drip of some sort, she assumed. 'You were such a champ,' he told her with a smile. 'You did just great.'

Good for me, she thought. *But what does that mean?*

'You barely lost any blood at all,' the nurse added. 'Two teaspoons at the most.'

Until now, she had never even thought about how much blood might be involved.

'Did the doctor say if—?'

'She said to tell you the procedure went very, very smoothly.'

'Really? Two verys?' She was starting to wonder if this was how they handled patients when the news was too horrendous to be presented by a nurse. She didn't need to be told that she was the world's best patient; she needed to be told that she had the world's most cancer-free insides. Was that asking too much?

The nurse smiled at her again. 'The doctor will be by later to tell you in person.'

'What did the pathologist say?'

'Can't help you there, I'm afraid.'

'Right . . . of course.' She remembered being told that it would take three days to get the results. She decided to focus on being grateful that she hadn't died on the table.

The nurse laid his hand gently on her shoulder. 'Get some rest, Mrs. Caruthers.'

'Please . . . Mary Ann.'

'Mary Ann,' he repeated.

'Thanks for saying hello, Seth.'

'C'mon. This is the best part of the job.'

'Just the same, thank you.'

Thank you, thank you, thank you.

The next time she drifted into consciousness, she heard DeDe and Dr. Ginny in quiet conversation across the room, so she kept her eyes shut and eavesdropped. It was scary to do this, but she wanted to make sure Seth hadn't been sparing her the truth.

'You'll need to get her up and walking,' Dr. Ginny was saying.

'Tonight?'

'Just down to the end of the hallway. Take your time about it, but do it. It'll help with the healing.'

'Okay.'

Ask her how it went, DeDe! No, don't ask her!

'I expect the incisions to heal rather quickly,' said Dr. Ginny. 'It helps that she was already so fit.'

'I know. It's so annoying.'

Dr. Ginny chuckled. 'It's just Pilates.'

'No, it's genes, dammit. Have you ever seen a picture of my mother? We were born to be hens.'

Their soft laughter was encouraging, if not especially informative.

Surely they wouldn't be laughing if the news had been bad.

*　　*　　*

She was awakened by a metallic rattling that sounded like medical machinery. She opened her eyes with a vague sense of dread, wondering if something had gone wrong and she was back on the operating table. But it was just DeDe, methodically removing dishes from a gingham-lined picnic basket and arranging them on the bed tray.

'Hey, missy,' she said, realizing her charge was awake.

'Hey, pretty lady.'

'Oh, they *did* get you blitzed, didn't they?'

'What's this?'

'Don't worry. It's not from the hospital. D'or dropped it by a little while ago. We have a nice home-made fruit salad and a lovely *Boeuf Bourguignon* from Fleur de Lys. Also yogurt and cookies for dessert.'

Just the sight of this fare made Mary Ann nauseous, but she did not have the heart to tell DeDe. 'Look at you,' she said instead. 'You're like Grace Kelly in *Rear Window*.'

DeDe snorted. 'More like Thelma Ritter.'

'Stop that. You're beautiful. We have to work on your self-esteem.'

A strained silence followed. DeDe looked misty-eyed, making Mary Ann wonder if catastrophic news was imminent.

'Dig in,' DeDe said at last.

Mary Ann took a bite of the fruit salad, and issued an appreciative 'Yum.'

'I'm so happy to be here with you,' said DeDe.

Mary Ann set down her fork, no longer able to bear the suspense. 'What have you heard?'

'You haven't talked to Ginny yet?'

'No.' She had stopped breathing altogether.

'Oh, Jesus . . . well . . . she said the cancer doesn't seem to have spread to your lymph nodes and your tissues look really good . . .'

'But?'

DeDe shrugged and grinned. 'No buts. None that *I* heard, anyway.'

'Seriously?'

DeDe took Mary Ann's hand. 'Would I lie to you, missy?'

There was a cursory rap on the door before an orderly charged into the room with a rollaway bed. 'Do you have a preference?' he asked DeDe.

Finding that question hilarious, Mary Ann giggled.

'Don't mind her,' DeDe told the orderly. 'She's high as a kite. Over against that wall would be fine, thank you.'

The orderly positioned the bed as directed. It was ridiculously narrow. The mattress was sheathed in a thick plastic cover that could easily repel any conceivable bodily fluid. Mary Ann heard it crackling as the orderly tucked in the sheets.

'You can't sleep on that,' she told DeDe as soon as the orderly was gone.

'Shush.'

'Well, at least get out of the damn Chanel and make yourself comfortable.'

'Not yet. We have to take a little walk later on, and I'm not going out there in my jammies.'

Mary Ann smiled at her knowingly. The Chanel was DeDe's own suit of armor, and apparently she thought she might still have use for it.

Dr. Ginny stopped by that afternoon and made DeDe's report official. They wouldn't be totally out of the woods, she said, until they got the lab reports, but things looked really good. As usual, Mary Ann found herself infatuated with the surgeon and her goddess-like aura of confidence. She envisioned her uterus resting in those strong, elegant hands, no longer capable of poisoning the rest of her body. She had not tried to picture what happened before that. She knew Dr. Ginny had made some very small incisions in her abdomen, but she wasn't sure if her uterus had exited that way or through her vagina. She didn't want to know, really. Not now. Not for a while. Maybe never.

'Thank you for her,' Mary Ann told DeDe, as soon as the doctor had left.

'My pleasure.'

'It was sweet of her to stick around.'

'Actually . . . I think she has another one here this afternoon.'

'Another what?'

'Hysterectomy.'

'Oh.' Mary Ann remembered how many notches Dr. Ginny already had in her oncological gun and reminded herself that that was why she was so good at her job.

'What's the matter?' asked DeDe, catching her crest-fallen expression. 'You jealous or something?'

She was, sort of. There was no denying it.

29

The Way She Wanted It

Ben was back in his studio, still pleasantly buzzed from his long swim at the Y, when Michael called from a job in the Marina to say that Mary Ann's surgery had gone very well. He had just heard the news from DeDe Halcyon-Wilson.

'That's great, baby.'

'I know, isn't it?'

'So she's getting out tomorrow?'

'Yep.'

'What do we need to do?'

'Nothing, apparently. Just let her rest and help her walk around a little. But here's the thing, sweetie . . . DeDe and D'or have offered to put her up for several days until she gets the lab results, and I was wondering how you'd feel about that.'

This seemed like a trick question to Ben. He wondered if Michael was testing his devotion to Mary Ann. 'How do *you* feel about it?'

'Well . . . they've got a huge house in Hillsborough . . . with a staff, I think . . . so she'd probably be more comfortable there.'

Ben hesitated. 'But?'

'Well . . . frankly, I think she'd rather be with us.'

'Has she told you that?'

'Well, I haven't spoken to her yet, just DeDe, but—'

'Why don't you ask her, then?'

'If I do, she'll think we're trying to unload her. I know how she is. And she'll agree to it whether she wants to or not.'

'Do you think maybe she asked DeDe to ask you because she's afraid of hurting *your* feelings?'

'No . . . I don't . . . honestly.'

'Then . . . we'll make her comfortable in the cottage. We've already told her she can do it, so we'll do it.'

Ben wondered what was going on here. Was Michael jealous of DeDe's attention to Mary Ann? Did he think he would somehow fail Mary Ann if he didn't insist upon taking care of her? Or maybe – and this was where it got murkier – he was trying to prove that he wouldn't desert her in her hour of need as she had once deserted him?

The truth, whatever it was, lay beneath the sediment of their shared history, and Ben had not known either one of them long enough to dig it out.

He wrestled with business for several hours, calling it quits around four o'clock. It was awful how the Zen calm achieved from making something beautiful with his hands could be so quickly erased by the demands of taxes and billing statements. But, over the years, he had learned to face the fact that art could not be practiced without the eventual use of numbers – not if you wanted to keep on doing it. His business had been successful for that very reason. At least it *had* been, before the recession.

He swung away from the computer, rubbing his eyes. Roman was watching him intently from his doughnut bed across the room, sensing even now, from the creak of Ben's Aeron chair and the slow, gray death of the skylight, that it was time to hit the road. The dog was already at the door, his tail thrashing like a flag in a red-state parade, when Ben removed the leash from the filing cabinet. Then, as an afterthought, he snatched the Chuckit! from his desk drawer, causing Roman to begin crooning with joy. That blue plastic ball launcher could mean only one thing: a trip to the beach or the park.

The beach would have been nice, given the clear skies, but Ben figured it would be chilly at Crissy Field and downright cold at Fort Funston, so he took Roman to the Collingwood dog park. When they came through the gate, he counted only three other humans on the field, though there were at least a dozen dogs. *Dogwalkers*, he concluded, with a shiver of disdain, since dogs being led around en masse brought a weird energy to the park. They just stood around looking bored and displaced, like school-children on a field trip, refusing to play with each other when they weren't ganging up on the rest.

Today, however, Roman had found a familiar face: Blossom.

While the terrier and the doodle wrestled, Ben spotted Blossom's doting dad sitting alone on a bench at the far end of the park. He had no choice but to acknowledge Cliff with a wave, but he was relieved when the old man seemed not to have noticed. After their exchange at the Y, he'd had enough Cliff for the day. He wasn't sure what they'd talk about this soon. For all his implied tragedy, Cliff just wasn't that interesting.

He looked back at the roughhousing dogs, grateful for a reason to turn away from the old man, but Roman quickly lost interest in Blossom and ran off to harvest a tennis ball. Blossom looked crestfallen for a moment, then left to join the listless dogs on the chain gang. When Roman returned to deposit the slobbery ball at Ben's feet, Ben obeyed the implied command and flung it across the compound. Roman was already halfway there when the ball hit the cyclone fence. He caught it in midair on the second bounce and pranced back to Ben, ridiculous and beautiful, his whole body shouting triumph.

Ben wondered sometimes what would happen if the capricious electricity in Roman's brain fired at a time like this. How would the other dogs react to a grand mal seizure in their midst? Or the people, for that matter, who might get the wrong idea about the foam on Roman's lips. Would he be able to stay by Roman's side, comforting him until the seizure stopped, or would he have to cope with a larger madness? And what about the postictal period? How would he clear *this* room while Roman went nuts?

They'd been lucky so far; the seizures had been at home – or at least inside – so the situation had never arisen. Maybe it never would. Maybe Roman's morning dose of potassium bromide would be enough to keep the beast within him at bay. The main thing was that the seizures not be allowed to come too close together. Otherwise they would begin to dig a sort of neural trench that would make it easier and easier for them to happen.

Ben knew he could easily dig a trench of his own. When it came to dealing with the epilepsy, there was a fine line between caution and constant dread, and it would cheat them both if he crossed it. He wanted to share his life with Roman. He would not be one of those fretful neurotics who robbed their dogs of all spontaneity and fun.

* * *

Roman retrieved the ball at least a dozen times before taking time out to slurp water from a bowl at the entrance to the park. Blossom, meanwhile, had joined Cliff at his bench at the end of the park. She was sitting at the old man's feet, barking insistently, though Cliff seemed oblivious to it. His hands were clamped to his knees, and he was rocking slowly back and forth, as if keeping time to his own private dirge.

He was crying, Ben realized. Sobbing.

Ben got up and walked casually in Cliff's direction. He didn't want to draw attention to the old man's state, but he couldn't ignore it, either. As he drew closer, he could hear Cliff's whimpering – a terrible sound, like an animal caught in a trap. He sat down next to the old man and laid his hand lightly on Cliff's back.

The sobbing continued, as if Cliff were still alone.

'Is there something I can do?' Ben asked finally.

The old man shook his head, then wiped his eyes with the sleeve of his parka. 'It's too late for that. It's too late for everything.'

'Would you like to talk about it?'

Blossom was barking again, so Cliff scooped her into his arms and petted her, obviously trying to compose himself. 'My wife is dead,' he said at last.

'Oh, damn . . . I'm so sorry.'

'I got the word this afternoon.'

'Was it . . . a natural death?' That came out sounding totally awkward, but Ben thought it would have been rude to ask if Cliff's wife had died of old age.

'I don't know what it was,' said Cliff. 'They didn't tell me.'

Ben was remembering what Cliff had said earlier at the Y – that his wife hadn't been 'with him' for a while. 'I take it she wasn't living with you?' he said.

Cliff shook his head. 'No. But that wasn't my doing. That's the way she wanted it. She started using drugs . . . a few years after we got married. She ended up needing the drugs more than she needed me. She just went off the rails and never came back.'

Ben nodded. *What could you say about that?*

'I tried to give her a good life.'

'I'm sure.'

'We had one, too, for a good little while.' Cliff pulled the terrier closer until she was licking the side of his face. 'Didn't we, Blossom? We were a family back then.'

Ben found himself moved by this flash revelation of Cliff's domestic life. 'How did you meet?' he asked, trying to draw the old man out of his suffering.

'She was working in a shoe store in West Portal. I was looking for some shoes. Prettiest thing you ever saw. Black hair. Green eyes.'

'How old was she?'

'Um . . . thirty.'

'And this was . . . ?'

'Ten . . . twelve years ago.' Cliff gave him a melancholy look that was tinged with a curious sheepishness. 'Think I was robbing the cradle?'

Ben smiled at him. 'Not in my book. Love is love. My partner is twenty-one years older than I am.'

Cliff absorbed that for a moment. 'That's right,' he said.

This puzzled Ben. 'You've met him, you mean?'

'No . . . but . . . I think I saw you with him here last summer. Handsome, stocky fellow? Gray mustache?'

'That's him.' Ben was still baffled. Michael almost never came to this park. He preferred Stern Grove, out near the ocean, where Roman could run in the grass.

'It's good to have somebody,' Cliff said, staring vacantly into the distance. 'I never saw my wife anymore . . . not for years . . . but just knowing she was still . . . out there made it a little easier to be alone.' There were fresh tears on the old man's face, but he didn't bother to wipe them away. 'Funny how that works.'

Ben scrambled for something positive to say and ended up scratching Blossom's silky belly. 'These little critters can be really good company.'

'Yeah . . . for a while. Then nothing works anymore. Not even love.'

There was a strained silence. Scratching the dog had brought Ben close enough to smell Cliff's rotten, gin-infused breath, so he leaned away as subtly as possible.

'Would you do me a favor?' Cliff said after a while.

'Uh . . . sure . . . if I can.'

'Would you see she gets a good home, if anything happens to me?'

'Oh . . . Blossom, you mean?' Ben knew very well what he meant; he was just stalling while he searched for an acceptable excuse. As much as he sympathized with the old man's situation, this was not a burden he was willing to assume. 'You know, Cliff . . . we don't have a whole lot of room at our house, and Roman tends to—'

'I didn't mean you. Just see that she's not left alone.'

'But . . . you understand . . I really wouldn't have any way of *knowing* if something happened to you.'

'Oh, you'd know,' Cliff said vaguely. 'Word gets around.'

'Still I don't think you should take that risk. It's better to contact the SPCA. They're a great outfit, and I'm sure they have provisions for that sort of . . . advance-need situation. If you like, I can look into it for you . . . get the number.'

It was excruciatingly clear that Cliff was feeling rejected. 'I know how to look up a number,' he said.

'Well . . . of course, I didn't mean—'

'I need to be alone now.'

'You bet. Of course.' Ben rose from the bench, now feeling like a total piece of shit, but glad to be excused anyway. 'Take care, okay? I'll see you soon.'

He didn't look back once as he headed for the gate with Roman.

* * *

It was almost dark when he got back to the house, so he poured himself a tall brandy and took it out to the garden, where a gibbous moon was rising in the lavender sky. He should have done something to help Cliff. He knew that. In his stumbling, shutdown way Cliff had been reaching out, and Ben had effectively ignored him. What was that about, anyway? Was it too personal an act to take responsibility for this old man's dog? Or at least make an effort to see to it that someone else did?

Yes. It was. No – it was too *familial* – and Ben didn't want to be an in-law to all that wretchedness and regret. Cliff was just a guy he knew from the dog park; he felt pity for him, but he was repelled by him as well, and he didn't want their casual connection to become something more formal. It was that simple.

The sad thing, Ben thought, was that Cliff had probably received this reaction his whole life. His social uneasiness seemed part of his very constitution. No wonder he was feeling the loss of someone who had actually married him, however briefly. If his wife had become an addict, Ben couldn't help wondering if the drugs had driven her away, or if Cliff himself, in his all-consuming cloud of despair, had driven her to the drugs.

Ben was a little drunk now, so he went into the kitchen to get the irises he had bought on his way home from the dog park. He wanted the cottage to be a welcoming place when Mary Ann got back in the morning. Finding a vase on the shelf above the stove, he filled it with water and fluffed the irises for a while. It felt good to commit this small act of generosity in the churning wake of the larger one he had just dodged.

When he put the irises on Mary Ann's bedside table, he saw a T-shirt on the bed next to a gift bag and a spiral of pink paper ribbon. The shirt read PINYON CITY: THE MIDDLE OF NOWHERE. He had seen that T-shirt before – lots of them, in fact – gathering dust in his favorite general store. It was touching to think Mary Ann had cared enough about their trip to the mountains, even while it was going on, to commemorate it this way. And the fact she had done so on her own made it seem that much more sincere.

He stuffed the T-shirt into the bag and put the bag with her other things on a shelf in the closet. Then he stripped the bed and hauled the linens to the laundry room. She would have clean sheets when she got back, and that would be a good way of saying that she was starting over now, that things could only get better from here on out.

30

The Anna She Remembered

The guys had been so sweet to her. They had built a nest for her on their sofa and plied her with chick flicks and foot rubs and goodies from the chocolate shop on Castro Street. Almost immediately, she and Michael had begun taking therapeutic walks around the track at Kezar Stadium, though she never stopped being aware of the absence she was carrying. When, on the third day, Dr. Ginny called to tell her the 'wonderful news' from the pathologist, she sat down on the bleachers at the stadium and cried in Michael's arms.

When the guys were at work, she busied herself with her Facebook friends, commenting on their cute pets and cake-smeared children. She didn't once mention the cancer, or even the fact that she was recuperating, since she didn't want an avalanche of Rumi poems from people she barely knew, however well-intended they might be.

Her silence on the subject was not like her mother's silence. She was building a new world for herself from the inside out, and she wanted to do so at her own pace. She had already phoned Robbie at NYU and apologized for texting him about his dad's affair with Calliope. Robbie had been incredibly sweet about it, saying she would always be his mom, that he understood her feelings, this was strictly between her and his dad. He didn't seem especially surprised when she told him that she would be hiring a lawyer. He didn't seem especially surprised about anything. She wondered if he had already known about Bob and Calliope, having heard it from his dad in a scotch-fueled buddy-buddy moment, and had been anxiously waiting for her to find out on her own.

But Robbie wouldn't do that, would he? He had always been her ally when things got iffy with Bob. Unless, of course, there were no sides to be taken any-more, because Calliope was already a fait accompli. Maybe he was just keeping his head down, bracing himself for the new administration the way his dad was doing with Obama.

'Are your classes fun?' she asked brightly, trying to show that she still cared about his life.

'Yeah. Pretty much. It's a little overwhelming.'

'I'm thinking of staying at the city apartment for a while . . . while things are getting sorted out, I mean. Maybe we can grab some coffee in the Village.'

'That would be great,' he said, though not convincingly.

'I've got a few more days here, but . . . it won't be long. I'm dying to see your new digs.'

'Yeah . . . well . . . it's kind of a mess right now, but—'

'I can help with that. We'll go shopping . . . get you some nice things.' She heard herself speak this obscenity in her own mother's voice, and it made her blood run cold. 'Sorry,' she added penitently. 'Clingy mom. Just what you need right now.'

Her energy had increased by the end of the week, so Michael took her with him to Mrs. Madrigal's house when he went to pick up Jake Greenleaf for work. Anna had been alerted of Mary Ann's arrival, so she – or someone – had laid out tea and sugar cookies on a red lacquer tray in the living room. Once Michael and Jake were gone, Anna made her entrance under her own steam, inching across the room in a pale blue satin kimono, as if to prove to her guest that she was still capable of doing it. Her white hair, encircling her head like a blizzard, was adventurously secured with two large tortoiseshell combs.

'You look wonderful,' Mary Ann told her as they were hugging.

Anna chuckled. 'What is it they always say?'

'About what?'

Anna's long fingers clutched Mary Ann's wrist. 'I need help with this part, dear.' She meant sitting down, so Mary Ann held the old woman's elbow as she eased into her armchair. 'What they always say,' said Anna, picking up the thread, 'is that there are three ages of man: youth, middle age and "You look wonderful." '

Mary Ann smiled. 'Well, just the same . . . it's true.'

'Thank you, dear.'

'Your hair has always been amazing. I remember those fabulous chopsticks you used to wear.'

Anna wore a look of amused chagrin. 'I'm afraid Mr. Greenleaf won't let me wear those anymore. I took a little tumble one night and almost harpooned the cat.'

This was very much the Anna she remembered: warm and self-mocking and completely present. And somehow that made it even harder to accept how frail she'd become since Mary Ann's last visit. The spirit was still there, blazing away, but her shrinking body seemed barely able to contain it anymore. Only two years earlier Mrs. Madrigal had somehow wrenched herself out of a stroke-induced coma with nothing to show for it afterward but a few more roses in her cheeks. But that was then, and she had changed considerably. There was no denying what time was taking from her.

'Help yourself to tea,' Anna told her. 'I can't trust myself with the pouring.'

'That's okay. I had coffee at Michael's. I'll take one of these, though. They look yummy.' She nibbled on a cookie, mostly so Anna could feel like a hostess.

'Are you holding up, dear?' Those Wedgwood-blue eyes were fixed firmly on Mary Ann, expecting nothing less than the truth, as usual.

'How much did Mouse tell you?'

'He said you have a clean bill of health . . .'

'Yes . . . well . . . yes!'

'. . . and you're leaving the . . . uh, Republican gentleman . . . because you saw him having an indiscretion on the Internet.'

Mary Ann grinned ruefully. 'Close enough.'

'So how are you holding up?'

'Oh . . .' Mary Ann made a mumbling noise that was meant to tell the truth without overtly complaining. 'I've had better centuries, I guess.'

Anna chuckled. 'Haven't we all?'

It surprised her somewhat to hear Anna say this. 'C'mon. You live in the moment better than anyone I've ever known.'

Anna shrugged. 'We don't have much choice, do we? But that doesn't mean I don't have . . . my special favorites when it comes to centuries.'

Mary Ann laughed.

'This one is too complicated for me,' Anna continued. 'Thank goodness for Mr. Greenleaf. I wouldn't know how to make so much as a phone call.'

'I know what you mean.'

'Are Michael and Ben taking good care of you?' Anna asked.

'Oh yes. More than I deserve.'

Anna frowned. 'What do you mean?'

Mary Ann felt a tightening in her throat. It was not that far removed from how she felt on mountain roads. She dreaded making this hairpin turn, but she had to, if she was ever going to get off the cliff. She was leaving in a few days, heading home to mop up the mess of her second failed marriage, so postponement was no longer an option. It was not unreasonable to think this could be the last time she'd ever see Anna.

'I treated you all so badly,' she said at last.

'*Who?*'

'All of you. Brian and Shawna . . . Michael . . . who was sick, for God's sake, maybe even dying.'

'How did you treat us badly?'

'By leaving. By running away and never looking back.'

'Twenty years ago, Mary Ann. You were following your heart's desire. I did that myself, dear, need I remind you. I left a wife and a two-year-old daughter without explanation.' Mrs. Madrigal's face clouded over. Mary Ann knew she was remembering Mona, the daughter in question, whom she'd lost to breast cancer back in the nineties.

'But you made up for it,' Mary Ann said. 'You brought her back into your life and made a home for her.' Now Mary Ann herself was remembering Mona, the flame-haired free spirit who had done a 'reading' of Mary Ann's garbage the morning they first met in the courtyard at 28 Barbary Lane.

There was another one she had carelessly lost forever, without even knowing the actual moment she had lost her.

Mrs. Madrigal gave her a meaningful look. 'Daughters, you'll find, are surprisingly retrievable.'

She was talking about Shawna now, Mary Ann realized. 'I gave it a shot,' she said with a sigh. 'I invited her out to Connecticut. It's perfectly clear she doesn't approve of me. Why should she? I don't approve of me myself.'

Anna fussed with the edge of her kimono, looking impatient. 'If you came here for a spanking, dear, you'll have to look elsewhere.'

In its own way this felt like an absolution, so Mary Ann smiled at the person who'd bestowed it. 'I came here to tell you I love you.'

'That's more like it,' said Anna.

Unscattered Ashes

Almost a week had passed since Shawna left the note at the house on Tandy Street, but so far no one had called. She had told the whole story in her blog, complete with a photo of Alexandra, but she'd thought it best to omit the address, since she didn't want her crusade to degenerate into an act of harassment. This ambiguous ending to her tale of the streets only enhanced its poignancy, she felt, and several of her readers had told her as much. Of course, there was still the issue of Alexandra's unscattered ashes.

Her relationship with Otto was getting wobbly. The first rumblings had come that day on Tandy Street, when he'd accused her of being capable of romance only in the abstract, or worse yet, only for the purposes of her blog. How could she have addressed that without being unkind? How could she have told him that her problem wasn't with romance per se but with Otto himself – or, rather, the thought of permanency with Otto. She loved what they had – the sex certainly, the laughs, the warm body at night – but she had never been able to envision whatever was supposed to come next. Outright rejection wasn't usually in her repertoire, but lately Otto had been forcing the issue.

'Hey, listen,' he said, without looking up. He was hunched over a burrito at the Roosevelt Tamale Parlor, his skinny shoulder blades jutting out of his shrimp-colored T-shirt like little wings. 'Remember my buddy Aaron with the awesome place in Bernal Heights with the open plan and the industrial skylights?'

'I think. Yeah. Sort of Rob Thomas-y.'

'I meant the apartment.'

'Oh … yeah … sure. We dropped off those tumbling mats.'

He finally looked up at her. 'It's all ours if we want it. He's going to Costa Rica for a job. All we have to do is pick up the rent … which, by the way, would be a fuck of a lot cheaper than our two rents combined.' He took a bite out of the burrito and waited.

All she could think to say was: 'There are clowning jobs in Costa Rica?'

Otto didn't smile. 'It's a very eco-friendly country.'

'And . . . what? . . . he's an eco-clown?'

'I don't know what he is, Shawna. Why aren't you answering me?'

'Because this isn't about the rent . . . and I don't know what to say to you.'

He looked crushed. 'Guess you just did.'

She reached across the table and took his hand. 'C'mon, dude. I love our two or three nights a week. I do.'

'What is it? Are you bored with me? Do you wanna be with a woman again?'

She rolled her eyes, trying to keep things as light as possible. 'If I do, I'll get one. And you'll be the first to know.'

He returned to his burrito for a while, coming back with his final shot:

'That apartment is really sick, ya know. There's even two bathrooms. It wouldn't have to mean anything.'

Yes, it would, she thought. *Yes, it would*.

They parted company after dinner. Not in any dramatic way, but Otto clearly wanted to sulk in private. Shawna walked back to her apartment and worked off her frustration by washing the dishes that had piled up in the sink. Why did he have to be this way? Why couldn't he just be content with what they had and not keeping angling for more? When people started making demands of each other, that's when the trouble started. Lucy had been that way in Brooklyn, and Shawna had grown sick of it.

She rolled a joint from her stash and smoked it contemplatively as she stared at Alexandra's ashes. She wanted this to be over now, so she considered driving to Dolores Park and scattering the ashes on the grassy slope at the upper end, where the gay boys liked to sun in the summertime. There was a great view of downtown from there, and the moon would soon be rising above the urban labyrinth that Alexandra had roamed for the last years of her life. To give her ashes on that swath of green, high above the fray at last, would be just the imagery Alexandra deserved. Dolores Park, Shawna remembered, had even been a cemetery in the old days, and the name itself meant 'sorrows' in Spanish.

It was perfect.

But as soon as she was in the car and heading for the park, that voice in her head, her own instinctual GPS, began directing her back to Tandy Street. She had been there only in the daytime, after all. There would be a much better chance of finding someone home after dark. How could it hurt to check one more time? She wouldn't even have to get out of the car if there were no lights on in the house. She could just keep on driving, say her good-byes to Alexandra, and be back at her apartment in time for Conan O'Brien.

As it happened, there *was* a light burning at the unnumbered house on Tandy Street. It wasn't in the front window but somewhere in the back of the house. Shawna couldn't see the window itself, since the space between the houses was so narrow, but something was illuminating the blind wall of the neighboring house.

It was much harder to park there at night, so she had to comb the neighborhood for a while to find a space. As she was walking back toward the house, it occurred to her that she had never confirmed that the unnumbered house was, in fact, 437 Tandy Street. It was too late for quibbling, though. If her cryptic note about a dead woman had landed in the wrong hands, at least she'd have a chance to explain herself.

Remembering the broken doorbell, she rapped on the door three times.

A dog – *that* dog from the last time – began to bark from somewhere in the back of the house. It was silenced very quickly by a gruff male voice yelling, 'Quiet!'

Moments later, the door opened. A large, stoop-shouldered old man stood there glowering at her, holding the little dog under one arm. He was wearing the red Snuggie she had seen through the window. It gave him an absurdly ecclesiastical look.

'I'm sorry to bother you at night,' she said. 'I'm the person who left the note last week.'

He just gaped at her, swaying. She realized he was drunk.

'You're Sheila?'

'Shawna.'

He beckoned her in with a wave of his ecclesiastical arm. This was too much for him to handle at once, so he lost his balance and had to steady himself against the door. When both the dog and the Snuggie escaped to the floor, Shawna was relieved to see that the old man was wearing something underneath: a short-sleeved white shirt and worn-shiny trousers. He was eightyish, she figured, but probably had not been handsome at any age. When she tried to pair him mentally with the stunning Alexandra, the most charitable she could be was *Beauty and the Beast*.

'Sorry I didn't call,' he said, closing the door. 'I've had some sorting-out to do.' He was slurring his words, so it sounded more like 'shorting out,' which Shawna thought was a good description of his emotional state. She could practically hear the sparks.

'I understand,' she said.

'I can't ask you to sit down. I have to go somewhere. There's something I have to do.'

'That's okay . . . really.'

'How did you know Alexandra?'

'I didn't, exactly. I brought her to the hospital once. I visited a few times. I just felt a sort of connection with her. She seemed like a good person.' *Why give him the gory details?* she thought. He was suffering enough already. 'She was your wife, right?'

He nodded dolefully. 'Once upon a time.'

'Before the drugs took over.' Shawna spoke these

words softly, almost reverently, not as a question but simply to finish his thought.

'Did she say anything about me?' he asked.

He looked so pitiful and ruined that Shawna couldn't bring herself to say no. 'She saved a letter you wrote her. A love letter. She must've loved you very much. You can have it, if you like. Well . . . you wrote it, but still . . . it means something.' She was glad Otto wasn't here to watch her scrambling so shamelessly for her happy ending. 'I have several of her things, in fact. Photos, mostly, but you're welcome to them.'

'That would be nice,' he said.

He looked so grateful that she was emboldened to go all the way. 'I also have her cremains.'

'Her what?'

'Her ashes. She was cremated.'

'Oh.'

'It's up to you, of course. There might be someplace you'd like to scatter them.'

He seemed to think about that for a moment. 'Where are they?'

'In the car.'

'Get them, please.'

She all but sprinted there and back.

He took the ashes from her on his doorstep, holding them close to his chest as if they might somehow escape from him.

'I'm so glad I found you,' she told him.

He went back into the house without a word.

32

Back Before Bedtime

'It gets dark so early,' Mary Ann was saying, apropos of nothing. She was hugging her knees in the window seat in Michael's living room, gazing out at the cottage in the garden. The sky above Twin Peaks was almost drained of its magenta stain.

'I hate winter,' Michael announced, slouching in a nearby armchair. 'Fucking Daylight Savings. Ben always gets home after dark.'

'Why doesn't he just leave early? He's his own boss, right?'

'Yeah, but . . . the traffic in the Mission is god-awful at rush hour, so it's better just to miss it altogether and sleep in later in the morning.'

'Makes sense, I guess.'

'He'll be home soon,' Michael added. 'He makes a point of it when he has a play date.'

She turned and looked at him. 'A what?'

'A play date. Some hot daddy he met at the Y.'

It took her a while to catch his drift, and then she couldn't think of anything to say except: 'How do you do that?'

'How do I do what?'

'Not be jealous.'

'Who says I'm not?'

'Then why do you agree to it?'

He shrugged. 'It's something we agreed on years ago. I think of it as the price of admission.'

She frowned. 'You make him sound like a ride at the fair.'

'Well . . .' He was trying to look devilish.

'Seriously, Mouse. Why?'

'Because men know how men are. I know how *I* was at Ben's age. You know, too, actually. You were there.'

She appreciated this nod to their wicked youth, but she still wasn't buying it. 'But if two people are in love with each other, if they *marry* each other, for heaven's sake . . .'

'. . . then they know enough not to make fucking the deal breaker. They know there's something much more important.'

She wondered if this declaration was a not-so-oblique reference to her situation with Bob.

'But there have to be rules, Mouse. There just do.'

'We have rules. Full disclosure, for one thing. And we're in bed with each other at the end of the day. Our commitment is for life, and we save our hearts for each other. That way we can have play *and* permanency. If monogamy becomes more important than fidelity, you're bound to get hurt. It's all the lying that clobbers you, not the sex.'

She raised an eyebrow. 'Ever tried watching it on Skype?'

He cringed. 'That must've been awful.'

'And, you know, Mouse, it wouldn't have been an improvement if he'd told me in advance that he'd be fucking Calliope that afternoon.'

'Maybe . . . but just having to keep something secret can drive a huge wedge between you. And in the end that just makes it easier to fall in love with someone else.'

'Okay, fine. Thanks for the input. Let's talk about something else.'

He seemed to realize how badly he'd stepped in it. 'I don't mean it's necessarily right for you, sweetie. It's not even right for lots of gay men. I just had to decide on what was important and trust in that. Otherwise love turns into a stupid Maury Povich show, where it's all about lie detectors in the end. I'd rather we had the freedom to play occasionally and concentrate on having the deeper stuff. You know?'

'And he gives you the freedom too?'

'Of course.' He grinned. 'Not that I exercise it all that often.'

'Why not?'

'I'm old . . . in case you haven't noticed.'

'You're not old,' she said, scolding him with a glance. 'You're my age.'

Ben came home not long after that. Perversely, Mary Ann found herself studying his gap-toothed face for telltale signs of extracurricular pleasure. It was the same old Ben, though, wholesome as cornflakes as he burst through the door with that loopy dog, kissing Michael before dropping a small paper bag on the coffee table.

'You guys feel like going out for dinner?' he asked. 'Some place in the neighborhood, maybe?'

'Sure,' said Michael, plastering on a smile for his husband. She was almost certain he wasn't as blasé about this homecoming as he pretended to be.

'Sushi?' asked Ben, looking at both of them.

'Great,' said Michael. 'Sounds good.' He glanced down at the bag on the coffee table. 'What's that, then?'

'Just some baby tangerines.'

'Yum,' said Mary Ann.

Michael looked puzzled. 'All by themselves?'

'They were a present.'

'Really?' Michael widened his eyes noticeably. 'For whom?'

'For us,' Ben said evenly, looking directly at Michael.

'From . . . ?'

'My buddy at the gym. He bought too many at the farmers' market and thought we might like some.'

'That was thoughtful of him,' said Michael.

Ben wriggled free of Michael's penetrating gaze and turned back to Mary Ann. 'Are you good with sushi? There's a new Italian place we could try.'

'You know what,' she said pleasantly, already feeling the suffocating tension in the air, 'you guys just go ahead. I'll curl up here with a book and some Yoplait.'

'You can't do that,' said Ben.

'Yes, I can. I'd like to, actually.' This was the truth, since she didn't want to get caught in their emotional crossfire tonight, however civilly it might be played out. Besides, she loved the idea of having the whole house to herself, knowing the guys would be back before bedtime. 'Go on,' she said. 'I'll have company.'

She meant Roman, of course, who was already sprawled out next to her in the window seat, as if in anticipation of their evening alone together.

Once the guys were gone, she accepted their long-standing offer to use their shower. Compared to the fiberglass cubicle in the cottage, this was a luxuriously roomy space, and the rain showerhead was the size of a Frisbee. Standing beneath a tropical downpour, she used their extension mirror to examine her incisions.

She was starting to think of those four little cat scratches as a sort of Map to the Stars' Homes. ('This is where Lucille Ball used to live . . . and over there is the former home of Ava Gardner.')

Her surgery had been like a clever burglary, where the house had been left so tidy you could barely notice that someone had broken in. That had certainly been a bonus, but, more than anything, she was grateful to her uterus for being such a pilferable item, such a sturdy, yet disposable, little carrying-case for cancer. She visualized the bad stuff being taken somewhere far away, somewhere she would never have to go again.

Something soft and fleshy brushed against her knee and made her jump. It was Roman, or rather Roman's tongue, a sensation she was learning to recognize. He had walked into the shower as if he owned the place, which he pretty much did, as far as she could tell. Michael and Ben had been giving him shampoos in here.

'Go on,' she said, giggling. 'That's very nice of you, but I don't need your help.'

The dog just gaped at her as if he needed convincing.

'Go, Roman . . . go find your monster.'

His monster was a hard-sided felt cyclops that he was encouraged to mangle in lieu of destroying the sofa cushions. Its white polyester innards were strewn all over the house. He had been through several monsters in the course of Mary Ann's stay.

The dog wagged his tail excitedly and left on his quest. She showered for another five minutes, dried off with one of their thirsty white towels and slipped into clean flannel pajamas. She had told the guys she would curl up with a book, but that had just been a figure of speech. She wondered how many people who said that actually did it, or if they ended up, as she had, back around the campfire of the Web, telling tales to strangers.

But she felt curled up, at least. It was so cozy there on her bed in the cottage, with her laptop at her fingertips and Roman's fleecy body radiating warmth against her leg. Facebook lifted her spirits even more, since there were seven new people soliciting her friendship, two of whom she actually remembered. One was a realtor named Shelley, whom she'd met on a Pilates retreat at Canyon Ranch; the other was someone she had known during her pre-Bob party-planning days in Manhattan. She told both of them about her surgery, calling herself a cancer survivor for the very first time. It felt remarkably good.

She had four private messages tonight. Three of them were just people thanking her for the add. The other was from Fogbound One, the faceless Facebooker who had spooked her by having known Norman Neal Williams all those years ago.

The message said: 'Did you like the T-shirt?'

It made no sense to her. The only T-shirt that came

to mind was the 'Middle of Nowhere' T-shirt from Pinyon City that the guys had left on her doorstep the night before her surgery. She had never even thanked them for it, and, for that matter, didn't recall having seen it since her return from St. Sebastian's. That wasn't especially remarkable, of course, since Ben had a way of tidying things up.

She wondered if Fogbound One had come to her by way of Ben's Pinyon City network. Maybe someone he and Michael knew up there had seen them buy the T-shirt. Or Ben or Michael hadmentioned it to someone who was using it now to presume an intimacy with her. It was annoying, at any rate, since the vagueness of the message was clearly meant to force a reply from her. She wasn't taking the bait. Fogbound One was one of those losers who glutted her news feed with reams of their favorite poems and quotations but had nothing much to say themselves. Besides, if this person had really been friends with Norman, why on earth would she want to share *anything* with them?

This was a no-brainer.

She went to her Friends list, scrolled down to Fogbound One and clicked on the x that would defriend this faceless nuisance forever.

The noise on the roof didn't surprise her – or Roman, for that matter. They were both used to the sound of raccoons crossing the compound on their nightly descent to the gourmet garbage cans of the Castro. They were huge creatures, sometimes four or five of them, so they sounded like sled dogs on the roof. Their chatter was a peculiar clicking noise. Mary Ann remembered that sound from her youth on Russian Hill, but these days it evoked the scaly green aliens in that Mel Gibson crop-circle movie.

Roman had a similar reaction to them, barking furiously at the first indication of their presence. She had learned to make sure all the doors were closed, not because the raccoons would barge in, but because Roman would chase after them. That would not be a pleasant scenario, she'd been warned. Years ago, Michael had owned a poodle whose eyes had, reportedly, gone completely red after a strangling – a *strangling* – by raccoons. These little bastards had *hands*, and were capable of ganging up on even the largest dogs.

The door to the cottage was already closed, so she held on to Roman's collar and spoke to him as soothingly as possible.

'That's okay, little boy. It's just those old meanies.'

The dog continued to growl under his breath until the clattering on the roof had stopped and the clicking sound had passed into the neighboring garden.

'See?' she cooed. 'All gone.'

Roman seized this golden opportunity to solicit love, sprawling on his back in an invitational pose. She rubbed his belly gently for several minutes, until both of them were almost hypnotized into a place of peace.

Then, without warning, the dog righted himself and began wagging his tail gleefully. He went to the door and tapped it once with his paw, asking to be let out. He was making the silly crooning noise he reserved for people he knew.

By now she had heard the crunch of gravel in the garden path, so she assumed that the guys were home. She got out of bed and opened the door. 'Go on,' she told the dog. 'Go give your daddies a kiss.'

But the person who had prompted the dog's ecstasy was neither Michael nor Ben but a hunched-over old man in a long black coat. He was holding the handle of a white plastic shopping bag. 'Here ya go, Roman,' the old man said gruffly, using his free hand to pull something from his pocket. The dog gobbled down the treat and sat waiting for another, as if the two of them had performed this ritual a hundred times before.

'Excuse me,' said Mary Ann, remaining in the doorway of the cottage. 'If you're looking for Michael and Ben, they're out at dinner.'

The old man said nothing. He was outside the range of the porch light, so it was difficult to read his expression. When he finally stumbled forward, he reached into his pocket again, pulled out a small black handgun and pointed it at her.

'We have to talk,' he said.

Those Damn Tangerines

'Just level with me,' said Michael. 'The tangerines were for you.'

They were eating at the Thai place next to the Edge. They both liked this place, but they could never remember the name of it, so they always called it 'the Thai place next to the Edge.' Ben had thought they might drop by the Edge afterward, have a few beers together, but the prospects of that were looking pretty dim right now.

'The tangerines were for both of us,' he replied calmly.

'What? 'Thanks for the sex. Here's some tangerines for you and your husband.' '

'That was the gist of it, yeah.'

'So you told him you were married?'

'Of course. I brought it up. I referred to my partner. I always do.'

'But he's single himself?'

'Seems to be. He's got some kid in Brazil that he's hot for, but I don't think he's here all that much.'

'You understand my concern here, don't you? Produce is kind of personal.'

'Personal?'

'You know what I mean. Domestic. It feels like courtship.'

Ben tried not to grin, but he did, a little. 'He was a nice guy, babe. He just tossed 'em to me afterwards. Said to take 'em home.'

'So he didn't mention me specifically.'

'No . . . I dunno . . . maybe not. Whatever. If I'd known those damn tangerines would cause so much pain I would have left them at the studio.'

'Is that where you did it? At your studio?'

'No. His condo.'

A long silence.

'Is that worse than my studio?' asked Ben.

'I don't know,' said Michael, giving him a lopsided smile.

Ben reached across the table and took Michael's hand. Manual communication almost always worked wonders on him. 'I'm yours, babe. You know that.'

'Do you know that song about tangerines?' Michael asked. 'From the sixties? "Would you like some of my tangerine? I know I'd never treat you mean." '

Ben said it didn't ring a bell.

'Claudine Longet,' Michael explained.

'Sorry.'

'She had a ski bum boyfriend named Spider that she shot.'

Ben nodded. 'Great.'

'Not that that's pertinent,' said Michael.

'That's good to know.'

Michael gave him a sleepy smile. 'I babble a lot, don't I? Don't you get tired of it?'

Ben smiled. 'Only when I'm trying to cook dinner.'

'I love you so much, Benjamin. And I'm trying to be better. I wanna celebrate whatever brings you pleasure. I wanna stop being the scared little boy and start being the wise old man who's found the love of his life and can finally . . . relax.'

'You're there already, babe.'

A long, contented silence.

'So,' Michael said playfully. 'Was it fun . . . Johnny-O?'

'Who?'

'Sorry. *Vertigo* reference. Even older than Claudine Longet. I just meant . . . you know . . . this afternoon. Was it fun?'

Ben knew this was always a ticklish question. 'It was okay. His body and dick were nice, but . . . he was a little too self-absorbed to be great sex.'

Michael frowned. 'That's too bad. I hate it when that happens.'

Ben grinned at the noble effort.

'See how well I did?' said Michael.

'You did,' said Ben, squeezing his hand. 'How 'bout a beer next door?'

They had several beers next door, enjoying each other in the genial crush of the crowd. After twenty minutes or so, Ben went off to pee and returned to find Michael missing. This threw him for a moment, until he realized that Michael was outside on the sidewalk, amid the usual knot of smokers, talking on his cell phone.

Ben joined him just as Michael was putting the phone away.

'What's up?' asked Ben.

'Just Jake. He wants to borrow our DVD of *Gods and Monsters*. We were talking about it at work.'

'We have to go home, then?'

Michael shook his head. 'Mary Ann is there. It's a good chance for them to have a little one-on-one.'

Ben couldn't quite picture that working.

Michael discerned his reaction and added: 'I figured she could be helpful right now. He's finally having his hysterectomy next month.'

'He can afford that now?'

'Anna's paying for it. I told him to do it when we're in Hawaii.'

'So . . . how exactly can Mary Ann help?'

'You know . . . moral support. He's nervous about the operation.'

'He still wants it, though?'

'Oh yeah,' said Michael. 'More than anything.'

A Man on the Verge

They were sitting on Mary Ann's bed now, but at opposite ends. The gun was still in the old man's hand, though resting in his lap, no longer pointing at her. That white plastic shopping bag lay between them on the bedspread, like a gift awaiting the proper presentation. To make the scene even more grotesquely implausible, Roman was sprawled on the floor, his tail wagging languidly, looking back and forth between the two of them, as if enthralled by their exchange.

'If it's money you want,' Mary Ann said. 'I can help with that.'

She was banking everything on his aura of melancholy defeat. He was drunk, certainly, but he

342

didn't seem out of control. *He doesn't want to hurt me,*
she thought. *He's just a pathetic old man at the end of his
rope.*

'I don't want your money,' he said.

'What do you need from me, then?'

His lip flickered, revealing teeth like crooked tomb-
stones. 'Recognition would be nice.'

'I'm sorry . . . what?'

'I'm the guy who sent you the T-shirt.'

She was looking at his long black coat now,
suddenly remembering its silhouette from somewhere else.

It was the man in Pinyon City. The one who had
howled at her in the snow.

'Oh . . .' she said, her palm pressing against the top
button of her pajamas. 'I wondered who'd given me
that. That was such a sweet gesture.' She was simper-
ing like a Southern belle, but it seemed the only way
to proceed in the face of such madness. She would
have to stay calm, stay ahead of him. She considered,
briefly, kicking him in the chest to get the gun away
from him, since he was old and seemingly feeble, but
his finger was still on the trigger, and she didn't trust
her recovering body to pull off the kick.

'You must be Fogbound One,' she said.

'Clever girl.'

'I really enjoy your poems.'

'They're not mine. Somebody else wrote them.'

'Still . . . they're lovely.'

'You shouldn't have lied about Norman Neal Williams.'

'What?'

'You heard me.'

'What was it . . . you think I lied about?'

'You said you didn't know him. You said you didn't date him.'

'Well . . . the name rings a bell, but . . . when was this?'

He looked at her with no particular menace – just sadness – and said her name three times like a charm: 'Mary Ann, Mary Ann, Mary Ann.'

Only it sounded like someone saying Shame, Shame, Shame.

And the terrible thing was: she bought it. She could own any crime this loony old prick with a gun could lay on her, because she'd gone through the world feeling guilty, and a little more penitence, at this particular moment, could very well save her life.

'I took you to Sam Wo's,' he told her. 'You hated the rude waiter. Said you'd never come back again.'

What?

'And you always hated *this*,' he added sourly, raising a large, mottled hand to his throat. She thought for a moment that he was going to hit her, but he just grabbed his stained clip-on tie and yanked it free from his collar.

That was as good as being flashed an I.D. She felt the truth burning in her veins. The only thing left to

344

do was home in that voice, peel back the overlay of alcohol and age, until she reached its deeply insecure and unmistakably dweebie core.

'*Norman?*'

He didn't say anything, just gave her a bitter, triumphant smirk.

'I thought you were dead.'

'That's *because*' – he swayed a little as he made his point – '*you* didn't stick around.'

'There was a cliff, Norman.'

'I know what it was. It's my goddamn name now.'

'What?' She noticed that the hand with the gun was twitching.

'Cliffs have ledges, ya know. Not that you would notice.'

'Were you hurt badly? Why didn't you come back to Barbary Lane?'

He snorted. 'Yeah. Right. Come back. After what you said about me and Lexy.'

Leave it alone, she told herself.

'You didn't care, anyway. You were glad to be rid o' me.'

'That's not true, Norman. We called the police.'

'And you told 'em where I fell?'

Her silence betrayed all he needed to know.

'See?' he said. 'Liar.'

'Please put the gun down, Norman. We don't need that to talk.'

'Oh, really? Cudda fooled me.'

'This has all been a big misunderstanding. You don't wanna do anything rash.'

'How do you know what I wanna do? Maybe rash is all I got.'

'No . . . Norman . . . it's never too late to talk things out. Today is the first day of the rest of your life.'

Jesus, she thought. Where had *that* come from?

'I tried to talk to you,' he told her. 'I wanted to explain about me and Lexy, but . . . you wouldn't let me . . . you stuck-up bitch.'

'When did you do this?'

Still holding the gun, he reached into the breast pocket of the coat with his free hand and produced a sheet of dog-eared paper, folded down the middle. She took it from him, opened it and instantly recognized one of her 8x10 glossies from her old TV show, circa late 1980s. Her hair was feathered and enormous. The inscription read: *Cliff – Thanks for the memories – Mary Ann.* It was obviously her handwriting.

'When did I do this?'

'After you got famous. I came to your show and sat in the audience. You didn't even recognize me.'

'Well . . . you know . . . it's hard with the lights and all.'

And I thought you'd been dead for a dozen years, you batshit pervert.

'They wouldn't even let me backstage so I could explain.'

'But this says Cliff. The name isn't even yours, Norman —'

'I told you. I changed it. What else could I do after what you'd been saying?'

'And you'd been here in the city all that time?'

He shook his head and said, 'Bismarck.' The name struggled out of him like a drunken belch.

'Okay,' she said calmly, deciding not to pursue that. 'We're here now. What is it you'd like to explain? I'm willing to listen, Norman.'

He seemed to believe this. He tidied himself up, brushing off his lapels with ridiculous dignity, like a man on the verge of clearing his name.

'Lexy loved me,' he said. 'And I loved her.'

'Okay.' *Forgive me, little girl. It's not okay at all.*

'You were with us,' he said. 'You saw how much she loved me.'

This time she just nodded.

'I even thought the three of us could be a family.'

'Norman—'

'No, listen.' He was shaking the gun again. 'I know I did some bad things. I know that, believe me. I shouldn't have put us in those magazines. I shouldn't have made money off our love. That was the wrong thing to do.'

She was starting to feel a familiar sourness in the back of her mouth. She wondered if he would kill her if she vomited on him.

'I felt really bad about it for a long time. What you

said was right. I realized that once I found the Lord in Bismarck. I asked for His forgiveness.'

'Well, you see? We're all capable of redemption. That's wonderful, Norman.'

I'm sorry, Lexy, I'm so sorry. I thought you were safe from him.

'Here's the best part, Mary Ann: The Lord brought me a miracle. He gave me a chance to make it all up to Lexy.'

'Really?' *Really?*

'I met her again when she was all grown up. Completely by accident. She was working in a shoe store, and she didn't recognize me. That was the miracle: I was able to be somebody else.'

'Well,' she said, struggling for some sort of common ground. 'We all need a chance to start over.'

'See! That's all I wanted to do. Just to be kind to her like a father, give her the love and financial support she deserved. The Lord made that possible for me!'

Mary Ann was thinking maybe college tuition.

'So I married her,' said Norman.

'What?'

'I married her. I took responsibility for my actions. I did the right thing. I'm not like you, Mary Ann. I don't throw people away like they're *nothing*.'

She had her hand on her mouth now.

'She was happy with me, too. We both were until . . .' He cut off the thought.

She knew she shouldn't ask, but she did. 'Until what?'

'Until she remembered me. We were making love one night and . . . Lexy remembered me.'

She took her hand off her mouth and just let it fly. She retched the way she'd expected to retch when DeDe brought that *Boeuf Bourguignon* to the hospital. When she finally straightened up, Norman was still sitting there with the gun, observing her with weary contempt. 'Just because you don't *understand* something, Mary Ann . . .'

She sprang to her feet 'No, I don't, Norman. I don't understand.'

'Where are you going?' He was pointing the gun directly at her, but her anger had somehow eradicated her fear.

'I need to wash my fucking face.'

'Sit down,' he told her.

'The sink is right there, Norman. There's no way I can get out.'

'Sit the fuck down!'

She obeyed him.

'Who are you cleaning up for, anyway?'

Good question, she thought. The coroner? Still, she seized a corner of the sheet and wiped her mouth with it. 'Where is she now?'

'What?'

'Where is Lexy, Norman? What happened to her?'

Another contorted smile. 'Thought you'd never ask.'

He lunged in her direction, making her flinch, until she realized he was reaching for that white plastic shopping bag. He pulled it closer and removed a pressed cardboard container about the size of a small jewelry box. He opened it to reveal a plastic bag full of something gray and granular.

'What are you doing?' she asked.

It's something chemical, she was thinking. *Lye maybe. He's going to blind me or poison me . . . or disfigure me.*

'Norman, please don't—'

'SHUT UP! This isn't about you! This is *my* moment.'

Still holding the gun, he used his free hand to yank the plastic bag out of the box and dump its contents onto the bedspread. Then, with priestly deliberation, he began to sprinkle the gritty gray substance over his body – his arms and legs, his chest, even his face, where it caught in the creases, forming a ghastly lunar landscape.

'How about that, Miss Fancypants?' He was mugging at her like a schoolboy. 'How does she look on me?'

'What do you mean?' She was almost sure she knew what he meant; she just couldn't face it. *Please don't let it be that. Please don't.*

'You thought it wasn't real love. But it was. It lasted all this time, and now it will last for an eternity. Lexy and Norman, together forever.'

'Norman, I would never judge—'

'Oh, but you have. That's why I wanted you here to witness this. That's why you can't run away this time.'

'Okay,' she said feebly. 'Just put the gun down.'

He frowned in confusion. 'What's the point of that?'

'So . . . I can prove to you that I'll stay without being coerced.'

'I told you,' he said irritably, 'it's not about you.'

He lifted the gun from his lap and placed the barrel against his temple.

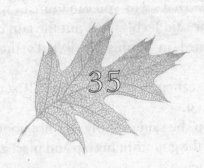

35

All The Man Stuff

It was only a short bike ride from Jake's place in the Duboce Triangle to Michael's house on Noe Hill, but the last few blocks were killer steep. Jake usually dismounted near the foot of Cumberland and pushed the bike the rest of the way up Noe Street. Tonight, however, his energy was flagging, so he dropped the bike and sat on the concrete stairs to rest. Seconds later his cell began jittering in his jeans.

The sensation moved straight to his heart when he saw who it was.

'Jonah . . . dude . . . wassup?'

'Hey, Jake.'

'You in Snowflake?'

'Yeah.'

There was a long silence, so Jake prodded him. 'So . . . what? You miss me or somethin'?'

'Dude—'

'Guys can miss each other, you know.'

'I know,' said Jonah. 'And I do.'

This seemed to be a serious declaration, and Jake could already feel himself blushing. He wondered if losing his uterus would eliminate that, and if, in fact, he even wanted it eliminated anymore. He wanted all the man stuff, for sure, but he wouldn't mind keeping the blushing. It was just his heart doing semaphore.

'That's cool,' he told Jonah quietly. 'I miss you, too.'

'It feels freakin' awesome, too.'

Jake laughed out of sheer joy. 'That's the *idea*, man.'

'It's my first bromance.'

'What?'

'You know . . . like Paul Rudd in that movie.'

'I know what a bromance is, Jonah. That's not what it was. There was a lot more goin' on than that. We made out for half a fucking hour.'

'Yeah,' said Jonah quietly. 'And Heavenly Father has forgiven me.'

'You're shitting me. Forgiven you for a kiss?'

'The thoughts were unclean, Jake. It was just a blessing that we didn't go any further.'

'So . . . as long as there's no peen involved, you're not being queer. Is that what you're telling me here? Is that what your fucking therapist told you?'

'Dude, c'mon. I think you're a great guy. Even though you're gay, I—'

'*Even?*'

'The Lord has forgiveness for everyone, Jake.'

'Fuck your forgiveness, dude. And fuck you for being too much of a coward to face your own truth. You wanted me bad and you know it.'

'My therapist said you'd say that.'

Jake hung up on him and sprang to his feet. He grabbed his bike and began pushing it up the hill toward Michael's house, since he needed physical exertion to calm the storm in his head. He was more pissed at himself, of course, than he could ever be with Jonah. Why couldn't he have left it alone? What had he hoped to make of that relationship? Why had he tried to build an eternity out of thin air?

He was a block away, on the steepest part of Noe Hill, when he heard the scream. There was little doubt as to its seriousness – and none at all when he heard the gunshot. He dropped his bicycle on the sidewalk and sprinted up the hill to Michael and Ben's house. There were lights on in the house, so he approached with caution through the garden. Beyond the French doors he could see Mary Ann sitting on the couch, hugging her knees and rocking back and forth. When he tried to get in, he found the door locked, so he kicked through the panes with his boot, prompting another scream from Mary Ann.

'It's okay,' he said. 'It's Jake. Are you all right?'

She nodded, unable to speak.

'Is someone else here?'

Another nod as she pointed to the garden cottage.

'Do they have a gun?'

'He's dead,' she said.

He crossed the garden to the cottage. The door was open, so he could already see the blood pooling on the floor. Moving closer, he saw the mound of the corpse, most of it covered with a long black coat. There was a sunburst of blood on the wall, and a hole in the side of the old man's head. Jake had never seen this guy before.

Jake heard a whimpering noise that made him jump. Roman came out of the bathroom with his head held low, as if he himself might have pulled the trigger.

'C'mon, boy,' said Jake, feeling sorry for him.

Roman made a slow, cautious exit, stopping only to sniff the corpse's pocket a few times before heading out the door.

Back at the house Jake called 911. He gave the dispatcher the address and told him: 'We have a suicide here. Gunshot.'

Then, thinking about it, he whispered to Mary Ann: 'That's what it was, right?'

She nodded.

He signed off and sat down next to her on the couch. She rolled over and began weeping against his shoulder, softly at first then with a ferocity that caught him off guard. She was like one of those old Greek ladies who fling themselves on coffins.

'It's okay,' he told her, stroking her hair. 'You're safe now. Jake's got you. It's gonna be all right.'

He was getting used to this man thing.

36

Bad Juju

They had given her a sedative. She had asked for one, in fact. She was tired of being brave, and oblivion had had a lot going for it at the time. When she woke up in Michael and Ben's bed, the house was full of familiar faces: Michael, Ben, Jake, even Shawna, who'd brought Mrs. Madrigal with her as soon as they'd heard the news. Mary Ann thought of Michael's *Wizard of Oz* joke when Roman pulled out of his epileptic seizure: 'And you were there, and you, and you . . .' Roman himself was there, in fact, curled up next to her feet on the bed. He'd had something of a trauma himself.

What struck her as peculiar was how remorseful they all seemed. Ben, after all, had not known the history of the old man in the dog park, and Michael had never met 'Cliff,' so therefore could not possibly have identified him as Norman. Shawna, of course, had less reason than anyone to feel responsible, since she hadn't even been born the first time Norman 'died.' She'd been totally in the dark about everything.

'I'm so sorry,' Mary Ann told her after the others had left for the living room.

'For what?' asked Shawna.

'This whole mess. You don't deserve to have this nightmare laid on you.'

'Actually,' said Shawna. 'I laid it on myself.'

This made no sense to Mary Ann. 'In what way?' she asked.

Shawna sat down on the edge of the bed. 'You don't follow my blog, do you?'

Mary Ann shook her head. 'Not a lot, no. I'm sorry.' She wanted to explain that the brazenly frank subject matter bothered her because she still thought of Shawna as her little girl, but she knew, better than anyone, that she had long ago forfeited the right to say that. '*Should* I have been reading it?'

'It might have helped,' her daughter replied with an odd little smile.

'I don't get it.'

Shawna was fidgeting. 'I've been more involved than you think.'

'You're scaring me now.'

'No . . . please . . . don't. It's all good. I'd just rather you read it when you're feeling stronger. Anna told me about the cancer. I'm glad you're kicking its ass.'

'Thanks, Puppy.' Shawna's baby name had just tumbled out unconsciously. 'Do people still call you that? Besides your dad.'

Shawna shook her head. 'He's never called me that, actually. He said that's what *you* called me.'

She doesn't even remember, thought Mary Ann. 'Would you mind if I still do?'

'If that's what you want. Sure.'

An awkward silence.

'They told you about me and Bob, I guess.'

Shawna nodded. 'For what's it's worth . . . I think it's for the best. I think you're gonna make a sick single lady.'

Robbie also used the word 'sick' in a complimentary way, but Mary Ann had never gotten used to it. As she basked in her daughter's smile she realized, with a sense of completely undeserved relief, that Shawna wasn't doing that awful snood thing anymore. 'I love your hair,' she told her. 'That's a nice cut.'

Shawna smiled. 'It's sort of yours, isn't it?'

As if to confirm this, Mary Ann touched the side of her own head. 'I guess you're right.'

'It wasn't intentional.'

'No . . . I'm sure.'

'I didn't mean it like that.'

'I know, Puppy. There's not a mean bone in your body.'

Shawna, surprisingly, reached out and took her hand. 'I know this sounds funny, but . . . I think this was all for a reason. I think it was meant to bring us together.'

Mary Ann rolled her eyes. 'Facebook might have been easier.'

'No . . . seriously . . . we had all the pieces all along. We just needed to talk to each other.' Shawna paused, studying Mary Ann's reaction. 'Do I sound like a total flake?'

Mary Ann shook her head. 'You just sound like Anna.'

'Well . . . duh.'

Mary Ann smiled. Mrs. Madrigal had left her imprint, all right.

'Tell me something, Puppy . . . did you talk to the police?'

Shawna nodded. 'We all did.'

'Did they say what that stuff was?'

'What stuff?'

'You know. That he sprinkled on himself. They were ashes, right? Cremated remains?'

Shawna stood up, suddenly looking flustered. 'Let's save that for another day. Tonight's all about getting bad juju out of the house.'

What did that mean?

'Seriously,' said Shawna, catching Mary Ann's anxious expression. 'It's all good.'

That was another thing the kids said today that

offended Mary Ann's ears. How could that possibly be true, after all? Nothing in the world had ever been 'all good.'

When Mary Ann finally joined the others in the living room, they had closed the curtains on the cottage side of the house, presumably to spare her the sight of what she had already seen. Mrs. Madrigal had settled into Michael's armchair; Jake sat at her feet; Shawna was fiddling with an iPod; Ben and Michael were serving a late supper.

'Pizza,' said Michael with a sardonic grin. 'Perfect for every occasion.'

She sat down on the sofa across from Anna. 'Are the police gone?'

'Of course,' said Jake, holding up the tube of the vaporizer. 'Or we wouldn't be doing this.' He handed the tube to Anna, who puffed on it demurely and handed it back. Mary Ann flashed on the pot plants Anna had grown at 28 Barbary Lane and the joints she had taped to every new tenant's door. No one in the house had ever disapproved of that gesture except Norman. For someone so wicked, he had been curiously square.

When dinner was over, Mary Ann followed Jake's example and sat on the floor next to Mrs. Madrigal. She leaned against the old woman's leg – just because it felt so right – and was duly rewarded with the silent benediction of Anna's hand on her head. Mary Ann wasn't talking much herself that evening – just listening, just being.

They stayed with her until almost midnight, laughing and playing music and telling stories about the old days. No one talked about the mess that had been made of the cottage, or the man who had made it. When Anna dozed off in the armchair, Jake woke her gently and helped her out to Shawna's car. Mary Ann's heart sank as they left.

Michael turned to her as soon as the door was closed.

'You're sleeping with us tonight,' he said.

She didn't put up an argument. She slept between them on their big matrimonial bed, like a child in flight from the boogieman. Death had been chasing her for weeks, she realized, but not in the way she'd imagined. It had found its intended quarry in the garden cottage and left her to live another day. What she would do with the time she had left was entirely up to her. As she drifted off in that bunker of warm, breathing bodies, it occurred to her that her fear of dying had left far too little room for the joy of living.

It's all good, she told herself. *It's all good*.

37

Treat

The flight attendant in first class was a gregarious sort who kept talking about how much he'd love to live in 'San Fran.' She hated hearing the city called that – it jarred her ears even more than 'Frisco' did – but he was fiftyish and kind of rugged-looking and, though she couldn't have told you exactly why, struck her as being straight.

'How long were you in town?' he asked, as he replenished her warm nuts.

'Just a few weeks.'

'Such a great place.'

'It is, isn't it? I used to live there years ago.'

'Lucky you.'

'Yeah. I'm thinking of moving back.'

'Oh . . . wow. You have family there?'

'Yeah.' The undeniable truth of this made her giggle. 'I do . . . yeah.'

'That's great.'

'I have to sort a few things out first.'

'So . . . you live in Manhattan now?'

She nodded. 'I have a little place in the Village.' Why mention Darien, after all? It would only make her sound married and boring.

'Where are you?' he asked. 'Just out of curiosity.'

'Charles Street,' she told him.

'I'm on Waverly Place.'

'Hey. Small world.'

'Isn't it?'

What was the protocol here, anyway? Exactly how brazen could you get with a flight attendant?

'Excuse me,' he said, touching her arm lightly as he headed off to deal with another passenger. She gazed out the window at the cartoon clouds and the endless blue, feeling like a giddy teenager again. He looked a lot like George Clooney, she decided.

When he returned a few minutes later, he knelt next to her and, without uttering a word, left his card on her tray. He had written his phone number on the back.

'Would your friend like a treat?' he asked.

She looked directly into his eyes. 'I'm sure she would love one.'

He smiled a languid George Clooney smile as he

reached into his shirt pocket for a dog biscuit. She took it from him without comment, leaning down to the Burberry-plaid carrying case at her feet and unzipping the panel on its side.

Blossom gobbled it up with gusto.

Tales Of The City

Armistead Maupin

THE FIRST VOLUME IN THE ACCLAIMED SERIES

'Maupin with all his elegance and charm, has found
a place among the classics'
OBSERVER

WELCOME TO THE legendary world of *Tales of the City*, and meet the
weird and wonderful inhabitants of 28 Barbary Lane.

There's sweet, innocent out-of-towner, Mary-Anne Singleton;
Michael 'Mouse' Tolliver, gay, proud but not yet out; Mona
Ramsey, who isn't quite sure what she is, and, of course, their
irrepressible, dope-smoking landlady, Anna Madrigal. If you
thought San Francisco in the seventies was all about sex, drugs
and having fun – you're absolutely right.

'A consummate entertainer . . . It is Maupin's Dickensian gift to
be able to render love convincingly'
THE TIMES LITERARY SUPPLEMENT

'An enormously talented writer, witty but always
sympathetic . . . By writing about what's seemingly different
Armistead Maupin always manages to capture what is so
hilariously and painfully true for all of us'
AMY TAN

www.armisteadmaupin.com

9780552998765

More Tales Of The City

Armistead Maupin

THE SECOND VOLUME IN THE ACCLAIMED SERIES

'San Francisco is fortunate in having a chronicler
as witty and likeable as Armistead Maupin'
INDEPENDENT

IF YOU THINK that a family has to be a man, a woman and 2.4
kids, just meet the residents of 28 Barbary Lane, and think again!
The divinely human comedy that began with *Tales of the City*
rolls recklessly along as Mary-Anne Singleton falls in love with a
man who has lost his memory. Michael 'Mouse' Tolliver plucks
up the courage to come out to his reactionary parents, in one
of the most moving letters you'll ever come across and
Mona Ramsey learns more about her missing father in a remote
desert whorehouse. Once again, Maupin is ahead of his time
in this intoxicating blend of compassion, humour and sheer
outrageousness.

'Like those of Dickens and Wilkie Collins, Armistead Maupin's
novels have all appeared originally as serials . . . it is the
strength of this approach, with its fantastic adventures and
astonishingly contrived coincidences, that makes these novels
charming and compelling'
LITERARY REVIEW

www.armisteadmaupin.com

9780552998772

Further Tales Of The City

Armistead Maupin

THE THIRD VOLUME IN THE ACCLAIMED SERIES

'An extended love letter to a magical San Francisco'
NEW YORK TIMES BOOK REVIEW

In *Further Tales of the City*, the third novel in Maupin's classic series, the residents of 28 Barbary Lane are leaving behind the delights of the flower-power seventies and moving into the darker, power-dressing eighties. Mary-Anne Singleton finds herself chasing a psychopathic cult leader across the continent; Mrs Madrigal kidnaps an over-ambitious anchorwoman in her basement; DeDe Halcyon Day has discovered the delights of Sapphic love and Michael 'Mouse' Tolliver is searching for romance at the National Gay Rodeo. Once again, readers will be entranced by the intertwining relationships and extraordinary coincidences, the romance and betrayals, that mark Maupin as one of the most dazzlingly entertaining and humane writers of our time.

'Maupin is a richly gifted comic author'
OBSERVER

www.armisteadmaupin.com

9780552998789